# Charred Heart

## Heart of Fire, Book One

## Lizzy Ford

ISBN-13: 978-1-62378-126-2

# Dedication

For Lisa Markson, who asked me to write her a book about a beefcake dragon shifter. It turned out to be one of my best books yet! Thank you for all the wonderful support you provide as a part of Team Lizzy. I couldn't do it without you, Leanne Jacobson, Stephanie Shaw and Emily Rae.

For cover model James Magnussen. Thank you for your patience, professionalism, and for being a gentleman to your newfound (rabid?!) fan base in Lizzyland. You've brought Lisa's dragon to life!

# Chapter One

C hace glanced up from the glass of amber beer as his closest friend, Gunner, approached their usual table in the corner of the bar. Unlike Chace, who was a dragon shifter, Gunner was able to transform into a panther the size of a car. He had dark hair and almond-shaped, brown eyes, a muscular frame, a gait worthy of a cat and two pints in his hands. He sat and placed one glass down beside Chace's untouched drink.

"You ate your pizza, which means you can't be too sick to drink your beer," Gunner observed.

"There's no excuse for wasting good pizza," Chace replied. "Just not thirsty."

"You really did it, didn't you?" Gunner guessed.

"Yeah," Chace replied. "I talked to him."

"And?"

Chace's eyes swept around the shifters' bar, the only safe haven for a dying race of supernatural creatures that were being hunted and killed off. The tables, chairs and flooring were all mahogany, worn but polished and clean, the ceiling and lattice work on the pillars resembling those of an English pub rather than a typical biker bar. The walls were decorated with autographed classic rock posters, and shadowboxes with guitars, drumsticks and other rock curios perched above the row of plush booths along one wall.

The bar fed off his magic and was full this evening, though its patrons were tense. Their talk consisted of worried murmurs and the occasional cursing.

"He'll give me what I want," Chace replied. "Doesn't seem to be any strings attached. Just wants me and everything I own, which is basically just my bike at this point."

Gunner sat down, frowning. "Why Chace?"

*Because I'm tired of watching people I care about die around me.* Chace debated what to tell his friend, who had been with him the longest of anyone still living.

"You remember Steven?" he asked.

"Yeah. He built your chopper, right?"

"Yep. I used to take it to him for maintenance every year for forty years, and he checked up with me monthly to make sure it was working well. He built it by hand," Chace mused. "He loved that thing like it was his own."

"*Used* to. I can guess where this is going," Gunner said. "He passed?"

"Last week. I got an email from his son. He left me spare parts in his will." Chace chuckled. "Think he liked the bike more than me, but he was …"

"… the last human friend who hadn't died. I get it."

They both fell quiet. Sometimes, Chace wondered where the years went, because they seemed to jumble up and fly by in a blink. And sometimes, he wasn't certain he'd make it through the end of a week, especially when someone like Steven died and made him question everything in his life all over again. He'd outlived every friend he'd ever had, up until he chose only to associate with other shifters. Every time he let himself fall for a girl or made a friend, he convinced himself that this time, it would work out. The curse would lift, and he wouldn't be left alone again.

*It never works out that way.*

"A thousand years, Gun," he murmured. "I've been alive a thousand years. Steven was eighty, and he left me spare parts, because he knew I wasn't going to die anytime soon."

"Oh, hell. Here we go again," Gunner joked. "It's the nature of who we are, man."

"It's the nature of who *you* are," Chace corrected him. "I was made a shifter. You all were born shifters."

"Doesn't matter, does it? We're all the same now."

"Except you can die in a fight with another shifter. Me? No such luck," Chace replied. "You expect to be immortal. I can't figure out why I'm not dead."

Gunner snorted in response.

"You know what I was doing when I turned eighty?"

"Sleeping your way across Finland?"

"Yes, but there's more." Chace grinned. "I was going to the funeral of my mother, who lived to almost a hundred. You ever see a Viking funeral?"

"On TV."

"They're spectacular." Chace allowed himself to think of the memory he didn't like recalling. He could almost smell the scent of burning wood as his mother's body was set afloat on a fiery Viking ship into the sea. The evening had been cold and clear, the sunset smearing brilliant pinks, oranges and purples across one end of the sky while the other end was deep blue and scattered with blinking stars.

He'd gone incognito, disguised as a distant cousin, for no one but his mother knew his secret at that point that he was immortal. Even she didn't know why the curse was placed on him. It was a secret he hadn't told anyone. Ever. He'd been a stupid, hotheaded fool when he was a kid.

"I want to be human again. I want my heart back. Anyway." He shook his head. "I went to see Mr. Nothing this morning, and he made me a smokin' deal. He'll lift the curse in exchange for everything that is mine."

"So … what is that exactly? Did you ask?"

Chace shrugged. "Don't care. The moment before he makes me mortal, I'm going to move my cabin one last time and just live out the rest of my years in peace. Beside, I only have my magic and my bike."

"When I met you, you were this hot-headed, cocky bastard." Gunner leaned forward, his face taut with concern. "You mellowed out over the years a bunch. But this decision sounds like it was made by the young dragon shifter who didn't stop to think before lighting things on fire."

Chace said nothing. A small part of him agreed, but he'd been more disturbed by Steven's death than he cared to let on. Long ago he tried to close off his emotions to the world. Maybe it was monthly chats and ritual trips to visit Steven that let the tiny man with a huge smile work his way under his skin. After a thousand years, Chace should be completely numb, able to rationalize death as a stage in the natural way of the world the way Gunner did.

But he couldn't, and he'd tried for years to philosophize his way into accepting death.

"I made the deal anyway," Chace said. "He's going to send a messenger tonight or tomorrow with one of his cards to let me know where to meet him for the final spell."

"You know we don't know anything about Mr. Nothing."

"We know he's older than even me, and that he's got the magic to do this. The deal is straightforward. Worst case scenario, he kills me." Chace shrugged.

"I don't like it."

"I don't either. What other choice do I have of ever having this curse lifted? The woman who placed it on me – she's been dead for over nine hundred years, Gunner!"

"I know."

"At some point, I'll outlive you and the rest of the guys we run with. No, Gunner, I'm done. What she did to me can't be undone any other way, and I've looked for a way to end the curse my entire life," Chace said firmly. "I turned a thousand last week, and that's when

Steven died. It's a sign."

"I hear ya." Gunner's voice was soft. "I don't blame you, Chace. I just don't trust Mr. Nothing."

Mr. Nothing had gotten his nickname because no one could find out anything about him. No one knew where he lived and yet, he was easy to find whenever Chace had wanted to talk to the elusive creature that had been around since he was made a shifter.

*Easy to find. Not easy to get answers out of.* Chace had nearly gone mad the first few years of the curse trying to get the shadowy figure that only appeared at night to tell him something about his newfound immortality or his magic.

To this day, Chace had no idea what Mr. Nothing was, aside from a shifter of some kind with great power. He suspected Mr. Nothing was a dragon, though he'd long since given up trying to get answers out of someone who didn't seem interested in anyone else.

Gunner waved to someone who had just entered, and Chace looked up to see the third member of their four-man gang. A phoenix shifter with a like-minded affinity for fire, Luke was blond like Chace, though his hair was short and his eyes dark, whereas Chace had blue eyes and kept his dark blond hair long in the way of his Viking people.

"Don't tell the others," Chace said to Gunner. "I'll let them know when everything is final."

"All right." Gunner didn't appear to be happy about keeping secrets from the other two members of their tight-knit crew.

"Thanks. I'm gonna go get changed."

"I'll put on some tunes. I think the shifters need something to cheer them up."

Chace rose. He agreed silently and took in the faces of those around him once more, trying to distance himself from his concern. As much as he tried to deny it, he knew they were his people, even if he'd started off as a human. They had nowhere else to go, and no one else to turn to. The shifter creed was simple: to live their lives quietly without harming anyone or bringing attention to their society. It was how they remained hidden, a secret subculture that the humans had no need to know about.

Yet someone had found out, and the shifter ranks had thinned considerably the past twenty years. Once numbering in the thousands, the several dozen men and women seeking refuge in his bar were all that remained.

Chace left out of the back door of the bar and stepped into the warm air of early evening. The distant drone of traffic on I-10 reaching him across the flat desert terrain.

He didn't want to feel worry or fear for the shifter family that adopted him when he had no one else, but he did. On one hand, the timing for him to decide to strike a deal with Mr. Nothing felt wrong, because he wouldn't be around to help the others, if they needed it. He'd airlifted a few other shifters out of their homes when they'd been too afraid to leave. Their fear struck him hard, even when he tried to remain numb to the world.

*You care too much to abandon them,* Gunner had told him once.

And he did. The brash, selfish, cocky young man who was cursed for being a fool had turned thoughtful over the years, compassionate and observant of his world. Even if he tried to keep everyone at a distance.

Chace focused on the small cabin that materialized out of thin air. Another creation of his magic, he had managed to take his home with him wherever he went over the years, the only real solace he had. It was the cabin where he'd been born and where his mother had lived up until her death. Only after returning to it after her funeral had he realized that his magic would let him take it with him.

There were days when he thought it was more alive than not with a mind of its own. Its magic and his were intertwined but not the same. It reacted to his emotions and commands, and yet, it had its own life as well, which had baffled him for many years until he finally just accepted it.

He walked in. The cabin had looked the same for many years. It had a simple floor plan consisting of a great room where everything was and a small bathroom he'd added a hundred years before. The great room held a king-sized bed with a wood stove, living room area, small office space and a storage corner where he kept what precious items he had.

Chace changed out of the dusty clothes he'd worn on his daily ride and into a fresh t-shirt and jeans, though he replaced his motorcycle jacket in case he had the urge for a midnight ride, like he did sometimes. Crossing to the storage corner, he paused.

"Would you stop rearranging my boxes?" he growled at the cabin.

It didn't reply. It never did, but the boxes returned to the order where he preferred them of their own accord. The tiny disturbance reminded him of how independent the magic of his cabin was, when it chose to be. It was like his magic, which obeyed him most of the time and then sometimes, responded too readily to his emotions and forced him to shift when he otherwise wouldn't.

"It's like living with a passive-aggressive woman," he said, amused. "You listening?"

The boxes suddenly flew off their shelves and tumbled to the floor at his feet.

"A thousand years old and less mature than me," he teased it. "Clean that up, please."

He turned away, knowing the magic would obey, but probably not until after he left. He didn't understand why his cabin was possessed or the link between it and his own independent magic.

After a thousand years, he no longer cared. In a few days, none of it would matter anyway.

He left the cabin, gaze going to the sky once more. A familiar yearning filled him, the call of the heavens clear in his thoughts. He found peace in the sky and in flying around.

Deciding he had time for a quick flight, he peeled off his clothing and tossed them on the porch. The transformation from human to dragon was brutal on his body – and irreparable on the clothing.

Pain roared through him, hot enough to rob him of breath. His flesh tore and his muscles were ripped from the bones. His bones then snapped and changed, forming the skeleton of his new shape, before sewing themselves back together. Tissue, muscle and skin adjusted and rearranged atop the new skeleton.

The first time he shifted, he thought he was dying. A thousand years later, he could control the pain with ease, even if he hated the bursts of agony and the twisting of his bones, skin, and insides that occurred when he changed shapes.

The process lasted mere seconds, and he unfolded his long wings on either side of his body. The translucent wings glittered dark teal in the moonlight, the same color as his thick scales and the fur edging them.

His senses were far more sensitive in his dragon form, and he breathed deeply and sneezed fire. The stream of yellow barely missed the bar. The scents from within were overpowering, and he shook his head then leapt effortlessly towards the sky. His wings caught him easily and propelled him upward.

He imagined the distance between him and the stars growing shorter as he soared upward, and he beat his wings hard, wondering if tonight was the night he got close enough to capture one.

Amused by his thoughts, he dipped his wings, caught an air current, and began playing, alternately floating in place and weaving in and out of the current, always intrigued by the challenge of how it tugged or pushed at his wings. He dove, wheeled and slammed on the brakes in midair, plummeting towards the earth only to unfurl the long wings and catch himself a couple feet from the ground.

Chace loved the sensation of the air ruffling his fur and tickling him, the cool air of evening filling his lungs. He loved the *freedom* of being a dragon most, the ability to take to the heavens whenever he felt the urge. He found peace in the skies, looking down at the miniaturized buildings, vehicles and cars. It gave him perspective, reminded him that his biggest concerns always looked tiny from far above.

Content with his short flight, he circled the bar lazily, slowly descending from the sky. The choice he'd made and the deal he'd bartered for with Mr. Nothing was done. The mysterious Mr. Nothing gave him time to think it over once last time, but Chace already knew his decision.

He was tired of seeing everyone he cared about die. He wanted to be human again, and nothing anyone said was going to convince him otherwise.

# Chapter Two

From the parking lot, Skylar watched the magnificent dragon circle and land somewhere behind the bar. Its size was stunning, and she convinced herself it was like the moon: it always looked bigger on the horizon, but it was just a matter of perspective.

Otherwise, she wasn't certain she wanted anything to do with the massive creature she was there to cage and deliver to the center where shifters were rehabilitated and integrated into society. It was too dark for her to tell its color with any certainty, but she guessed blue. Its wingspan was close to sixty feet, unless her eyes were tricking her, and its body the size of an SUV from the distance.

A flicker of recognition went through her, an unexpected sense of familiarity with the dragon. It was like a tiny flame lighting in her blood. Did the other slayers experience this when they found the shifters they were tracking?

Skylar approached the biker bar, not enthused about walking into a seedy, filthy, scary place she didn't want to be to confront a creature much bigger than she was. It was close to midnight, and the bar was hopping. Classic rock and smoke rolled out of the door, propped open to let in the cool night air.

"Looks like he's here," she whispered under her breath. The sensitive microphone she wore disguised in the choker at her neck was sure to pick up her voice. She scratched the back of her neck absently. It was the spot that grew itchy whenever a shifter was nearby.

"This guy has been a bitch to track, but I think we finally got him," replied the voice of Dillon via the small bud in her ear. Dillon's tone was always clipped and irritated, a reminder that he was more than a coworker – he was also her ex-boyfriend.

"You mean *I* finally got him," she replied.

A dragon slayer, Skylar was tracking one of the most elusive shifters they'd ever met. It meant he was old. Experienced. Not likely to go down easy, which was why she had a team of two more shifter slayers waiting in the parking lot. The three of them could handle anything. She wore tight leather pants and a snug, soft t-shirt that clung to her body in all the right places. Her steel-toed boots would crack a skull and the slender, golden lasso in her pocket would tame even the strongest dragon.

If she got it over his head, of course. That's usually where slayers got into trouble, because it wasn't exactly easy to lasso someone discreetly, especially if they knew what was coming at them.

An image popped into her thoughts, one that made her pause.

*A dark-haired woman sat beside her at a table in a large kitchen. Morning sunlight filtered through the curtains of the window over the sink, and music played softly somewhere in the house.*

*The woman beside her was gorgeous with blue eyes and a smile that filled Skylar with warmth.*

*"We are the dragons' protectors," the woman said.*

*"They're so big, mama! How do I protect them?" Skylar heard herself respond. She was no more than six or seven at the time.*

*"You only have to protect one. You'll get your very own dragon."*

*"Woooooow. When?"*

*"When the time is right. You must learn how to guard them from*

*harm, first."*

*"I want to learn now!" Skylar leapt out of her seat. "I want my dragon! Where is he?"*

*"You'll know him when you meet him, Sky."*

"Yo, Sky. You're standing there like an idiot." Dillon sounded amused.

Skylar blinked, unable to understand the strange vision. The dreams were becoming more vivid, more like coherent memories and less like disjointed nightmares. It was too real to be a dream, but her mother had died before she turned a year old. And what was this business about protecting dragons? She was a *slayer!*

"Sorry. Just uh … whatever," she said, embarrassed. It wasn't the first strange memory she'd experienced. The woman – her mother? – had been in her dreams for three days straight.

Forcing herself to refocus, Skylar wove carefully through the row of motorcycles lining the parking lot in front of the bar. Located off the highway, the bar was convenient for those travelling, but a potential nightmare if something went wrong. The nearest town was twenty minutes down the highway, which meant if she got shredded by dragon talons, she'd be dead before she made it to a hospital.

*Assuming the dragon is satisfied with just shredding me,* she added silently. Skilled and lethal, she knew the difference between life and death was often discipline and instinct. She'd been trained how to try to calm down a dragon, but sometimes, there was just no reasoning with a furious fire breather.

"Bring him in. If you can't – "

" – slay him," she finished. It was the dragon slayer's motto, one of the few traditions that survived the thousands of years of the cat and mouse games the shifters and their slayers had been playing. "Although technically, no one has had to kill a shifter in like, a hundred years. Wish me luck."

"I wish you skill," Dillon replied, amused. "If any of us had luck, we wouldn't be doing this shit. Keep him calm and talking so he can't shift."

"Amen, brother," she muttered. "Going in."

With a deep breath, Skylar stepped into the smoky, hot bar. She looked over the people quickly enough to get a feel for where he might be but not long enough to draw attention. Rough riders were squeezed around tables, hovered over pool tables and stationed at the bar. The music was louder than their combined voices. While most of the tables were full, it wasn't as crowded as she expected from the number of bikes out front. There was room to maneuver if she had to fight.

Her instincts – the same that led them to this bar after years of searching – tugged her in one direction, towards a relatively quiet corner. She didn't let her gaze linger longer than to discern that there were four men at the table. Walking to the bar, Skylar tried to engage her senses, the ones inherited by the dragon slayers in her family, to sense which exactly he was.

"I'm standing right here and I still can't pick him up consistently," she said, ducking her head to keep those around her from noticing she was talking. "I'm getting all kinds of weird vibes, though."

"We got a partial description. Blond-ish brown hair."

"Hopefully he's the only blondish-brown haired guy here." She leaned against the counter as the bartender approached. "Guinness."

"Pint or half-pint?" He looked her over skeptically.

"Pint. I can hang," she said and winked.

"If you say so."

She watched him tilt the glass and pour then place the beer on the counter, where it'd sit for five minutes until the air bubbles had settled near the top. Skylar watched the room behind her through the mirror lining the back of the bar area, her eyes straying from the rows of high end liquor to the reflection of the men in the far corner where she felt the slightest tingling of intuition.

"Narrowed it down," she said into the microphone. "I think."

"Alone?"

"With friends."

"He know you're there?"

"Shit, Dillon," she returned. "I'm not even certain which one he is. But no, don't think any of them have looked my way." *Unlike the furry grizzly bear at the table beside them.*

The dark-haired man was more beard than face and staring straight at her.

"Here ya go," the bartender put the drink on the bar before her.

She handed him a ten and took a sip, enjoying the rich flavor for a moment before turning to face the room. With her back against the counter, she noticed for the first time that the bar wasn't scary like she first thought. The clientele looked rough, but the bar itself was well cared for.

Rather than take comfort in the contradiction of a nice biker bar, it made her uneasy.

*Just one more sign this dragon is just … weird.*

The latest to try to track the elusive bigfoot of the dragon world, she and her team had pooled their resources for a chance at doing what no one else in the past thousand years had been able to: capture the mythical Teal Dragon, named for the color of wings he was thought to possess. At a thousand years old, he was probably the largest dragon ever to exist as well.

Which meant his talons would be the size of her hand at least.

She sipped her beer, eyes settling on the corner where she could almost sense someone.

*Just my luck. Three of them have blond hair.*

"You, um, got any more info on what he looks like?" she whispered between sips.

"Tall."

"Never mind. I'll figure it out."

"Maybe if you get close enough, you'll be able to sense him."

"Or get my head bitten off."

"Either way, right?"

The only female among the three, she was the natural choice for flushing a male dragon shifter out of a bar. There were moments when she didn't think Dillon was involved for the sake of helping the team bring in the elusive dragon but for bringing in the Teal Dragon on his own. Which meant he wouldn't mourn her, if she did get her head taken off in the process, especially after how hard she dumped him a month before.

"I am the only dragon slayer here," she reminded him. "You wouldn't get near him if my head gets taken off."

"I'll take my chances," came the arch response.

She rolled her eyes.

Skylar debated for a moment then decided to take the long route to the restrooms at the back of the bar. She pulled out her phone and pretended to be texting, tilting the glass of beer at an angle where it'd slosh over the rim if she bumped someone. Or tripped. Whichever she decided to do to get to her target.

Her concern grew as she approached the four in the corner. To make it appear that she was walking a natural route, she'd have to veer before reaching their table, but she couldn't yet tell which was the one she needed to spill beer on.

If anything, *all* of them were radiating some small source of shifter magic, old enough to be too faint to identify whose was whose, yet present nonetheless. Like a small burst of scent from an air freshener if she stood in just the right place to smell it.

"You're new here."

The dark-haired man who had been staring at her interrupted her attempt to concentrate.

"Just passing through," she replied.

"You alone?"

"Look, I'm not interested okay?" she snapped, facing him. "So, just … back …off."

The man had gotten out of his chair at her words and stood close to seven feet tall. He was huge, the bulges of his biceps like small bags of potatoes and the unfriendly glint in his dark eyes borderline animalistic.

Skylar looked up, startled by his size. It took her a moment to realize that he, too, was radiating the subtle magic of a shifter.

*Five of them? What the hell is this place?*

The mountain of a man snatched her phone first then the choker at her neck, crushing them in hands as big as her head. He grabbed her arm and yanked her close, flipping the earpiece out of her ear. His grip on her arm hurt, and she sensed now was not the time for heroics. He was glowering and angry. It was the time for talking her way out of here.

"Um, you spilled my beer," she managed in a light tone, testing his viselike grip on her arm.

"You know what I do to scum of the earth like you?" he snarled.

"Down, boy. We're expecting her." The low, sexy growl of the newcomer behind her was accompanied by an arm sliding around her waist and the warmth of a hard, male form at her back.

She elbowed him back instinctively.

"Trust me. I'm the lesser of two evils." His whisper tickled her ear and sent shivers down her spine.

Caught between him and the angry mountain of a man, Skylar decided to take her chances with the man she couldn't see. She nodded once.

He pulled her into his strong body, the grip around her firm and possessive. He wrapped his other arm around her shoulders, drawing her fully against him. The top of her head rested just below his chin, and she could judge his impressive width and size by the body pressed against her. Her shoulders fit inside his perfectly, and she glanced down to see the roped forearms of the arms around her.

The angry man who was more beard than human released her slowly, eyeing the stranger holding her.

"We don't welcome her kind here," he said.

"She was invited." As he spoke, the man behind her eased back a step, maneuvering her body with him.

Skylar tried not to let her confusion show as the angry man studied her once more. Finally, he stepped away and resumed his seat, albeit unhappily, as if he was looking forward to eating her this night.

"You know you're in trouble, right?" the man behind her asked without releasing her.

"I, um, thought we could … talk," she said, heart racing from more than fear. How did he know who she was? What did he plan on doing with her, now that she had no chance of calling for backup and was wrapped in his thick arms?

"You were supposed to bring it with you. It better be in your pocket."

Skylar racked her brain, unable to understand what he was talking about.

"Sure," she said slowly. "It totally is."

"Good."

"Can you let me go?" She made an attempt to move away but was held in place. She was incapacitated and couldn't reach the lasso, let alone the emergency beacon in her shoe.

*Is he even the right guy?* Her senses told her nothing.

"When you tell me where it is."

"Or …" she started, thoughts racing. "We could just talk this out."

"Problem, Chace?" the mountain of a man asked, eyeing her.

"Not sure. Do we have a problem?" Chace asked her casually.

*Shit.* Skylar tested his grip again. It was unyielding.

"Maybe …" she pushed at one arm unsuccessfully "… we can just … work things out …"

The huge man rose again. She froze then twisted in Chace's grip. He loosened it enough for her to turn then tightened it instantly when she faced him, trapping her against his body.

For a moment, Skylar didn't speak, not expecting to find the man who held her to be quite so stunning. Chiseled jaw and cheekbones, large, intelligent eyes the color of the ocean's depths, perfect, full lips, long dishwater blond hair held loosely in a band at the base of his neck … he resembled a Viking god, at once too perfect to be real and yet, she was too aware of being pressed against the length of his hot, strong body.

*Thirty three percent chance I got the right blond guy.*

"… in private," she finished, eyes drawn to his sculpted lips. Unsettled, she was nonetheless certain she stood a better chance with him alone than with the huge man waiting for a chance to crush her head the way he did her phone. It was hard not to be aware of the body pressed to hers or the fact that one hand was resting just below the small of her back, an erotic pressure point.

Chace was studying her closely, and she held her breath, hoping that whoever he thought she was, it wasn't bad enough to turn her over to the angry shifter behind her.

"Just us," she added, lowering her voice for his ears only. "I'll make it worth your time." Unable to free her hands to touch his face, she stood up on her tiptoes instead, touching her lips to his.

Strange fire shot through her, stirring her blood and making her shudder. More images from her dream popped into her mind, distracting her momentarily, despite her desire.

"You okay?" Chace asked.

His attention was on her, and he held her gaze, the dark blue depths of his eyes unwavering. For a moment, she thought she'd pissed him off worse. He was hard to read, though he'd gone still when she kissed him.

"Yeah," she said breathlessly.

His eyes dropped to her lips, and he lowered his head, kissing her. The light pressure of his lips lingered longer than her peck, and instinctively, she responded to him. His lips were warm and soft, and she didn't recall a boyfriend whose kiss she'd experienced in such detail. A kiss was a kiss.

From Chace, though, it was something more – a spark of chemistry she wasn't expecting. She found herself leaning into him at the combination of his hard body, the arms wrapped around her, and the gentle yet insistent pressure of his lips.

He withdrew long before she was ready, and raised his head.

"Okay. You win. We'll do this in private," he said, the timbre of his voice lowered after the kiss. "But if you think I'm giving you a chance to run ..."

"I won't," she replied, recovering her senses. "Scout's honor."

"Girl scouts don't come to biker bars." Without awaiting her response, he released her and stooped, tossing her over one shoulder.

"Is this ... necessary?" she grunted, face red from the rush of blood to her head but also from the knowledge her ass was stuck in the air.

"Later," he said to the three at the table, who wore smirks in various stages of amusement.

*Never coming back here, even if everyone in this bar is a shifter!*

She still didn't know if Chace was the one she sought. Frustrated and uncomfortably turned on after the brief kiss, Skylar hung over his shoulder like a laundry bag and waited, trying to keep track of where they went.

It wasn't far – through a door into the cool night and into a small building behind the bar, one she hadn't noticed when they surveyed the bar area earlier in the day. He locked the door upon entering then set her down without completely releasing her.

Chace steadied her then left one hand on her hip, keeping her close to him.

Skylar glanced around, surprised to see the comfortable, one-bedroom cabin. A small wood stove was in one corner, a kitchenette in another, and a king size bed taking up the space opposite the cozy living room area. The cabin was neat and pleasant, the wooden floors covered with thick, colorful rugs and the walls bare.

*This place wasn't here when we were doing surveillance earlier.* How did a cabin just magically appear out of thin air?

"You wanted to talk. Talk." His words drew her focus back to her danger.

Skylar tried to brush his hands off her. He responded by closing the distance between them, one arm going around her to draw her into his body once more. Distracted by the feel of the handsome stranger, she drew a deep breath.

"Talk. Not touch," she said, pushing at him.

"You kissed me first." He pulled her back against him.

"I didn't really want my head crushed by gigantor in there," she said.

"Start talking."

Skylar gazed up at him, aware she had no idea what it was he wanted from her. How long would she need to stall him for the guys to come rescue her?

He leaned past her towards the door.

"No!" she exclaimed, shifting between him and the door. "Why talk when we can ..." her eyes went to his lips again. After only a moment's hesitation, she took his cheeks in her hands and kissed him again.

Chace froze, as if undecided.

Skylar nibbled on his lower lip then deepened the kiss, parting her lips in a silent invitation.

His arms both wrapped around her, and his hot tongue darted into her mouth. She dwelled on the taste of him, marveling at the feel of his plush lips and the heat of his velvety mouth.

What started out as a means of distracting him grew into something else, as desire bloomed within her, and fire raced through her body. Skylar wrapped her arms around his neck, surprised at how easy it was to lower her guard for this stranger. Being in his arms felt comfortable. Natural. Even when he'd held her in the bar, she hadn't felt threatened by his strength or the sexy purr he used to address her.

Chace pulled away. Like her, he was breathing hard.

"Are we gonna talk or ..." he trailed off then spread kisses down the side of her jaw.

*Any minute now, guys.* Skylar found herself starting not to care if Dillon showed up or not.

She pushed Chace's leather jacket off. Flinging off the coat, he kissed her again, this time more demanding, deep and hungry. The thought of being rescued began to melt away, and she slid her hands up his shirt, across the supple skin covering his hard chest and abs.

How long had it been since she felt such need for anyone?

Had she ever? It was melting her reasoning and the instincts that told her she came her to find the most elusive shifter in history. Now that they were alone, she sensed a trickle of magic from the man before her, not enough for her to figure out if he was the one she sought or not.

She found herself too infatuated with his scent, like honey and a bonfire, and the sensation of his soft skin beneath her hands.

He whipped off the shirt to reveal a body that had been molded to perfection, with a layer of honey-golden skin poured over taut muscle. From the wide shoulders, thick biceps and chiseled chest to the ridges of his abdomen and the lean width of his hips, he was built to excite and thrill.

Over his heart was the simple, black dragon tattoo. Stunned, she stiffened.

*What the hell do I do now?*

"Nice tat," she said. With morbid curiosity, she placed her hand over his heart to see if what the others said was true: that shifters didn't have hearts.

There was no heartbeat, but the flame she'd felt in the parking lot sparked even higher inside her. It was affected by the proximity of his magic, and she grew even more distracted by the unfolding of a new instinct, one that compelled her to him.

"We really gonna do this?" he whispered, warm hands sliding beneath her shirt. He paused when she hesitated, his cheek pressed against hers and their bodies supported by one another's.

Chace raised his head to meet her gaze. There was genuine warmth in his eyes, something she didn't expect to see from a one-night-stand or from a heartless shifter.

Her body was screaming yes, her instincts humming with burning insistence that left her baffled. She didn't just need his body. She needed *him* and to make him hers.

*He's my dragon.* The sense filled her with a strange peace, one that told her she was supposed to be here, now with this shifter. It also confused her, the impulse to wrangle him down and take him to the rehabilitation center strong but rapidly melting beneath the heat of his kisses and the idea he was somehow hers already.

*I can lasso him in the morning,* she decided, torn between the two warring instincts.

His touch made the newfound instinct stronger, even if her logical mind told her to walk back into the bar and wait for backup.

With Chace's wide hands on her abdomen and the thick ridge of his arousal against her lower belly, she found herself unusually intrigued in him and not at all interested in waiting for her team.

"Yeah," she replied. "You're right. I'm no girl scout."

"Thank god." His hands skimmed up her body.

She laughed, raising her arms as he lifted her shirt off.

# Chapter Three

He unsnapped her bra next, his hands roaming her body as if to memorize every contour. He cupped her breasts in his palms and flicked his thumbs across her nipples, sending tiny sensations of pleasure through her. Skylar let her hands explore his body, unable to understand why this moment seemed more real to her than any other moment with her former lovers. She couldn't breathe in enough of his scent and marveled at the tight skin covering thick muscles that were firm beneath her touch. He was so strong and so gentle, a combination that awed her.

She shivered while he played with her breasts and leaned into him, relishing the smoked honey scent of his skin.

He started a trail of hot kisses down her neck and collarbone, paused to suckle her breasts until she groaned, then continued downward, his hands resting on her abdomen. He slid her pants down, over her hips and thighs then carefully worked each foot free until she stood naked.

She closed her eyes, absorbed in the moment, enthralled by the heat of his wide palms and how delicate he made her feel, just by touching her.

"I want to taste you." His voice was thick with need, his hands roaming her legs.

"I won't talk you out of it," she replied with a small laugh.

Steadying her with one hand, he lifted one leg over his shoulder and gripped her ass. He shifted closer until his nose tickled the sensitive skin of one inner thigh. His tongue flickered into her, lighting at first, and then more quickly, tasting her.

Skylar wound her fingers through his long hair, her breath quickening at the sensation of his mouth. His tongue left her core and traveled between her nether lips before he paused to flick the aching clit.

Skylar groaned at the flutters of pleasure, willing him to linger.

He did for a moment, sucking and circling the swollen button before he planted kisses on her lower belly. He stood, kissing his way up her body. Her leg fell away from his shoulder, and she waited impatiently for him to finish his journey and for his mouth to find hers again.

When it did, she wrapped her arms around him, kissing him with hunger that demanded satisfaction. The feel of his bare chest against hers drove her wilder, made her want him more, to explore his body until she was certain she had tasted every inch of him.

Skylar rubbed his erection through his jeans then unsnapped his pants and pushed them down. She let him work his own feet free, more interested in taking his large dick into her hands. Touching him gently, she slid her mouth over the soft, bulbous head and then down over the shaft as far as she could. He pulsed in her mouth, growing harder, longer. She squeezed him hard between her lips.

"Thank god you have no gag reflex," Chace said somewhat breathlessly. "You know how rare that is nowadays?"

It was a struggle not to laugh until she'd freed his erection from her mouth. Skylar chuckled and stood, leaving one hand between them to stroke him while she renewed their intense kissing.

Chace maneuvered into a wall, pressing her against it. She released his dick and wrapped her arms around his neck once more, enjoying his body pressed fully against hers.

His mouth left hers, nipping and licking his way down her jawline and side of her neck while one of his hands slid between their bodies and into her core.

She wriggled against him suggestively, and he nipped her earlobe in response.

"You ready?" he whispered.

"Oh, yeah," she replied.

"I've always wanted to do it standing up. You game?"

She laughed. "Sure!"

His hands slid to her hips, and he turned her to face the wall and pressed her against it once more. At the feel of his hard dick against her ass, she spread her legs instinctively, needing him inside her.

One of Chace's arms went around her torso to steady her. He dipped the fingers on his other hand inside her once more before they were replaced at the opening of her core by his erection.

Skylar pressed her backside to him to hurry him, and he chuckled, kissing her neck and down her shoulder. He made his way back and kissed the back of her neck.

His bite there was much harder than she expected, and her breath caught.

Skylar's eyes opened enough for her to see the hand he had pressed to the wall beside her head had black fingernails that had lengthened, resembling small talons.

"Chace …" she murmured, unsettled by the display and the pain in her neck.

Any concern she felt disappeared when he entered her, and she gasped at the friction and sensation.

"Yeah?" he asked in response. The hand on the wall went back to her body, the nails tracing down her side in a strange mix of pleasure and pain that baffled her. It paused when it reached her lower abdomen to brace her for his movements.

He moved in and out her, a slow rhythm that erased any conscious thought she had about sleeping with a shifter. The pain in her neck faded and disappeared, and she settled her hands against the wall.

Chace's hand slid lower. A flutter of alarm went through her at the thought of his long nails in her most sensitive region. But his touch was light, the nails eliciting exquisite bursts of pleasure-pain before he slid a finger against her clit and held it, letting the movement of their bodies guide where it went.

"Chace," she complained. "I need to touch you, too."

He withdrew at her words and spun her, claiming her mouth and lifting her onto his hips. With his hands on her ass, he lowered her onto his erection once more, and she wrapped her arms and legs around him. She ground against him, wanting to mold their bodies together as close as possible so she could feel him from the inside out.

He pressed her to the wall once more, bracing his hands on either side of her and moving in and out of her faster this time, the intensity of his kisses making the world slide away, until all she knew was his body and hers.

He gripped her bottom again and moved them away from the wall towards the bed and dropped with her into it, his body covering hers and hips working fast. The full length of him pressed against her was almost her undoing, and she kissed him with the desperation and yearning that coursed through her system. A hot new sensation was forming at the base of her belly, one that promised to be explosive once released.

"God you feel so real," he murmured, burying his head in the nape of her neck.

"I *am* real," she said with a husky laugh.

"I know. I mean ..." he drifted off.

She wanted to tell him she felt the same, except her body was growing taut, her ability to speak and reason gone. She communicated with her body instead and arched beneath him, clinging to him in an effort to keep their bodies together.

"Ahh, yeah. You're getting even tighter," he whispered against her ear. "I want to hear my name when you come."

Her eyes closed. He pressed her to the bed while her body

strained against his. For a moment, Skylar had the sense that time stood still. Her body was too tense for her to breathe, and she was drowning in the smoky-honey scent and flavor of his skin.

The tense moment cracked, and her body bucked.

"Chace!" she cried hoarsely before sharp pulses of pleasure rolled through her like the waves of a hurricane pounding the shore.

Soon breathless, she relished the feel of him quickening his pace, his breathing fast and his kisses harder. He relinquished her mouth, and she was able to see his eyes and the flames burning where his pupils should've been.

*I shouldn't be sleeping with a shifter.* The instinct caught no traction, and she traced her nails down his back then gripped his hard ass.

"You like doggy style?" she asked with a wicked grin.

One minute she was on her back, the next, he'd flipped her onto her belly. She gave a breathless laugh, her body still shuddering from the intensity of her orgasm. His hands were all over her.

Skylar shifted onto her knees then hugged one of his pillows to balance herself and lifted her ass in the air.

"I don't even know you and I love you!" Chace breathed. "Sorry, hon, this is gonna be quick and rough."

His words sent a thrill through her. He gripped her hips then penetrated her fast, pushing himself fully into her with a groan before he eased out and began to thrust. The new position sent tremors of intense pleasure through her, nearly driving her again to climax.

He leaned over her, his thrusts steady. One of his hands rested against the headboard while the other slid down her stomach and to her clit.

"Think you got one more in ya this round," he whispered.

Skylar shivered, not yet recovered from her first orgasm. He touched her gently despite the mini-talons, the flick of his nail against her clit making her gasp. The meat of his finger replaced it, but he continued alternating between the two, the distinct pleasure of his nail and the hard pressure of his finger sending her barreling again towards ecstasy.

Her body shook at the combination of his touch and the friction of his quick, deep thrusts. Skylar buried her face in the pillow as her body grew taut once more, her need to be sated overwhelming everything else.

He began to pump harder, faster, ratcheting up the intensity of the sensations shooting through her.

This climax was hard, slamming into her with such force that tunnel vision formed. She cried out again, a sound that didn't sound human to her ears, but which was soon drowned out by the sound of Chace's release.

Unable to support herself, she collapsed, her body trembling and bucking from the orgasm. Chace's body went with her, and he lay on top of her, panting hard, with his dick still clenched tightly in her seizing sheathe.

She struggled to catch her breath and not pass out, overwhelmed by the senses that were intoxicated by him and the intensity of her climax.

Chace pushed her hair from the side of her face and kissed her tenderly. His hands ran down her sides.

"I think we need to do that … again," he breathed. "And again and again."

Her laugh was more of a gasp as she tried to catch her breath.

"We can see how many times you come tonight," he offered. "Make a game of it."

She twisted beneath him. He lifted himself enough to give her room to turn over then lowered his body back on top of hers. She took his face in her hands, admiring the masculine planes and shadowed dips of his chiseled features. He rested his forearms near her head and ran his fingers through her hair.

Had she ever met anyone this stunning let alone dreamt she'd sleep with someone who looked like him?

Skylar gazed up into the dark blue depths of his eyes, unable to recall a time when she'd felt more comfortable and at peace with someone else. His erection was pressed to one thigh, already growing hard again while her body calmed from the double-climaxes.

"You're gorgeous," he said, almost absently. "Your eyes are like the sky, and you taste like Christmas."

"I don't know what that means," she laughed, tracing her thumb over his soft, sculpted lips. "You're very sweet for someone I think can get any girl he wants."

"Yeah," he agreed. "You feel different. I don't know why."

"It's the extra ten pounds I put on last year."

He laughed, the flames at his pupils dancing. She stared into them, mesmerized by them the same way she was by a normal fire. He nuzzled his cheek to hers, and she closed her eyes, listening to him breath. She draped her arms around him loosely, the thrill of his skin and hers preventing her blood from settling completely.

"Round two?" he whispered, tracing a nail down the side of her face.

The black talons were longer, but this time, she regarded them with intrigue and anticipation.

Her body responded with a surge of hot desire.

"Oh, hell, yeah," she murmured.

# Chapter Four

E arly the next morning, Chace sat on the edge of his bed, wearing his jeans and nothing else. He glanced at the woman sleeping soundly beside him. He never expected to feel satisfied, rested and fully sated for once, maybe even for the first time in a thousand years, since he fell under the worst curse in the universe.

She was sprawled out on her belly, body covered by a sheet as she slumbered like someone who had been kept up for hours making love. With long, curly, auburn hair and amazing blue eyes, she'd snagged his attention the moment she walked into the shifters' bar, clearly out of place but unafraid. Her skin was touched with olive coloring, her body a few inches below six feet and toned with rounded hips, a tight ass and shapely legs. Even now, he found himself wanting to push the sheet down so he could feel the soft skin of her round ass and slide his fingers into her hot core again.

His only deterrent: he had no idea who she was.

The woman he was expecting and the woman who showed up weren't the same, which meant he was going to be late for the appointment he was supposed to be at.

His eyes strayed to the contents in his hands, the two belongings she'd carried with her that he'd dug out of her pockets. He was expecting to find a familiar appointment card. Mr. Nothing always sent beautiful *human* women like this one to the bar to deliver the cards with locations and times of where they were going to meet. It was a dead giveaway that she was there with a message, and to leave her alone.

There was no card. No identification, nothing to tell him who this chick was or why she just happened to wander into a shifters' bar. The way she surveyed the room was too purposeful for her to be there for a drink, and she'd been wired. She'd clearly been looking for someone, though who, he wasn't sure. He'd drawn the short end of the straw to rescue her from Max, the huge, bearded shifter who acted as the guard dog for the shifter bar. A bouncer with a temper, he usually snapped people's heads off rather than tossing them to the curb.

After a night of fantastic sex, Chace was glad he had rescued her, until this morning.

*Figures the first girl I meet who makes me feel human again is probably here to make me disappear, like the rest of the shifters.*

The silky, woven gold cord in her pocket was one of the two belongings. He had no idea what it was, except he wished he'd found it in time to tie her up last night. Setting it aside, he focused on the small, round GPS tracker. It was flat enough not to make a bulge in her pocket, but he knew it on sight. He'd found one in the saddlebag of his bike last week.

Whoever placed it there, placed *her* at the bar last night, too.

There was a light tap at his door.

Chace rose, dissatisfied with finding no answers to the questions he had about the girl and why she was in his bar. He pulled on his heavy boots and crushed the tracking bug beneath a heel before going to the door and opening it.

"Long night?" Gunner, asked. The panther shifter with golden skin was dressed as if for a ride, his dark hair captured beneath a do-rag. He was clad in a faded, worn t-shirt that outlined his muscular upper body and featured the gang's logo – the dragon tattoo that was over Chace's heart.

"Yeah," Chace said with a distracted half-smile.

"Mr. Nothing give you a date?"

"No idea. Wrong girl."

Gunner frowned.

"She's got no ID or wallet, no birthmarks or tattoos, nothing," Chace mused. "Guess we're pulling up stakes and moving again."

"Maybe Max is right. Maybe we should stay and fight it out. Whoever these people are, they're persistent," Gunner said.

"It's not our way. Our shifters are dropping like flies. I know we're pacifists, but do you ever get tired of running?"

"Sometimes. Not enough to make a deal with Mr. Nothing."

"When you're a thousand years old, you'll think differently."

"I guess."

"I'll be out in a minute." Irritated with Gunner's reminder about how little they knew about Mr. Nothing, Chace returned to his cabin.

*You're destined to relive my heartache for the rest of your years.* It was the last words he'd heard from the jilted lover who put the curse on him a thousand years before.

He wished now he'd known to ask how many years that would be. He was devastated every time he let down his guard, and so he no longer did. His deal with Mr. Nothing was his business.

Chace forced himself to relax, aware he was tense enough to snap. He pulled on a t-shirt and his riding jacket, gaze lingering on the woman in his bed.

He really, *really* wanted to spend the day with her in bed. It was unusual to experience the depth of sensations he had with her last night. He'd been unable to do so since being turned immortal. While his senses were engaged with every woman he took to bed, he couldn't really connect with them the way he had this stranger.

*It's because she'll probably be the last.* This rationale made sense. He'd only been waiting for the appointment card to tell him where to meet the elusive creature offering him what he wanted most, when this girl arrived.

Chace considered her. What made him want to stay when every fiber in his being knew it was a mistake? Just that she might be the last woman he ever slept with, since Mr. Nothing was probably going to kill him?

He snatched his helmet and stormed out of the cabin, glancing upward at the bright morning sky as he went. There were only four bikes left in front of the quiet biker bar: his, Gunner's, Luke's and that of the other shifter that ran with them - Wyle. The other three were talking quietly, mounted up and waiting for him.

Chace lifted his chin in greeting but didn't speak, frustrated already with his day. He pulled on his helmet and buckled it, then gunned his bike to life.

And then he became aware of something else. He listened to the low growl of his chopper while testing his body.

His heart was beating. Racing, actually, and it made him almost ill. The sensation was one he hadn't experienced in a thousand years. He didn't remember it being so ... awful.

Had Mr. Nothing started to carry out their bargain, even though Chace missed their meeting?

Or was something ... wrong with him?

He barked a rough laugh at the ridiculous thought. Although unpleasant, his heart was supposed to beat. It was what the bodies of normal humans did. His magic was still present, though, which left him even more confused. Worse, he was having too vivid flashbacks of his night fucking the strange woman, memories that made him want to drop everything to crawl back into bed with her and wake her with kisses. His dick was already hard, his position atop the bike uncomfortable.

"Get a hold on yourself, Chace," he snapped quietly. *I gotta get out of here.*

Without waiting for the others, he roared away at top speed, not caring if he slammed into a wall or flipped the bike going over a rock.

It wasn't like he could die anyway and right now, he needed to get as far as he could from one certain woman.

# Chapter Five

*S*he was sitting in the backyard, under a huge maple tree whose leaves had turned dark purple with the changing seasons. She was about nine or ten in this dream. There was a Golden Retriever puppy in her lap with soft fur, a fat belly and a tongue that just wouldn't stop licking her arm. Skylar balanced him carefully, attention caught between the wriggling pup and her mother's daily lesson.

"To find a dragon, you listen to your intuition," her mother explained. "It will lead you to him."

"My intuition doesn't say anything," Skylar complained.

"It will when the time is right."

"Mama, is it true dragons don't have hearts?"

"Yes and no." Her mother fell quiet.

Skylar looked up from the puppy and waited.

"Dragons have a heart, but it's not alive. It only starts to beat like yours and mine, when he finds his other half."

"That's pretty. How does he find it?"

"You bring it to him." Her mother smiled. "And then he's yours to protect."

"Then I'll have my own dragon," Skylar said in awe.

Something thunked to the ground, yanking her out of the dream. Skylar stretched leisurely, comfortable in the satiny, warm sheets that smelled of smoky honey. The woodsy, sweet scent was addictive.

*I need air freshener like that.*

The errant thought jarred her, and she lifted her head, recalling she wasn't at home in her own bed. Sitting up, she looked around for some sign of the stranger named Chace. She was alone in the peaceful, quiet cabin, well rested but too content to want to move much after the explosive night with the shifter. Her inner thighs were too sore for her to keep her legs together and her lower abs aching.

The dream lingered, the odd conversation with a woman she'd never known staying with her the way the others had recently.

A box from the far wall had been what woke her when it fell to the ground. Her attention shifted to the foot of the bed, where her clothing was neatly folded. The golden lasso and crushed tracker rested on top of her panties.

"Dammit," she murmured and sighed.

The man she hadn't been able to sense, who made love to her with the tenderness of someone who had a heart, ended up being the shifter she sought. Did he know who she was, and that's why he decided to seduce her?

If he hadn't last night, he did now. Why did he leave the lasso? As a taunt? A reminder that he beat her at her game? Was this how he managed to outwit every dragon slayer for a thousand years?

Skylar tossed off the sheet and rose, getting dressed with jerky movements. Not only had she had the opportunity to lasso him, but she'd had hours to do it. Right now, she didn't know why she hadn't, except being around him made her feel ...

... *like he belongs to me.*

Shoving the lasso in her pocket, she left the cabin.

It was a warm midmorning in southern Arizona with clear skies. The steady thrum of vehicles on the nearby highway greeted her, but it was what she didn't see that made her stop in place.

The bar was gone. No sign of it was left. No parking lot, bikes, or building. Nothing. The only vehicle in the area was a familiar Ford Explorer with two men leaning against it.

They both started forward at a jog when she stepped out of the cabin, and she walked to meet them, quickly creating some feasible story as to how she spent the night with the shifter they were after and still managed to let him get away.

"You look like shit," Dillon said, slowing when he drew near. His light eyes took her in critically. "We assumed someone crushed the ear bud."

"Wow. So he knew you were there and knocked you out or something?" the other man, Mason, asked. He frowned in concern, dark eyes on her.

The two slayers were fit and lean, dressed in heavy boots and clothing like hers, stylish but practical enough for them to fight in. Mason's skin was as dark as his shades while Dillon was the opposite – too pale to stay out long in the harsh southwestern sun.

"Um, yeah," she said at their expectant looks. "Guys, there was something really weird about that bar." She rubbed her face and glanced at the mascara on her fingers. *No wonder they think I look like shit.* She was almost relieved she didn't have to own up to sleeping with her target, especially to Dillon.

"First, where were you? We searched this whole area twice this morning," Mason demanded.

"In the cabin behind where the bar was," she replied, twisting. She fell into stunned silence.

There was nothing behind her. Her footsteps started suddenly in the dirt a few feet behind her, as if she'd dropped out of thin air into that very spot.

"I swear there was a cabin there!" she exclaimed.

"This is how he's evaded slayers for a thousand years," Dillon said in a hushed tone. "He's able to bend his magic."

"There's no cabin, right?" Skylar voiced. "I'm not going crazy?"

"No, you're not," Mason assured her. "The bar disappeared this morning. We never saw a cabin."

"Tell us exactly what happened," Dillon directed her.

She was staring into the space where she'd spent the night with a shifter.

Had she imagined it all? Was she really knocked out and dreaming?

A subtle shift in the wind tossed her hair in her face, and she smelled his smoky honey again.

*God he smells so good.* Skylar drew a deep breath of the scent, reassured that she wasn't crazy or dreaming about spending the night with a nonexistent man in a building that disappeared.

"First," she started. "There was more than one shifter at the bar. That place reeked of them. Almost got my head taken off by this huge one with a black beard. He crushed my phone in his hand. Like *crushed* it." She held out her hand and squeezed it into a fist to emphasize her point. "There were these four guys at a table nearby. Three blonds, Dillon, no thanks to you for the help."

"We're going off fourth hand information here. It's not like I know who he is," Dillon retorted.

*But I do. Intimately.* Skylar shook the memories away. "One of them grabbed me while I was trying to figure out what to do with the big guy. And that's it. Woke up in a cabin that doesn't exist."

"You're so damn lucky," Mason said with a shake of his head.

"That's it?" Dillon crossed his arms, studying her closely. "Some guy grabs you and … boom. Done."

"Not some guy, Dillon," she continued smoothly, aware of her ex-boyfriend still felt jilted about being dumped. "A shifter. I couldn't move let alone grab the lasso."

"I still can't believe that place was crawling with shifters," Mason mused, focus on the spot where the bar had been. "We had no idea they congregated like that. All our training says they're solitary creatures."

"I'm telling you. This place was filled with them," she insisted. "Maybe they managed to find a magic refuge or something."

"Or it's all that's left of the shifters, and they banded together for safety," Dillon said.

Skylar frowned, uncomfortable with the thought of the man she slept with just disappearing into the rehabilitation center – called The Field – like the rest of the shifters who were caught. Something more than his scent was staying with her. The memory of his warm gaze, perhaps, or the way his touch sent trickles of fire through her. Or the talons that scratched her with an erotic mix of teasing and pleasure, the bite at the back of her neck that made her feel as though his fire magic was racing through her.

She touched the back of her neck, where he'd bitten her. It itched. He didn't break the skin, and she debated why he'd started off with her facing a wall with her eyes closed, unless he was accustomed to women freaking out when they saw his talons start to form or the flare of fire in his eyes.

Why hadn't she been freaked out? Because of her training? If so, then why didn't she do what she was supposed to and bring him in?

She'd been nearly incapacitated by desire at that point, drowning in the sensations of his body and hers. If he morphed into a building-sized creature, she was too besotted to have cared. Was it purely physical attraction?

*We are the dragons' protectors,* the woman in her dream had told her. Maybe this was why she somehow chucked all the slayer training she'd ever received out the window?

"Earth to Skylar." Dillon snapped his fingers in front of her eyes. "You need some coffee?"

"Yeah," she managed, irritated to feel the desire in her belly and the moistness forming at her core. *Something about that shifter really got to me.*

"Now that we know we're looking for a bar that magically appears and disappears, we can find him again, right?" Mason asked, upbeat. "I mean, how many of those are there?"

"How do you suggest we search every highway exit in the country for one?" Dillon replied acidly. He started back towards the SUV.

Mason hung back with Skylar, unconcerned with Dillon's moods. Skylar captured her hair and tied a scrunchie around it, eyes going again to the spot where she'd last seen Chace.

"You like that opening I gave you not to admit you slept with him?" Mason teased warmly.

"What?" She faced him, surprised.

"Um, yeah. I'm not an idiot. I know Dillon is still convinced you'll change your mind about him. Thankfully, he's in denial or he'd notice that you're glowing like someone who spent eight hours getting fucked good and hard."

Her face grew warm. "If you say anything, Mason …"

"I won't." Mason smiled. "All night?"

"Insatiable," she replied. "Just … bam. Under his spell, sprawled out on the bed begging for it. I even saw his talons and was still just … what is wrong with me?"

"Nothing. I had a run in like that with a female shifter once," he admitted.

Walking towards the vehicle with him, she waited curiously to hear his story. Mason was quiet for a moment then shook his head.

"I get it. Best night of my life." He gave her a secretive smile. "That's all I'll say. There's a lesson there, though."

"Don't get that close?"

"Yeah. And …"

She held her breath, hoping he'd say something that made the dreams and weird events from the night before make sense.

"It made me see things differently," Mason said cryptically. "I've been doubting myself a lot lately. I hate it."

"Hurry up!" Dillon called curtly from the driver's seat. The SUV was rumbling softly and his window was down.

"Coffee first, Dillon," Mason replied cheerfully. "Then we figure out how to find a magic bar."

*And a certain dragon shifter who just rocked my world then threw it all in my face.* Skylar hopped into the back seat. The more she thought about it, the more foolish she felt. She'd fallen straight into the shifter's lap, and he'd had his way with her then walked away, probably giggling about how he pulled the wool over her eyes.

"Actually, can you take me home first? I need a shower," she told them, unable to escape the effects of the smoked honey scent on her skin. It was making her body fevered and her attention too scattered.

Mason was right. She knew better now. If she got a second chance at the shifter, she wouldn't fall under his spell again, no matter how sexy he was.

The other two talked strategies on the way to her apartment while she stared out the window, unable to get her thoughts straight after her night with Chace.

Everything felt … off today. Dream-like. Or maybe, like she was a stranger in her own world. She'd been uncomfortable since the strange dreams started, sensing she was missing something without understanding exactly what.

The night with Chace only seemed to make her instincts more restless, as if his magic did something to her.

Lost in her thoughts, she got out of the SUV without saying farewell to the guys and went to the stairwell leading to the third floor of the apartment building. She mechanically unlocked the door and walked in, pausing in her living room.

Everything was in its place. She wasn't a clean freak, but she at least kept things straightened up from stacking the books she kept on her kitchen table to the basket that held the four remote controls to the shoe rack by the doorway. The kitchen counters were free of excess appliances and the furniture of the living room neatly arranged in front of a wide screen television.

She went to the pictures on the walls, wanting to find one of her mother, whose face was clear in her dreams. Her consternation grew as she walked down the hallway lined with pictures. None of them were of her family or even of her before six years ago, when she turned thirteen.

The pictures were of her growing up as a teenager with most of them being more recent. Mason was in some and a few other slayers she met at the rehab center in several.

She'd seen the pictures every day she'd lived here. Why did they suddenly not seem … right?

"What did you do to me, Chace?" she grumbled and shook her head to clear her thoughts.

She crossed to her bedroom and glanced around.

*If I picked out the furniture, it'd be a sleigh bed in natural wood. None of this dark wood stuff.*

Skylar paused once more, startled by the thought. Hadn't she picked out her own furniture in the first place?

"Why does this feel like someone else's apartment?" she asked the dwelling.

It didn't answer, and she went to take a quick shower, no longer comfortable in her own home.

# Chapter Six

*Two weeks later*

Chace looked over the bar and its patrons. The classic rock blared like usual, but it did nothing to ease the tension in the faces of those within the only refuge for shifters left. Their numbers used to fill a space four times the size of this one. Now, there were half a dozen tables empty within the small bar, a sobering indication of how quickly they were dwindling.

He instinctively glanced towards the door whenever someone new walked into the bar. He wasn't sure why he expected to see *her* again, even knowing he'd moved the hangout spot across the country to try to prevent any of them being tracked.

The men and women in the bar were uneasy, adding to his sense of foreboding.

"They feel it," Gunner said from beside him, untouched beer in hand.

"Yeah," Chace agreed. "Our next move might need to be around the world."

Gunner's dark gaze flickered to him.

"One every two or three days is disappearing," said Luke, the burly, blond-haired phoenix shifter with a sharp eye and quick smile.

Chace sipped his beer, eyes going to Max, who was eyeballing everyone who entered the bar. The restless bear of a man was even less friendly than usual, and Chace assessed it'd take all four of them to pull him off any stranger that walked through that door.

Not that Chace wanted to pull him off any stranger.

His one-night-stand hadn't seemed like someone who could bring down a shifter. She hadn't been armed, and yet, she had to have been part of the crew that was tracking down the members of his shifter family. It scared him to know she'd walked right into their midst and weaseled behind his defenses. He hadn't taken a chance on sleeping with any woman since, and his temper was beginning to show it. Unlike Gunner, who was proudly chaste, Chace loved sleeping around.

The bartender caught his eye and waved him over.

"Be back," he said, standing. Chace wove through the crowd. As the unspoken leader of the shifters, he felt the gazes of everyone on him and knew they were secretly imploring him to tell them about their danger.

But he couldn't, because he didn't know. Besides, he never wanted to lead anyone. He wanted to be alone with his misery the rest of his life, however short he hoped it was.

"This was left for you earlier today by a blonde chick," the bartender said, handing him a familiar appointment card. "She said she had instructions that you weren't supposed to get it before ten o'clock."

Chace snatched it, relieved Mr. Nothing didn't bear a grudge for being stood up two weeks before. It was ten, and he frowned at the time marked on the card for their meeting.

*Ten minutes. Great.*

"Thanks," he said to the bartender.

He made his way back to his table but didn't sit, instead holding up the card his friends were bound to recognize.

"Mr. Nothing," he said. "I'll be back in a few."

"You want me to come?" Gunner asked, standing.

"No, I'm good."

Chace didn't wait for Gunner to reseat himself but turned away, striding out of the bar into the cool night.

This time, they were in the northeastern part of the country, near the coast. The scent of the ocean was thick in the cold wind blowing off the Atlantic. Chace breathed in deeply, enjoying the flavorful smell and chill in the air. The moon hung low in the dark sky, lighting up the parking lot of the bar.

He tucked his hands into his pockets and walked along the dirt road. They'd avoided their normal exits near the highways for the past two weeks, hoping to make it harder for their pursuers to track them. Five miles away was a sleepy coastal town, and the bar was between two farms.

He walked for about five minutes then stopped. The wheat in one field was silver in the moonlight, rippling in the ocean breeze, while the fields of the other farm were barren and smelled of freshly turned dirt.

The faint magic of a shifter reached him a moment before Mr. Nothing spoke.

"I see you got the message this time."

"I did," Chace replied, turning to face the mysterious shifter that had never been seen in his other form.

Tall, slender and lean, Mr. Nothing had dark hair and eyes and wore all black – a turtleneck and slacks.

"Your mind is set?" Mr. Nothing asked. "Nothing has altered your choice?"

"No," Chace said firmly.

"Once made, this choice can't be broken."

Chace said nothing at the reminder. His instincts – and his friends – were against what he chose to do. Tired of running, hiding and outliving everyone he cared about, he didn't see any other choice. Besides, he couldn't get over the idea that maybe he had been the one who drew those hunting down the shifters. As the oldest, he was the strongest, which meant his magic was probably a dead giveaway and pulling their hungers to them.

"I was ready two weeks ago," he answered.

Mr. Nothing was quiet for a moment.

"Release from the curse," Chace said once more. "For all that is mine." *You're definitely getting the short end of this stick.*

"As agreed."

"Let's do this."

A shadow snaked away from Mr. Nothing and pooled at Chace's feet before it began to swirl around him. He resisted the urge to shift and fly away, instead watching the shadow warily creep up his body. It didn't touch him, yet he felt the chill of its nearness, a reminder he didn't know what Mr. Nothing was or why he was so powerful.

The shadow swirled around him until it reached his chest then paused over the tattoo of a dragon over his heart before it continued upwards. The cold, dark fog crossed his eyes then floated into the sky, leaving his body completely.

"I don't feel any different," he said, testing himself mentally.

"You won't until the right time comes."

"What does that mean?"

"It means, Chace, that I will determine when to let you go."

Dread sank into Chace's stomach. "We have a deal."

"We do." Mr. Nothing approached. "But, in all fairness, I don't think you're thinking this through. You just gave me everything that is yours. You seem to think it only includes you and your possessions. What about the bar?"

"What about it?"

"The protection it offers comes from your magic. No you, no bar."

Chace's breath caught at the idea of turning the shifters out of the only refuge they had left.

"I'm one of you," Mr. Nothing said before he could speak. "I don't want to see our kind decimated, which is why I want you to do something before I honor our deal."

Cold trickled through him at the calm words. They weren't the request they sounded like.

"What if I refuse?" Chace snapped.

"I'll close the bar. Or worse, maybe I'll tip off those who are slowly bringing down the others one by one."

"You would do that to your own kind?"

"I would do that to get the most powerful shifter in existence to take action, like you should have years ago when the shifters began dwindling in number."

"I'm no hero. I just want this all to end."

"Then so be it. You just disappear and our kind ends up extinct."

Chace's jaw clenched. It was obvious that he cared enough for the others to offer them refuge. Mr. Nothing knew it was a pressure point. While he did care, he'd stopped short of helping anyone directly, not interested in violence or a cause when all he wanted was peace.

But he couldn't let Mr. Nothing take away the only safe place the shifters had.

"What do you want me to do?" he asked through clenched teeth.

"Simple. Stop those who are hurting our kind."

"I don't know who they are."

Mr. Nothing held out his hand, and a familiar object materialized. A small, fine rope of gold.

"You've already met them," he said.

"That little girl takes on shifters and makes them disappear?" Chace asked, amazed.

"That little girl is a shifter slayer. You have no idea how many of our kind she might've brought in. I want you to bring her to me then do whatever you want to the rest of the slayers."

He felt a stir of anger and something else, the inexplicable desire to deny his one nightstand was involved. Or maybe, to protect her from Mr. Nothing. But why? If she was what Mr. Nothing said she was, he should have no mercy whatsoever.

"So I do this and then I'm free?" Chace demanded.

"Yes." The image of the rope disappeared in a puff of golden smoke.

Chace's gaze lingered, sensing there was more and even angrier with himself for blindly taking some woman to bed without verifying who she was first.

*Gunner's right. No more sleeping around with random chicks.*

"You're a predator – act like it. Track her," Mr. Nothing added. "She'll lead you to the others who are taking down the shifters."

He made too much sense. Chace debated silently.

"You're not going to let me go, are you?" he asked finally.

"When I no longer have a use for you or you get in my way."

Chace felt a familiar tingle, the flare of fire down the back of his neck and the heat within his body that indicated he was getting ready to shift. While he was able to shift at will, he wasn't able to control the involuntary shifting that was often spurred by emotion. And right now, he was pissed.

"Find the girl, get her secrets, bring her to you," he said.

Mr. Nothing stepped back, sensing he was ready to morph into his secondary form.

With no control over the magic, Chace didn't know what size he'd end up. He'd been as small as a mosquito or as large as a warehouse, depending on what the magic wanted.

Unwilling to take the chance he went big and ruined his favorite jacket, Chace stripped off his clothes, overheating to the point of panting. He dropped on all fours and waited while the magic worked its way through his system. He transformed from human to dragon quickly. The twisting of his insides stopped, leaving him to figure out how big he was this time.

Chace shook his head. In his dragon form, he opened his eyes, his senses a hundred times more sensitive to the world than when he was in his human form. The ocean breeze ruffled the fur between his scales and lining his wings, tickling him to the point he sneezed fire.

"Intriguing." Mr. Nothing remained a few feet away.

By the way Mr. Nothing towered over him, Chace guessed he was the size of a bat this time. Unable to talk, Chace still understood when someone addressed him, though the bombardment to his senses often distracted him.

He leapt into the air and hovered in front of Mr. Nothing's face, using his dragon abilities to confirm that Mr. Nothing was a dragon in his other form.

Mr. Nothing smelled faintly of fire and something else, a familiar scent, like that of wet fur. Chace's infrared vision picked up nothing, not even a stray hair on the man's clothing, while also confirming that Mr. Nothing lacked the familiar pooling of heat around where his heart should've been.

*Why am I suddenly different?*

"Go. Fly. Then return to our kind and protect them," Mr. Nothing said, swatting at him.

Chace maneuvered around the quick movement with ease, his instincts engaged. He hovered a few feet above Mr. Nothing, trying once again to figure out more about the dark shifter. At last, he gave up, sensing Mr. Nothing expected to be scrutinized and somehow managed to hide who and what he really was.

With the ocean breeze ruffling his fur and the open night sky around him, Chace vaulted towards the stars, surrendering his human thoughts to the sensations of soaring, tumbling and floating in the cold night sky. When the magic released him, he'd think about Mr. Nothing's ultimatum. For now, he needed the release that only flying gave him.

As he flung himself into the air currents, he became aware of something else. He'd missed out on the chance of asking Mr. Nothing about his heart.

In his dragon form, he was even more cognizant of his beating heart. It no longer made him nauseous, but it was still freaking him out.

Chace balanced himself in the air, letting the currents hold him aloft as he double-checked his heart, unable to prevent his fascination with it. He *heard* his heart beating with his enhanced senses. He sensed that somehow, he was different now.

*What did Mr. Nothing do to me?*

# Chapter Seven

"Two and a half weeks, and we've got nada," Mason complained, pushing away the notebook on the table before him.

Seated with her two partners at a Starbucks, Skylar's gaze rested on the laptop and pile of paper alongside the venti sized cups of coffee they'd been nursing for an hour.

She automatically scratched the back of her neck, the same spot where the damn shifter had bitten her just over two weeks before. She began to wonder if dragons had some sort of rare bug that gave her a skin infection that wouldn't go away.

*Scale flu?* She scratched harder, annoyed. It was worse today than it had been since the first day she got it. She'd slept horribly in her apartment since that night, too, plagued by the weird sense that she didn't belong there. The dreams weren't helping either. Each one was more vivid than the last, shedding more light on a life she didn't recall.

"Would you stop?" Dillon snapped at her. "You're being paranoid."

"You know I get itchy when I feel someone watching me," she grumbled. *Or apparently, when I sleep with a dragon.* "Maybe I'm allergic to dragons?"

"Like you are to commitment?" Dillon returned.

She glared at him. His dark eyes didn't leave her, and she saw the latent anger burning deep within them.

"Oh, snap. Time for more coffee," Mason interjected before she could retort. "Dillon's turn to buy."

The tall dragon slayer shoved back from the table and rose silently, stalking to the counter.

"Thanks, Mason," she said, forcing herself to calm down. "What an asshole."

"You saw something in him to date him for four months."

She shrugged. "Hot body and I was bored."

"I'm hot and you ignore me," Mason pointed out. "You like 'em complicated."

"You are sexy," Skylar said and then laughed. She made a show of looking him over. Mason was athletic and friendly, attractive, with a quick wit that never failed to make her laugh. "Think I learned my lesson about dating coworkers though."

"Yeah. Never fuck a shifter and never date a coworker," he replied. "You'll regret both, but for different reasons."

She glanced at him, unable to read the meaning behind his measured tone. She'd begun to think that no one was going to match Chace in the bedroom and wondered if Mason felt the same after his night with a shifter. She was about to ask when Dillon returned with their drinks.

"Americano for the lady, mocha for the wuss and double espresso for me," he said, setting down the drinks one by one as he spoke. "Any breakthroughs while I was gone?"

"Not a one," Mason reported soberly. "We've got people looking for guys that meet the description Sky provided."

"I can't take it anymore," Skylar said, scratching the back of her neck until it hurt. "I'll be back." She rose and walked to the bathroom, automatically glancing through the windows to the busy sidewalks. It was midmorning in Chandler, a suburb of Phoenix, where they'd met after a few days of exhausted, wasted effort attempting to find the elusive shifter bar.

A man standing still among the people strolling the streets caught her attention. He was taller than those around him, with wide shoulders, piercing blue eyes and blond hair.

*Chace.*

A ripple of warmth went through her, though she wasn't certain if it was caused by the memory of their night together or the sense that warned her when a shifter was around.

Skylar backtracked. He was gone, a quick flash she wasn't certain she'd seen. She lingered for a moment, searching the streets outside with her gaze. It wasn't possible for him to disappear so quickly and there was nowhere to hide.

The itching was back.

Chalking it up to two solid weeks of nothing but trying to track the elusive dragon, she continued to the bathroom. Skylar locked the door behind her then crossed to the mirror. She lifted the low ponytail she sported this day to see the spot that was driving her crazy.

"What the hell?" She stared. Beneath the red scratch marks was a streak of black. "If that bastard gave me some sort of plague …"

Leaning forward, she hesitated then picked at the black. It was raised but didn't scrape off under her nails. The skin around it, however, did. With trepidation, she peeled back the layer of itching skin and held it out in front of her, disgusted. She dropped it into the garbage can beside the sink and leaned forward again.

More of the black was visible, curves and straight lines too perfect to be some sort of horrible rash. It was beginning to take the shape of something, like a tattoo.

"This is the most disgusting … thing …" she drifted off and dug into the skin of her neck, pulling away small sheets of skin to reveal the black lines of a tattoo and the fresh pink skin surrounding it.

Finally, the itching stopped, a sign she'd reached the last of the bad skin. With dread forming in her stomach, she craned her neck to see the tattoo. It wasn't big, about three inches across, but the sight of it made her world stand still.

Dragon. The black tattoo was identical to the one she'd glimpsed on Chace's chest. He hadn't just flaunted her and left, he'd marked her somehow, though why, she had no idea.

Panic stirred as she sought some rational explanation for the mark on her neck. It was at the back of her neck, easy for her to hide with her hair. But she'd still know it was there, even if no one else did.

"Okay. Maybe it's his way of saying *screw you, Skylar*," she reasoned.

Unconvinced, she pulled out her phone and texted Mason, asking him to join her in the women's restroom. Dillon would tell her she was crazy, but Mason would do it. She unlocked the door and paced in the small space. A moment later, the door cracked open.

"Not that I care, but are you decent?" he called drily.

She yanked the door open and motioned him in then closed it and locked it.

"Girls' bathrooms are always nicer," Mason said, glancing around.

"Look at this, Mason," she said pulling up her hair and turning. She looked down and arched her neck for him to see.

Mason was quiet for a moment then stepped close enough for her to feel his body heat. He touched the marking with a thumb.

"Weird," he said quietly. "I, uh, take it he bit you there?"

"How do you know that?"

Stepping away, she heard the sound of his jeans being unzipped and turned. He'd pushed his shirt up high enough for her to see how flat his abs and lower belly were. Her gaze drifted downwards.

"You shave everything down there?" she asked, smiling.

"Yep."

Her gaze went to the black mark he wore on the sensitive skin just above his penis. It was black, in the same simple design style as hers, of a great cat.

"I thought for sure my dick was gonna fall off when it started itching. Then when the skin fell off …" he shook his head. "Anyway, she bit me there."

"But what does it mean?" she asked.

"Maybe they do this to everyone they sleep with?" Mason shrugged and pulled his pants up, zipping them once more.

"We would've seen that before, if so. Somewhere in the library or in all our training." She sighed and touched the back of her neck. The new skin around the raised tattoo was silky soft. "I mean, is this gonna kill us?"

"I don't think so. I've had mine for like two months."

"We could ask Caleb," she said grudgingly, referring to the oldest of the slayers and the head trainer who had brought in hundreds of shifters before retiring to teach new slayers.

"Or not," Mason muttered. "He flips out when we fail to make quota. He'd ban us if he found out we slept with a shifter."

"Especially me," she agreed. "Pretty sure Dillon told his daddy that I dumped him. So, what do we do?"

Mason met her gaze, thoughtful.

"Nothing?" he guessed.

She sighed and nodded. "Does the itching stop now?"

"Should. Mine did."

"Maybe we should drop by Caleb's just to see if we can dig through the historical records. Discreetly."

"Sounds good. Let me suggest it, though, or Dillon will think something's up." Mason winked and opened the door, walking out of the bathroom.

Skylar rolled her eyes and counted to ten before following him. She looked out of the window without seeing any shifters waiting for her. Dillon stood when she approached the table and gathered up their files.

"We're going to my dad's," he informed her.

"Whatever you say."

He ignored her. Mason gave a trace of a smile and handed her the cup of coffee.

Skylar trailed them out and down the street, reaching the car before the tattoo itched faintly again. She rubbed it and looked around, sensing that this time, it was a shifter making her itch and not irritated skin.

She saw no one following but couldn't shake the sense someone was.

Climbing in the truck, she kept her eyes on the streets as Dillon took them a circuitous route through the downtown and suburbs towards the east, away from Phoenix. The housing divisions thinned out. Dillon turned down a gravel road leading to several large estates hidden past low, stone gates and desert landscaped front yards.

He pulled into the familiar driveway leading to his father's home and drove to the sprawling Santa Fe style house. He stopped the car in the crescent driveway.

Skylar got out, grimacing at the heat of the late summer sun.

Not looking forward to the visit, she nonetheless suspected Caleb was the only one who might have the answers she needed in his library. She and Mason followed Dillon inside the house.

"Going to the library," she said before Dillon could maneuver her into meeting his sour father. She strode down the hallway to the left, hearing Mason's soft footfall behind her.

The library was quiet and empty. It was the largest room in the house, taking up one whole wing. Books lined the walls from ceiling to floor while a central glass cabinet displayed hundreds, if not thousands, of small stone animals and creatures. A black one caught her attention, and she walked through tables to the glass cabinet. One of the charms inside was of a black dragon that looked too much like the tattoo on her neck for her comfort. Her eyes swept over the cluttered collection. They were all animals or mythical creatures like dragons, unicorns and griffins. She'd seen the collection every time she entered Caleb's house but never paid too much attention to it, assuming the man in his prime had a weird fetish for collecting animal charms.

Today, however, the collection was making her uneasy, and she didn't know why.

"Where do you want to start?" Mason asked, standing a short distance away and looking around the massive library.

Skylar reluctantly left the case to stand beside Mason.

"Needle in a haystack," she responded, overwhelmed by the size of their task. "So what if we just stop hunting these guys?"

"They burn down cities and attack innocent people, yadda yadda," Mason said. "Like our instructors told us about the legends from our past."

"Yeah. Powder keg. If we don't keep them in check, no one will," she recited the canned words her trainers used to tell her.

"We give them a chance to turn themselves in."

"Sometimes I think it's too generous, if they're that dangerous."

"Could be. Guess we gotta be fair."

"Sometimes what we do doesn't make sense," she grumbled.

"Heaven forbid we question what we learn at The Field," he agreed, referring to the training and rehabilitation center where all slayers and captured shifters went.

"I guess we don't have a choice. Born to be what we are."

"On that cheerful note, grab a book and start reading!"

Skylar went to the nearest bookshelf, aware the collection was arranged by topic. She breathed in the rich scent of books, admiring the different members of the collection. Some were hundreds of years old bound in wood while others were newer additions with modern dust jackets. Multiple languages made their search even more complicated.

"Tell me what you need, and I'll tell you where it is," Caleb's smooth, low voice came from the entrance of the library.

Skylar turned to face him, not expecting to find the eyes of Dillon's father on her. Dillon was built much like his father, though he lacked the hardness of experience that characterized Caleb's features.

"We're having trouble tracking them," she said.

"Dillon should've given you everything I gave him about tracking, and you had a source giving you information. You found them, didn't you?" Caleb asked.

"And lost them again," she said. "What we did last time isn't working this time. The source stopped talking." She faced the shelf again, reading through the different subjects slowly.

Caleb was quiet. She held her breath, hoping he left them alone or at least, gave them a few references. She didn't hear his silent step or register he was behind her until he lifted her ponytail.

Skylar started to whirl. The most experienced shifter slayer with hundreds of rehabbed shifters under his belt reacted faster than her. Bracing his forearm against her shoulders, Caleb shoved her up against the shelf. His other hand lifted her hair enough for him to run a finger over the tattoo.

"Interesting," he said.

She slammed her elbow back, and he released her. With a glare, she spun to face him.

"He marked you. Did anyone else see him do it?" Caleb asked.

She gazed at him for a long moment, before deciding he was probably the only one who might have the answers she and Mason needed.

"I don't know," she said truthfully. "There were tons of shifters in the bar where this one grabbed me." She touched the tattoo absently.

"There's only one dragon shifter left and one dragon slayer in existence. The rest have been tracked and rehabilitated," Caleb said. He crossed his arms. "I'd say he's got a plan."

*That's not good.* "What does the mark mean?" she ventured.

Mason joined them.

"It means he can track you."

"Why?"

Caleb shrugged. "Maybe so he knows you're coming for his head?"

"So this Chace is the last dragon and Skylar is the last dragon slayer," Mason said. "Now he knows when she's looking for him."

Skylar shifted, her instincts wriggling. She didn't know why the idea of Chace being the last bothered her. Or was it the thought of killing him? She'd been trained for this, but she hoped that he'd come willingly. Her instructors at The Field assured their students that only one shifter in the past hundred years had refused to come willingly and been killed.

Chace hadn't seemed like the stone cold, heartless killer that shifters were supposed to be but neither had he seemed like someone interested in being rehabilitated. He'd let her go after marking her. If he wanted to ensure his own life, why not end hers?

"You want to find him, make him come to you," Caleb advised.

"How do you recommend I do that?" she asked, surprised.

"He marked you for a reason. It doesn't just happen."

She exchanged a look with Mason, who had grown pale.

"Sky!" Dillon's excited voice came from the hallway. "We got your dragon. He's setting fire to buildings west of Phoenix."

For a moment, she was too startled to move. Adrenaline kicked in and she bolted towards the door.

"Don't forget your tools!" Caleb called after her.

She waved to indicate she had the golden lasso and the slender knife made from a dragon scale, the only weapon that would kill a dragon, if he didn't come quietly.

The idea of seeing him again filled her with a different kind of thrill, one that left her insides humming with warmth.

Dillon ran to their vehicle, and Mason was quick on her heels. The three of them piled into the SUV and within minutes, they were back on the highway, cutting across Phoenix to the western suburbs.

"So he just started burning shit down?" Skylar asked, leaning forward from her spot in the front seat.

"Looks like it," Dillon said tersely. "Someone radioed it in. He's targeting some sort of storage building or warehouse or something."

"Wow," Mason said. "I wonder why."

"Maybe he snapped," Dillon said. "Pops said when that happens, they're beyond the ability to save."

Her pulse raced.

"You up for this, Sky?" Dillon asked.

"Yeah, totally. I've waited my whole life for this."

"Hopefully he's in his human form. Otherwise, it might be hard to get him," Mason said. "He's gotta be the size of this SUV."

"I told you he was big." She swallowed hard. She hadn't considered what she'd do if she had to corner him in his dragon form. Shifters were hard enough to work with as humans. She'd helped the others corral other shifters, but never anything as big as a dragon. The biggest they'd seen was a bear the size of a Ford Focus. But this dragon was old. Ancient even, which meant he was probably closer to the size of a VW wagon.

She began to pray her eyes had been tricking her when she first saw him flying over the bar, the night they met. She'd convinced herself he wasn't as big as she initially thought. Mason's words reminded her that she'd thought him far bigger than they assessed.

All her training at The Field was going to be needed to capture him.

"Not chickening out, are you?" Dillon bated.

"No. Never. You guys will be there to back me up anyway, right?"

"Definitely," Mason replied.

Dillon was silent.

*At least I have Mason.* Skylar sat back, unease drifting through her.

They saw the smoke from the fire miles before they reached it. Local fire engines were already at the scene when Dillon pulled up, and they joined a few onlookers crowded near the truck.

Skylar engaged her extra senses, trying to pick up the elusive shifter's essence among the sensations around her. The tattoo itched once more.

"This looks like a normal fire. Split up?" Dillon suggested. "Don't engage, just look?"

"Yeah," Mason agreed. He pulled a small case free from his pocket that contained ear buds and tiny microphones. He handed one of each to them.

Skylar placed her ear bud in then loosened her ponytail to hide her ears. She clipped the microphone to her bra strap then reached to the back of her neck.

"Would you stop scratching?" Dillon grumbled. "It drives me crazy."

"Hey, at least we always know when someone is watching us," Mason said cheerfully.

"Exactly. I'm like an itchy radar system," Skylar agreed. She looked around at the warehouse area, trying to pick up some sense of where she should start looking.

A faint instinct guided her to the buildings on the far side of the compound, away from the fire and excitement. Just as quickly, the sense was gone.

"I'll try that way," she said, pointing. "Meet back at the car in like an hour?"

"Yeah. Stay in contact," Dillon said.

She nodded, distracted by the attempt to track him. With a glance over her shoulder, she trotted towards the far side of the compound. Dillon was circling the fire to get to the buildings behind it while Mason headed towards the other building in this aisle.

She slowed when she reached the walkway between two buildings and paused halfway down, instincts unsuccessfully trying to locate the dragon shifter.

*Hell, I slept with him and didn't pick him up consistently.* She shook her head, not wanting that memory to return.

"Nothing yet," she said softly.

"I'm not even sensing a shifter at all," Mason seconded.

"Nada here," came Dillon's voice.

She reached the end of the walkway and stepped out into the open area between the chain link fencing and buildings. Walking to the fences, she scanned the desert and the road just beyond a patch of saguaros and squat mesquite trees.

"Think he jumped the fence?" she asked.

"Or flew over it," Mason said with a quiet laugh.

"You know what I mean," she replied.

"Is it just me or is this shifter super complicated?" Dillon complained.

"Yeah, seems about right," Mason agreed.

She rolled her eyes, reading Mason's tone. With Dillon on the line, though, she couldn't retort the way she wanted to.

Instead, she turned and stopped short of moving.

"Oh, shit," she breathed.

Chace was leaning against one of the buildings with his muscular arms crossed, watching her like a hunter ready to pounce. His head was lowered, his dark blue gaze piercing, and his deceptively relaxed form a breath away from snapping. She knew how lean and strong he was from exploring his body with her hands, but seeing him in full daylight made her a little less sure about getting the lasso over his head. She wasn't going to win in a wrestling match, not with his long, lean limbs, the thick biceps and thighs, and the width of his shoulders and chest. He'd have her pinned beneath him in seconds, the way he had two weeks ago in bed.

The sight of him sent a streak of cold fear and a shot of hot desire through her, and the tattoo on her neck grew warm. As she had the night they met, she sensed her desire to lasso him and drag him to The Field melting under his intensity. What was it about him that made a lifetime of training simply ... disappear?

Not expecting to find him, it took her a moment to recover.

"I see you got my invitation," he said when she didn't speak. His honeyed growl was about as welcoming as his stance, and she had a hard time reconciling the bristling shifter before her with the tender man she slept with.

"So you wanted me to find you," she said.

"You've been following me, haven't you?"

"Yeah."

"What now?"

"Well." She swallowed, self-conscious under his direct gaze, and withdrew the lasso. "I'm supposed to bring you in."

His gaze fell to the gold rope in her hand. "With that?"

"Yeah."

"You can give it a try."

"You're coming in voluntarily?" she asked, not expecting his response.

"If that *thing* works, sure. Is it magic?"

*How does he know nothing about slayers?* "Wow, okay," she said. "It goes around your neck."

He lifted his chin in a silent summons but didn't move from his spot or change his unwelcoming stance.

The idea of getting close enough to lasso him suddenly didn't seem like such a good idea when he was regarding her like she was a wounded gazelle. After a brief hesitation, she approached him and stopped as far as she could while still being able to reach him.

"What happens next?" he asked.

"This controls your magic, and I take you in to The Field," she replied, holding up the lasso. "May I?"

The arms dropped from their defensive position across his chest, and he straightened.

"If you can track me, why invite me here?" she asked, waiting for him.

"Track you?"

She frowned, gazing up at him. "You didn't know that?"

"News to me."

"And you know nothing about this?" She shook the soft rope.

"Nope. After you lasso me, what do you do?"

*Something isn't right here.* She paused. The lasso would make him almost human, unable to shift or use his magic. She'd seen it used on the few shifters she helped Mason and Dillon catch.

"I take you to the oldest of my kind, and he resettles you when you're no longer a threat to people," she answered. "How do you not know this?"

"How can a dragon slayer not track a dragon?"

"We did. We just lost you again after ..." she cleared her throat, face warm. "Let's get this over with." She stretched forward and draped the lasso over his head. It settled around his neck. "That's it."

She was close enough to draw his honey-bonfire scent into her senses, and she did so, ensnared by it like she had been when they slept together. Her body grew uncomfortably fevered.

"Hmmm." His eyes narrowed, his gaze turning lethal once more. "So this takes away my magic."

She nodded. "No more burning down buildings or terrorizing humans."

"Interesting. What if it doesn't work?"

"It's never *not* worked," she replied then stepped away. She spoke into the microphone. "Hey, guys, we're ready."

"Great work. Meet back at the truck," Dillon replied.

"So, what happens if the dragon captures his slayer instead of vice versa?" Chace asked.

She raised an eyebrow. "I'm not understanding the question."

"Let's say a dragon decides to capture his slayer. He lures her into a secluded spot, lets her think she's won then just … turns the tables."

His words made her pulse fly. Her gaze swept over his muscular body once more.

"Why would he want to?" she asked.

"Maybe he thinks there's something weird going on. Like that you slayers aren't who or what you say you are. Too many inconsistencies surrounding you."

*Why does this almost make sense?* She wanted to ask him more, aware of the instincts that had been trying to tell her something similar over the past two weeks.

*We are the dragon's protectors,* her dream-mother had said. It was the exact opposite of what she'd been taught at The Field.

"It's not possible with the lasso on," she reasoned aloud. "He would've had to act before that. And hypothetically, if she couldn't get the lasso on, she'd have to kill him."

"Hypothetically, how would she do it?"

Skylar's gaze dropped to the lasso. It was the one Dillon's father gave her, the one used by previous slayers to capture dragons almost as old as the one before her. There was no way it wasn't going to work, and there was no way Chace could take it off, now that she'd placed it around his neck. Everything she'd learned at the field supported her belief.

*Don't be silly, Sky. You just think he's sexy – that's why you're confused.*

"With a dragon scale dagger," she replied. "It's the only way."

"I'm assuming our hypothetical dragon killer has one with her."

"Of course. She never leaves home without it."

If the clench of his jaw was any indication, he wasn't happy with her words. Aware she was staring too long into the dark blue depths that lulled her into a sense of security like the waves whose hue they shared, Skylar started away.

"No more questions. Let's go," she said curtly over her shoulder.

"What if the lasso doesn't work?"

Exasperated by the barrage of inquiries, she turned.

"It's not possible for …" she drifted off, gaze falling to the lasso lying on the ground. The scent of fire was in the air, and the golden rope lay half in ashes at the shifter's feet.

"All right. My turn."

Her eyes flew up to his face at his calm words. She braced herself and whipped out the scale dagger, ready for him to tackle her.

He didn't. Instead, he backed away into the open area, his nails lengthening and eyes flaring with flames. His skin rippled, his body beginning to expand within his clothing until they were stretched taught around bulging muscles while fire curled out of his nostrils.

"I'll give you a head start," he offered.

"I'm trained for this. I'm not going to run."

"Offer's on the table." He grunted then dropped on all fours.

The rippling of his body continued, and she watched with mesmerized horror as his body began to grow and morph. Scales emerged from his skin while small nubs appeared on his back behind his shoulders. They expanded rapidly, turning from nubs into feathers into wings.

He was growing at a rate that alarmed her. Within a blink, his body was the size of a small car. Seconds later, bigger than an SUV – and still rapidly changing.

Gripping the hilt of her dragon-scale knife hard, she nonetheless found herself stepping back.

"Guys, we got a problem," she whispered, craning her head back to watch the shifter go from expanding width wise to height wise. "A really, big … *huge* problem."

After a full sixty seconds, Chace unfurled his long wings and shook his head. Scales were still forming along his body, though his piercing blue gaze settled on her.

"How big?" Mason asked.

"I'd say building-sized," she breathed, unable to believe her eyes.

Chace wasn't large – he was massive, his feathered wingspan over half the length of a football field. His wings shimmered a dark, metallic teal, and his body was thick, solid, easily the size of a small building. He stood on four legs thicker than she was wide, each of which ended in a paw three feet across with razor sharp talons half that size. A large head with fangs longer than her thigh was perched upon a short neck while deep-set eyes were lined with lashes longer than her fingers.

The huge creature before her was magnificent, beautiful in a terrifying way. The sun made his wings sparkle as if with magic, and the mesmerizing hue of his eyes was only magnified by their size.

*I've seen a dragon before.* A great one with dark blue wings even larger than Chace's. The image in her mind was nothing more than a flash of a great beast flying over her head belching fire. *It's not possible.*

Chace's growling distracted her from the errant thought. He tossed his head once more. Smoke curled out of one flared nostril, a warning sign that jarred her out of her transfixed surprise. She'd seen that before and innately knew it was time to run.

"I'll take that head start," she said, hoping he at least understood her words, even if he wasn't able to speak. "So … like ten minutes? An hour?" She backed away as she spoke, praying he gave her enough time to escape being burnt into a crisp.

He shook his head.

Uncertain what that meant, she turned and bolted between the buildings. A whoosh of air made her look up, and she saw him hovering above the buildings, watching. Expecting him to fry her up good, she hunched her shoulders and ran to the end.

"Holy shit!" Mason's exclamation reminded her that the other two were nearby. "He's … he's … what the hell?"

"Yeah and I think I pissed him off," she said.

Rather than run out into the open, she stopped and tested a door leading into one of the buildings. It opened, and she hurried inside.

The storage building was only half full with an open bay opposite the stacked pallets. She tucked the knife away, at a loss as to how she was going to get close enough to use it against that large of a creature.

"Dillon, I really need to talk to your dad about now," she said quietly. "He burnt the lasso to a crisp."

"You're shitting me," Dillon responded. "It's not possible."

"We didn't think he'd be bigger than a truck, either," Mason pointed out. "Sky, he's circling the building you're in. Totally freaking everyone out."

She looked up at the corrugated roof far above her. Scared yet furious at herself for running, she wished she'd spoken to Caleb more about what to do if she pissed off a dragon shifter.

"He's torching the other buildings around you. You're about to be trapped in there," Mason said grimly.

"Shit, shit, shit!" she muttered. "I can't get close enough to stab something that big!" She sprinted to the other end of the warehouse, to the side closest to the fence. Wrenching the door open, she was relieved to see no flames between her and the only escape route. About to make a run for it, Dillon's next words stopped her.

"He's cornered the people!"

Skylar's hand stayed on the doorknob. The thought of hurting innocents made her sick – it was one of the reasons why she hadn't fought her fate as a slayer too hard. She stared at the desert outside the fence. If the dragon was occupied, she had a chance to run.

*I see you got my invitation.*

He drew her here for a reason, and he'd had a chance to fight her or light her on fire. What if this, too, was a play to get her outside the building?

Even if he didn't intend to let her live, how could she run instead of trying to help innocent people?

Knowing she couldn't just walk away when she was the only one who could possibly fight a dragon, Skylar spun and searched the interior of the building. She had to get his attention somehow, and being stuck in a warehouse wasn't going to help.

A metal stairwell on one side of the building led to a catwalk above and a door she guessed led to the roof. Skylar raced to it and ran up the stairs, reaching the roof door breathless but determined to try to distract the dragon from his quest of hurting people he shouldn't.

Wrenching it open, she trotted onto the roof, eyes drawn first to the fires blazing on either side of her before she spotted the massive dragon.

He'd cornered a few people against a building and was pacing fluidly back and forth in front of them, as if trying to choose which one to eat first.

Mason and Dillon were at the SUV, Dillon on the phone while Mason stood to the side, as much at a loss about what to do as she was, since the lassos hadn't worked.

*Chace brought me here for a reason.* Skylar told herself this over and over. She strode to the edge of the warehouse's roof, heart flip-flopping almost painfully in her chest.

*Let's say a dragon decides to capture his slayer.*

Then again, the idea he wanted to capture her was almost worse than being fried.

"Hey!" she shouted, waving her arms. "Chace!"

For a moment, she didn't think he was going to respond. Mason looked up at her.

"What're you doing, Sky?" he asked.

"Saving lives, hopefully," she replied then yelled, "Chace!"

"You got an escape plan?"

"I don't think he wants me dead."

"That's not a plan."

"I'll figure one out."

The dragon paused in his pacing and swung his head around to see her. She waved her arms over her head once more. After a moment of consideration, he turned and bound once towards her then leapt deftly into the air, lifting his massive body like it weighed nothing at all.

The vision of a dark blue dragon tore through her mind again, too crisp and clear to be a dream. An ache went through her, an indication she knew – or should have known – why the blue dragon was so vivid.

Skylar's heart pounded in her ears. She moved away from the edge of the building, silently panicking. The dragon hovered in place, staring at her. He didn't spit fire at her, which she took as a good sign.

"You … you said you were going to capture me, right?" she called. "I'm here." She held her arms out.

"Are you nuts?" Mason belted in her ear. "You can't remember to put the lids on jars of peanut butter. You can't handle a dragon!"

"I'm capable of taking care of myself, Dillon," she replied. *Hopefully.*

Chace lightly landed on the rooftop, wings still outspread, as if he was prepared to fly at the drop of a hat. He lowered his large head to her level, letting her see just how sharp the long fangs were.

Skylar backpedaled until she hit a ventilation box and stopped.

Chace was growling again, a rumble deep in his chest.

"You invited me," she reminded him. "If you plan on … eating me, just do it. Otherwise, let's leave innocent people out of this." *Like I'm in any position to tell a dragon what to do.*

Chace's wings rippled in response. He lifted himself into the air, causing a small gust of wind to sweep by her.

"Or you could just fly away, and we'll forget this whole thing happened," she added, skirting the ventilation box.

Chace hovered closer, and she sensed he was about to act. Though far from the roof door, she decided to make a run for it anyway.

Skylar whirled and ran. Before she made it two steps, she was snatched up in a talon. She squeezed her eyes closed, waiting for him to crush her. He didn't, but she was soon aware of another sensation: that of flying.

Opening her eyes, she stared at the warehouse area as the buildings became smaller, distant and the ground far, far away.

*Oh, god. He's going to drop me!*

She waited for it, terrified of the dizzying height to which he took her before he began flying westward at a speed that made the terrain below pass as quickly as if she was in a plane. Wind flattened her hair against her head while his uncomfortably tight grip kept her arms pinned at her sides. She'd never gotten air sick before, but the knowledge that there was nothing between her and instant death except for an angry dragon shifter made her want to vomit.

Instead she closed her eyes and tried to focus. If she could get to the knife, she could stab him.

Then fall screaming to her death.

*Okay. Maybe wait til on the ground.* She tried to pretend she was hang gliding or standing on a cliff with the wind rushing past her or … something. Anything to take her mind off the dragon carting her off to some unknown place.

The images behind her eyelids were almost as distressing. The dreams were no longer constricted to her sleep.

*Skylar stood on a hill overlooking a large farm that was ablaze, from the farmhouse where she'd spent her summers to the cornfields that ran in each direction as far as she could see. Her gaze followed the billowing smoke upward toward the sky, where she saw the great blue dragon circling high above. Sun glinted off his dark scales, creating small rainbows around him.*

*She was eleven or twelve in this vision.*

*"Mama, where is he going?" Skylar asked.*

*"C'mon, Sky. You have to get out of the open. They'll see you!" her mother said urgently.*

*Skylar retreated from the hilltop to the car waiting down below on a dirt, country road. Her mother was shaking, her face covered in soot.*

*Skylar looked down at her hands and saw them, too, covered with soot and streaked with blood. The sight left her rattled.*

*"Are we going home now?" she asked anxiously.*

*"No, baby. We can't go home. They'll find us there. We just have to keep moving," her mother said and got into the car. "Get in, Sky."*

Skylar sensed Chace turn and risked a peek below, more than happy to leave the disturbing daydream alone. The desert had given away to greener areas: mountains filled with pine trees. Chace was lazily circling one mountain, descending slowly as he did. Clearly, he wasn't going to drop her, which left her insides tight and knotted not to know what his intentions were.

The circles made her nauseous again, so she closed her eyes, waiting for the horrifying ride to end. Abruptly, he released her. She didn't have time to scream; the fall to the grassy earth was about a foot.

Her eyes flew open, and she quickly tried to get her bearings. It was cooler here than in the desert, the air clear and crisp. She was on a grassy plateau surrounded by pine trees and …

His cabin. The same one that had been behind the bar.

*What the hell?*

She hopped to her feet and faced the massive dragon, whose

wings were folded. He lifted his head towards the cabin.

She wanted to refuse, but faced with what was outside, she decided against it.

Skylar fled, shoving open the door and slamming it shut behind her. The cabin was cozy and homey like she recalled, his subtle scent in the air. Shaking from adrenaline and fear, she sat down on a chair, eyeing the door fearfully.

"You guys there?" she asked.

"Oh, thank god!" Mason exclaimed.

"You're alive? For reals?" Dillon almost managed to sound concerned.

"So far," she said wryly. "No idea where I am. We flew west for like, ten minutes and are now on some mountain."

"I'll see if I can Google it," Mason said.

"What the fuck is going on?" Dillon demanded.

"Damned if I know," she admitted. Recovered enough to take in her surroundings, she stood and drew her knife, going to the door. "I've got one plan. After that, I'm out."

"Knife?"

"Yeah."

"If the lasso didn't work, I wonder if the knife does."

She looked down at the grey-black knife that looked like stone. "Dammit, Dillon. Can you be supportive for once?" There was a note of panic in her voice, one she hated to hear.

The screen door of the cabin creaked open, and she steadied her breathing. Her focus was all over the place, affected as much by emotion as the bombardment of sensations from flying.

"Be back, guys," she whispered and crept to the door.

Skylar stood behind it, praying for all she was worth that the dagger would take out whatever came through the door.

It opened, and she waited.

# Chapter Eight

W hen his leg appeared past the door, she shoved the door closed and lunged.

Chace responded with reflexes unlike any she'd seen, twisting. The blow aimed at his heart scraped his bicep instead. He snatched her wrist and used her weight against her, yanking her hard.

Completely off-balance, she had no choice but to fall into the direction he pulled her. He bent her wrist until she released the weapon then snatched both wrists, and hauled her into him, trapping her in his arms. She shifted one leg back between his to regain her balance, surprised at what she felt along her thigh.

"Jesus, are you … *naked?*" she asked.

"Oh, now you're a girl scout," he growled. He held her in place the way he had in the bar the night they first met.

The body behind her was warm and solid, assuring her he wasn't a dragon any longer. Except that, right now, she was recalling how delicious he looked naked and how much she'd enjoyed his body.

"They don't make dragon-sized clothes, do they?" she asked in the awkward silence.

He didn't respond but pinned her hands above her head against the wall in a familiar pose. He leaned into her, his body resting against hers as his wide palms and long fingers ran from her wrists down her arms and to her chest.

*Don't be turned on. Don't be turned on.*

She should want to cage him, not to strip her clothes off and join him!

His hands went over her breasts and down her stomach before the circled her body to her rear end. He ran them up her back next, her shoulders, then pulled her ponytail to the side. At first, she thought he was looking for the tattoo, until he flipped the ear bud out of her ear.

"Where's the mic?" he demanded.

"Fell out while flying," she lied.

His hands went to her breasts again then slid into her shirt. He pulled the mic free from her bra strap and dropped it to the ground beside the receiver. He continued searching her, feeling her hips and down each leg.

His touch left her body. She was fevered once more from the brusque treatment. He swept up the electronic devices and stepped away.

She stayed where she was for a long moment, not at all certain she wanted to know what came next. Her gaze drifted towards the door.

"You, um, didn't even lock it," she said. "Not afraid I'll run?"

"There's only one way off this mountain, and that's me. Unless you want to jump."

She turned in time to see him pulling up a pair of jeans over the perfect, round globes of his ass. He zipped the jeans. They hung low on his hips, and his upper body was bare. The muscles of his back rippled smoothly beneath the taut sun-gold skin, and she assessed he could probably take her as a human or a dragon.

Could she ever look at him without remembering what he really was?

As if hearing the thought, he faced her. He finished wrapping a rubber band around his hair then dropped his thick arms to his sides, studying her with the same predatory look he'd given her at the warehouse. It made her want to take her chances jumping off the mountain.

"Who's on the other end?" he started, holding out the electronic devices.

She shook her head, not about to rat out her friends, no matter how scared she was.

"You've got about ten seconds to start talking, slayer." Chace dropped both and crushed them with his heel.

She was having a hard time coming up with anything at all in that moment, torn between fear and the heat blooming in her belly at the sight of his supple skin.

"Time's up." He started towards her.

She darted towards the door and had made it a few steps outside the cabin when he tackled her. She didn't have a chance to fight him. He rolled off her and snatched her arm, pulling her over his shoulder while simultaneously standing.

Her legs were pinned in place, and she slapped at his back. There was nothing for her to grab for leverage.

He set her down and whirled her, wrapping one arm around her to hold her against his chest.

She stared down at their feet, trying hard to backpedal away from the cliff. Hundreds of feet straight down was a valley between two peaks. The valley was filled with jagged rocks and the occasional pine tree that looked like a fuzzy green dot from their height.

Chace braced one leg against a tree hanging out over the edge and shifted forward.

With her feet hanging over nothing but empty space, Skylar clawed at his arm, struggling to find a handhold in case he decided to drop her. She stretched back and locked one arm around his neck.

"Let's try this again," he said. "Who are you working with?" He worked her arm free of his neck, overpowering her with ease, and pinned it to her body.

She said nothing, staring at the rocks far below.

His grip loosened, and she started to slide.

"No!" she shouted, struggling to free one arm to grab something.

"There we go," he said, satisfied. "Now that you're talking ..."

His arms tightened again, but she couldn't shake her frantic need to find something stable to grab.

"Your name," Chace said.

He was close enough for her to feel his words tickle her ear. Unlike her, he was completely in control, unconcerned with dangling over a cliff's edge. The heartbeat at her back was steady and strong, his breathing even.

*Heartbeat?*

"Skylar," she managed. "Nielson."

"You're a dragon slayer."

"The last."

"Interesting," he said, his arms loosening. "So if you're gone ... the dragons are safe."

"You didn't bring me here to kill me!" she said, squirming again. She stretched with her foot to reach the edge. He shifted farther out in response.

"Knowing you're the last might've changed my mind. I can keep my kind safe this way."

"You're the last, too!" she shouted, wrenching one arm free and clutching at his forearm.

"What?"

"There are no more dragons. Just you." She was slipping down his body faster.

"Keep talking," he said.

"I just wanted to bring you in. Not to ... kill you. We found your bar and then things went ... off track. You wanted me to ... find ... you ..." She gasped.

He released her. Unable to reach the ledge or the tree, she clung to his arm with both of hers and dangled helplessly over the cliff's edge.

"The last time I checked, there were five dragons." The note in his voice terrified her.

"Not anymore," she said then rushed on. "I didn't hurt them. You're my first."

"The other shifters? You've been hunting them down, too, haven't you?"

"It's not how it works. I can only track you," she said quickly. Her eyes went to the rocks awaiting her. She looked away fast, trying not to panic. "Dragon slayers hunt dragons. Cat slayers hunt ... cats."

"How many kinds of slayers are there?"

"I don't know," she mumbled.

He gripped one wrist, prying her hand free from his arm and holding it.

"Six!" she shouted. "Six!"

"There is no reason on the entire planet I should let you live," he said in a hard tone. "Your kind kills mine!"

"No! We only protect normal people from attacks by shifters."

"Where do you get this shit?"

"It's the truth!" she said in a mix between desperation and frustration. She sensed him debating.

Finally, he straightened, drawing her back towards the cliff. He lifted her by the wrist he held until her tiptoes were able to reach the edge of the cliff between his legs. He didn't move but snaked his other arm around her to pull her against him.

She'd never been so happy to perch precariously on a cliff. Skylar heard herself panting and wrapped her arms around him, not daring to let him go. His muscular chest was warm beneath her chilled cheek, his scent winding through her senses.

"If we go inside, you gonna talk?" he asked gruffly, lifting her chin to see him.

"Scout's honor."

His eyes narrowed, and he leaned forward, knocking away her feet from the ledge.

Letting go of the tree of a man keeping her from falling, she took his face in his hands and pulled it down to her.

As she had before, she sought to distract him with a simple kiss. Pressing her mouth to his, she didn't expect him to respond so fast. Chace's lips were soft but demanding, and she instantly caved, opening her mouth for him to taste her while she kissed him hard and deep. His velvety tongue was hot, the pressure of his lips – combined with her surging adrenaline from the near-fatal fall – rendering her response far more passionate than she intended.

"I'll make it worth your time," she whispered, pulling away and resting her cheek against his. "Again. You know I can."

He said nothing for a moment, didn't move. They breathed the same air, and she felt how fast his heart was beating.

*Why does he have a heartbeat this time?*

Uncertain what he was thinking, she nuzzled his cheek and traced kisses down his jaw then claimed his lips again, this time in a slow, deep kiss.

Despite his declaration, he responded with the same hunger that was working its way through her system.

At last, he took one step back then another, until her feet were firmly on the ground. His grip grew slack and he withdrew from the kiss.

"Let's get one thing straight," he said, meeting her gaze. "Of the two of us, I'm the one who can fly. Don't think for a moment that I won't throw you off the mountain, if you piss me off again. Got it?"

She nodded, afraid to say anything that might see her at the bottom of the valley.

He took her arm and led her back to the cabin. She stepped inside, and he closed the door behind them. She was about to sigh in relief when he spun her and kissed her again, this time harder.

Fire spread through her the same way it had the first time they made love. She leaned into him, not caring what they did, so long as she wasn't hanging over a cliff anymore. She let her trembling hands skim over his bare chest and down the muscular arms. He gripped her ass and pulled her hips against his. His erection was hard against her, and his fingers slid around her wrists.

She didn't register the cold metal for a moment, too caught up in the sensations of his body against hers. She wanted her clothing gone, so she could feel her skin against his and to run her fingers through his long hair once more.

He lifted her hands above her head then ran his palms down her arms, her chest, her sides, taking her hips to hold them against his. Enjoying the sensation, she left her hands up while he explored her body, enjoying the sensations.

"You can*not* kiss your way out of this one," he whispered, pulling away.

Scattered from a mix of desire and the saturation of her senses, she didn't understand what he meant, until he shifted away. She went to lower her arms and looked up, startled to find her wrists were shackled together and suspended by the chain between them on a hook over her head.

She yanked at it.

"Sorry, Skylar," Chace said from a few feet away. "Can't have you trying to escape or call for help."

Stunned he'd tricked her, she lowered her gaze from the ceiling to him. His eyes glowed with desire but also fire, and his talons had begun to grow. She swallowed a retort, the sudden urge to hide somewhere filling her.

He moved into her personal space once more, smelling more of bonfire than honey. She was able to see the unnatural flames in his pupils clearly, and he radiated heat, the way he had before he shifted into a dragon earlier.

She discreetly pulled at her bonds, afraid of what happened if he turned into a dragon. She was trapped in place, able to move about a foot in either direction but no farther.

Chace traced a lengthening talon down the side of her face and neck, leaving a trail of fire that tickled and burned. His finger continued down her collarbone and arm. He held her gaze while he touched her lightly.

The finger slid under her shirt and traced a path from the small of her back to her belly. The nail was sharp enough to sting, and her skin quivered.

He lowered his head and kissed her lightly, and she felt the teeth that were lengthening, as if he was getting ready to shift. Terrified yet turned on, she responded to him timidly this time, too aware of the heat of his chest and the talon making its way up her body towards her breasts.

"Don't try anything," he warned against her mouth.

She said nothing, shivering under his light touch. The tender man who made love to her two weeks ago was gone, replaced by this stranger, who seemed all too aware of how much control he had over her body and its reaction to him.

Chace moved away, stalking towards the door and out. He slammed it behind him, and the screen door creaked closed.

Skylar breathed a sigh of relief. Her legs were quaking, the sacred hollow between them wet while her body was tense with fear. Looking up, she stood on her tiptoes and tried to shake her hands free. The hook was too deep for her to lift her chain over the edge.

She studied the area around her. He'd hung her in a perfect place – right in the middle of everything but too far from anything she could stand on. She stretched and leaned towards the closest thing, an ottoman, but wasn't even able to graze the small piece of furniture.

"Come on!" she said angrily. "This is not how it's supposed to happen!" She gave up for a moment then tried again.

*What the hell have I gotten myself into?*

# Chapter Nine

C hace understood why Mr. Nothing pointed him in the direction of the shifter slayer without fully knowing how to deal with her.

This time, his shifting was involuntary, an instinctive reaction to his emotional turmoil. He'd never hurt anyone in his life and yet, dangling the helpless girl over the cliff, it had taken every piece of his willpower not to drop her. He was torn between wanting to strangle her and to make love to her, an emotional powder keg he didn't think possible before meeting her.

That she was so nonchalant about hunting down and slaughtering shifters who were just trying to live normal lives infuriated him. Distracted by the intense attraction between them, the chemistry that made him topple into bed with her without bothering to ask her name, he didn't know what to think.

*Skylar.* It was a perfect name for someone whose eyes were the color of the heavens.

What part of what she said was true and what part was a lie? He was too angry to try to figure it out.

Chace barely registered the pain rippling through him as he morphed. He needed to feel the sky, to release the emotion inside him before he threw the only lead he had to what was happening to the shifters off a cliff.

He launched into the air and hovered beside a tree, trying to gauge his size. Unless the pinecones had grown huge over night, he was about the size of a dragonfly this time. He alighted on a pinecone for a moment. The scent of pine and nature soothed him somewhat, and he let his dragon senses absorb everything around him. He needed to replace the womanly scent of Skylar and the memory of how soft her skin was. All she did was piss him off, and he didn't think he'd be able to stay human long enough to question her, if he didn't erase all traces of her from his system.

The calm of nature worked into his system slowly, and he released the anger that was boiling over. When he felt under control again, he left the pinecone and soared upward. Too small to deal with the wind currents high above the mountains, he kept to the treetops and explored the mountain where he'd placed the cabin with his magic.

Eventually, he managed to center himself and fluttered back towards the cabin. He landed gently on the windowsill and peered into his home, wanting to gauge his instinctive response to see if he was ready to deal with her yet.

She'd managed to make a mess in the time he was gone, a true accomplishment, given that he'd laid out strict orders for the cabin's magic. He'd told the cabin to make room for her to go to the restroom only but to keep everything else out of reach. Somehow, she'd managed to knock over a chair, pushed the ottoman out of place, smashed a vase that used to be on the stand next to the couch ...

Her wrists were bleeding. She was working hard to get free, no doubt anxious to get away from the monster she considered him.

*She has no mercy for our kind,* he reminded himself. His eyes followed the blood from her wrists down her forearms, and he forbade himself from feeling bad about it, not when she was helping slaughter shifters.

But he still did. She was frantic, a trapped animal, one whose lies about not hurting the others he was almost able to believe, even if he didn't want to. He'd seek out Mr. Nothing again later, but right now he wanted to know more about the woman in his home.

His magic returned to his control, settling within him. Chace flew away from the window, back to the jeans he'd left in the grass when he'd shifted.

His dragonfly body expanded, the tearing and reshaping of sinew, muscles and skin making him grimace. At last, he was human again. He waited for his wings to be absorbed into his body then tugged on his jeans and drew a deep breath.

As long as he stayed calm dealing with the slayer, he wasn't going to run away to morph.

Chace took another moment to settle the last vestiges of his anger then strode towards his cabin. He flinched at the sound of something else smashing to the ground a second before he opened the door.

Determined, he entered his home and surveyed the damage.

Skylar twisted to face him, apprehension crossing her features. She was gorgeous, with large blue eyes lined with feathery lashes, high cheekbones and an oval face with olive complexion framed by dark hair. Above average height and trim, he'd intimately experienced the lean muscles of her body. Remembering how well they fit together made his blood stir.

He found himself looking too long and closed the door. She'd been in his place for all of an hour, and already, he was struggling not to breathe in her heady scent.

Chace crossed the room to the stove, aware the mountaintop got downright cold at night. He ordered the magic in the cabin to clean up her mess and right all his furniture where he preferred it.

Her gasp confirmed that the furniture was moving back into place, as if possessed. Chace straightened from placing wood into the fireplace, debating. After a moment, he grudgingly ordered the magic of the cabin to make her wrist chains so they wouldn't hurt her.

When he turned, she was staring up at her hands, puzzled. The interior of the metal cuffs were lined with pink fleece and their edges topped with pink feathers.

*Pink? Really?* There were days when even his magic cabin pissed him off. It was a reminder that he and the magic coexisted – intertwined but still independent.

Irritated, he moved towards his prisoner. She moved away instinctively. Chace preferred to be in contact with her and gripped her hips, pulling her into his body. Her tight ass settled against his hips in a way that was almost too distracting while her frizzy hair tickled his chin.

"Stay," he ordered.

She mumbled something he couldn't hear but didn't move. With her body resting against his, he reached up and tugged at the chains. The magic obeyed his command, and her shackles went through the hook holding them up. He wrapped one arm around her shoulders to keep her in place then lifted one arm to see the damage.

She'd rubbed the skin right off her wrists. It looked as though she'd tried to pull one hand through a cuff. It was raw and red all the way to her thumb knuckle.

"This is just foolish," he said with more heat than he intended. "You've got nowhere to go, and the cabin won't let you out anyway. Why would you do this?"

Her breathing was erratic, her body tense.

"I'll fix you up once and that's it," he said.

"You have a magic cabin." There was both awe and confusion in her voice.

He placed one arm around her waist to keep her warm, soft body close and maneuvered her close to the fire, jostling her without letting her fall.

He sat on a stool then motioned for her to sit in front of him on the ground. She glanced around then did so, seating herself cross-legged.

Chace took one hand and summoned the supplies he'd need to fix her up. They appeared on the table beside him, and she winced.

"How many shifters have you helped slaughter?" he asked. He felt her gaze on him, her consternation clear.

"None."

"But you admitted to helping others track them."

"Yeah. We haven't had to kill any, though. We just take them in."

"To where?" He pulled one hand free of its manacle and carefully began to clean her forearm and wrist of blood.

"What are you doing?" she asked.

"Fixing you up."

"But why?" The exasperation in her voice was enough to make him look up. Meeting her gaze was dangerous, because the familiar bloom of desire flared to life within him.

"Obviously, I don't want you dead," he said, amused.

That just seemed to confuse her more, and she shook her head.

"Where do you take the shifters?" he asked again.

"Somewhere where they can be rehabilitated and made safe for human society," she replied.

"Rehabilitated?" he repeated, lowering his hands. "What right do you have to do that?"

"What right do you shifters have to set buildings on fire and kill innocent humans?" she retorted.

"I have never hurt anyone. Not at the storage facility in Phoenix or anywhere else!"

"Whatever." She yanked her hand back from him. "Don't bother to fix me. You'll just fry me anyway when you get what you want." She stood and went back to the hook in the middle of the cabin. The manacle didn't respond to her, and she tugged at it in frustration.

His magic was slipping again, getting ready to turn him into his other form whether or not he wanted it to. Chace closed his eyes for a moment, willing himself to calm down. The fire was already growing, a sign he hadn't been able to make it five minutes with the slayer before his emotions got the best of him.

"Sorry." There was a tremor of fear in her voice. "Just, um, don't flip out."

He was tense enough that her soft touch on his forearm made

him snap. Chace snatched her arm and twisted, yanking her to the ground and holding her in place beneath him with his weight. He pinned her wrists above her head

Fear fluttered across Skylar's expression. She didn't try to fight him but gazed up at him with blue eyes that helped ground him, her breathing irregular and face flushed. Her tongue flickered out to wet her lips, drawing his gaze towards the plush lips he'd experienced several times already.

The tension between them was thick, his body remembering too clearly what it had been like to lie on top of her like this before, except without clothes. Her large breasts were pressed to his chest, her rounded hips against his crotch. He was inches from the mouth whose flavor made him want to dive in head first, even if she meant to kill him later.

"No dragon craziness," she whispered. "Okay? Just … stay like this until you're … uh, calm."

Chace liked the way her body felt too much to argue. He lowered his head to her neck. She flinched, and the pulse at her neck was rapid.

"I'm not going to hurt you," he said, sensing her fear. *Something about you drives me insane.*

Closing his eyes, he focused on the musk of her skin and the peach essence of her hair, letting it wind through his senses the way the world did when he was in his dragon form. It stirred his blood in a different way than he was used to, tugging at his magic like his emotions did – without releasing it. He listened to her uneven breathing for a long moment before he realized something very, very different was going on inside him.

The magic was receding. In his thousand years as a shifter, it had never backed off. Some days, he was able to postpone the inevitable shifting until he was some place safe and private, where no one would see or get hurt. But it had never, *ever* calmed of its own accord like this.

Was it … could it be *her?* The dragon slayer who came to kill him?

*That makes no sense.*

"What are you doing?" he asked.

"Right now? Praying you don't eat me." Her light tone indicated she tried to joke, but he heard her fear. "Sex makes you calm. If you need a little peck on the cheek or something, I'm game. Rather that than be turned into fried chicken."

"Don't tempt me." His body surged with desire in response to her tongue-in-cheek offer. He wasn't at all certain he'd have the same sense of humor in a similar situation, but her disarming delivery and soft tone took the edge off his tumbling emotions.

He digested her words, realizing she was right. Once before, the night they'd met, she'd managed to soothe the dragon side of him while they made love. Was it her or was it what she said? Sex? Physical contact? Something else?

It didn't seem possible that she was so unaware of what shifters were really like or what effect she had on him. Was she that crafty of a liar? Reviewing what little he knew of her, he was having trouble convincing himself either way. She'd taken his bait at the warehouses and surrendered to save the innocent people she was convinced he went around eating for dinner. That took guts, especially after he burned through her lasso.

But she openly admitted that she'd kill shifters if they didn't go with her voluntarily.

"Something isn't right here," he said finally.

Whatever she was and whatever she lied about, she was scared right now, and no part of him pitied her. Fear was the least she deserved for hurting his kind.

Chace assessed his magic once more, unable to accept that it had just decided to go dormant. A glance at his hands indicated that his nails were back to normal.

Unable to account for what was causing his magic to retreat, he eased off Skylar's body, straddling her hips and releasing his grip on her hands. He sat back and gazed down at her, not at all certain what to think of someone who seemed both unaware of the horrors she committed yet determined to continue doing them.

She moved slowly around the lethal predator, and sat up, pulling her legs out from under him.

"Fix your wrists," he told her curtly, motioning to the first aid kit on the table behind her. "Then it's back to hanging from the ceiling."

"Great. Can't wait." The sarcasm in her voice was lost in its breathless quality. Her hands trembled as she reached up to grab the kit.

"This rehabilitation," he started. "You brainwash people? Pull out their fangs?"

"I don't know," she said, focus on her wrists. "My job is just to find you and turn you over. I don't think the rehab program is that bad. We all go through some form of it before we're allowed to integrate into society."

"What do you mean?"

"Slayers. We're born with magic that lets us find you guys. We have to be trained, too, so we can use our magic right. It's done in the same facility as the rehab program. We call it the reprogramming tank."

"Reprogramming." He wasn't able to keep the anger out of his voice. "I wasn't born a shifter."

She looked up at him. "Really?"

"Yeah, really," he replied.

"Maybe that's why I can't track you," she murmured pensively. "Or rather, I can only when I'm near enough for you to turn me into fried chicken."

"Good to know."

Her gaze flickered to him then away again quickly.

"If I leave, do I need to tie you or will you stay here?" he asked.

"Well ..." she glanced around. "You're totally freaking me out."

*At least she's honest.* It was a strange combination: honesty and lethality.

He said nothing, though, watching her expertly and quickly dress her wrists. By the smooth, practiced motions, he began to think that this was part of her training.

"What did your family think of your reprogramming?" he asked, unable to pinpoint what was off about her. "You leave the house normal and come back with a taste for blood?"

"I don't have a family," she replied easily.

"You did at some point."

"They died when I was young. Probably got eaten by moody dragons," she said pointedly.

*This keeps getting weirder.* Something wasn't right about her story, and he wasn't entirely certain she was going to be any help. After all his years alive, he knew a thing or two about the darker side of humanity. She didn't question the story she'd been fed, but he did.

"What if you did have a family?" he pushed. "What if your reprogramming just made you forget them?"

"You think I was brainwashed," she said, a troubled expression flickering across her features.

"Sure looks that way. I've got a thousand years of knowledge under my belt, and this shit you're saying makes no sense. You've never questioned any of this?"

"Yeah." The expression she gave him was thoughtful. "But what does it matter? My job is to keep you from eating people."

"I don't …" His magic stirred with his anger.

She froze, staring at him, fear in her gaze again.

Chace stood and crossed to the door. This time, the magic ignored his silent plea to leave him alone. What made it listen while he was lying on top of her and not the next time he asked?

"By the way, this is not a dragon scale." He yanked open a drawer of the small desk near the door and pulled free the weapon she'd tried to use against him. "This is sandstone. Dragon scales aren't rigid like this. They shift and bend. They have to – it's part of my defensive mechanism."

He snapped the stone knife in his hands and dropped it on the desk.

"Okay. Chill, dragon" she whispered. She set aside the first aid kit, her wrists bandaged.

Chace sensed she was debating making a run for it. He reached down and took her forearms, pulling her to her feet.

"Don't," he warned her.

The connection of her skin made the magic inside him pause while it incited his blood.

"Being good," she responded. "Just tie me up and do your thing."

"Ditching the girl scout thing again, I see," he observed, unable to help the smile that tugged free.

"If that what it takes," she retorted, face growing red. "I definitely didn't *not* enjoy it last time."

She ducked her head, confusion on her features. She seemed hard to ruffle, confident and unflappable with a quick wit, which made her blush all the more charming. He had a feeling she'd respond to his kiss just as eagerly as she had before, even if she was also scared of him transforming into the human-eating beast she considered him.

He willed the manacles to reform around her wrists then lifted her hands above her head quickly enough to put her off balance. Her body collided with his, and sparks of a different kind of fire went though him. Her breath caught, her gaze on his mouth, and they stood frozen for a moment.

Chace waited for the hook to move and slide under the chain between her bound hands then traced her arms and sides again, his palms settling on her hips.

Her breathing was erratic, like his, the faint scent of her arousal apparent to his delicate senses.

Skylar met his gaze, studying him closely. "You're starting to turn again."

"I could just leave," he said, the offer clear.

"You could," she agreed, the light of need in her eyes. "Or you could untie me and I can help you calm down."

*I need to keep my distance.* He hesitated.

It was enough of a pause for her to lean forward and brush her lips to his again.

"Is this some ruse to escape?" he asked.

"One way to find out," she said cheerfully.

Chace withdrew, eyeing her. She was smiling.

"I have an idea," he decided.

Before she could ask him about it, he kissed her, hard and quick, his arms wrapping around her. She responded with the hunger he anticipated that made his arousal turn near-feral.

"Let me down," she ordered softly against his mouth.

"Hell no."

He kissed her quiet then shifted his hands down, tracing her hips and ass before moving to unfasten her pants. He broke away to push them down her body and took off her shoes to slide them completely off.

"Come on, Chace!" she urged.

Instead of standing, Chace knelt and took her bare ass in his hands, pressing his nose to the apex of her thighs.

"Just tell your magic cabin to …"

His tongue flicked between the folds of her sex to reach the swollen clit.

She gasped.

Chace lifted one of her thighs over one shoulder then the other, willing the cabin to make sure the cuffs didn't hurt her wrists again while she dangled from the ceiling.

He buried his face into the soft, slick center of her womanhood, hungrily drinking from her core then tracing the path between her opening to the tiny button of a clit with his tongue. Her scent drove him insane with need. This time, though, he needed to make her come, to feel her body shudder around him and hear her call his name the way she had weeks before.

Her firm thighs clenched his head, her heels digging into his back as she strained to intensify the sensations.

*This is heaven.* Chace licked and lapped at the clit, listening to Skylar's gasps and murmurs to guide him. He released her bottom with one hand to slide fingers into her core and moved them in and out slowly to match the rhythm of his tongue stroking the sensitive skin between her nether lips and suckling the clit.

"Let me down, Chace!" Her demand was breathless, more of a groan. "I want you inside me."

He almost relented, unable to think of anything he wanted more than to feel her slick, tight, hot sheath gripping his dick. He forced himself to stay where he was with this head between her thighs, savoring her sweet flavor and gently torturing her with his mouth and teeth. His fingers worked her G-spot at a slow, unrelenting pace while his lips and tongue swirled, sucked and tickled the sensitive clit.

Her body stiffened around him, her thighs clenching his head while she tilted her hips towards him and arched her back in a sign she was close to coming. He slowed his pace and received a kick in the back from one heel in response.

"I can stop now," he teased, lifting his head from the core of her womanhood.

"Please don't!" Her voice carried a desperate note.

He freed his fingers from her core and gripped her ass hard to hold her in place, leaning forward to taste her again then run it along the sensitive path to her clit. He licked her hard and slow.

Her tense body shuddered in anticipation with each flicker of his tongue. He circled the straining clit then sucked hard.

"Oh, god!" Skylar cried as her orgasm broke.

Chace lifted his head as her body began convulsing. Her breathing was ragged, and he slid a finger into her core again to feel her tight sheathe ripple around it.

Her body climaxing was almost too much. Her scent intensified, her soft gasps turning him on almost beyond control. He waited as long as he could for her pleasure to calm then slid her thighs off his shoulders and stood.

Her face was flushed, her eyes glowing.

Chace wrapped one arm around her and kissed her hard, one

hand sliding down her belly once more towards her core. He slid fingers inside of her, loving the sensation of her orgasm as it gripped his fingers in waves.

His magic had retreated again, but it was the woman in his arms who had his attention. She was kissing him passionately, silently trying to cajole him into staying. Every part of him wanted to slide his hands around to her perfect ass and pull her onto his hips then drag her into bed for the next day, week, month, year. However long it took to satiate the inhuman need to claim her.

But her strange claims about rehabilitation nagged at him, made him think he wasn't the only one who was oblivious to what was going on. She, too, didn't know a thing about what really went on beyond the surface of the slayers' duties.

*One of us has to figure this shit out.*

Reluctantly, he dropped his hands and moved away, determined to find someone to help him unravel this mystery.

"You aren't going to finish what you started?" she asked, dazed and surprised.

"The cabin will let you put on your clothes and clean up in the bathroom," he answered shortly. "But you can't leave."

Chace dressed fast and left, before the beautiful woman with sexiest body he'd ever seen and the calming touch could completely derail him, make him stay in bed with her for days instead of uncovering what was going on.

*I need to keep my distance.* With a sinking feeling, he began to wonder if it was too late for that.

# Chapter Ten

M r. Nothing didn't respond when Chace went searching for him in the last two places they'd met. Fed up after a few hours of waiting, Chace went to the bar, hoping at least Mr. Nothing would eventually respond to the text he sent.

He sat in his normal corner, tapping the sweating glass of beer before him. It was his favorite amber ale, available only during autumn. Normally, he drank it like others did water.

"So you're saying these slayers are behind the disappearances of our shifters, who have been taken somewhere to be brainwashed," Gunner said slowly.

"But the slayers themselves are also brainwashed," Luke added.

Chace's eyes flickered from one to the other. Gunner appeared equal parts thoughtful and concerned while Luke's brow was furrowed in confusion. Max sat with them, the burly man on edge.

"Yeah," Chace said. "Allegedly, it's been this way for thousands of years. I've been alive for a millennium, and I've never heard of a dragon slayer or any slayer at all."

"Me neither," both replied.

"So we agree. Something ape-shit weird is going on here."

"Nothing wrong with apes," said Max defensively.

"Sorry, Max," Chace replied, amused at how sensitive the primate-shifting man could be. "Bat-shit weird sound better?"

"Yeah," Max replied. "I'll handle this."

"No, thanks," Chace replied. "I need answers, not blood everywhere."

"Mr. Nothing told you to find these people, right?" Luke asked. "Why not just ask him for more information?"

"He didn't want to be found today."

"Like Mr. Nothing is a friendly neighborhood librarian?" Gunner retorted.

Chace sipped his beer, listening to them talk while his thoughts strayed to Skylar. He hoped the fleece interior of the cuffs didn't chafe her wrists then remembered he hadn't started the wood stove. He'd started to then gotten distracted. She was probably freezing.

What was wrong with him? She deserved nothing but to become the fried chicken she kept talking about.

Except it bothered him that she, too, was likely involved in something that left her a victim of some organization bent on capturing and killing shifters. His mind returned to how – a few short hours ago – he'd had her thighs wrapped around his head while he devoured the sweet, slick nectar of her core. Every time he touched her, it got harder to walk away. When he *tasted* her, leaving was almost painful.

*I have to keep away from her.* He had no idea what it was about the woman that ensnared him and wouldn't let him go. Was this how slayers worked? They seduced their prey as a means of controlling them? Because right now, the only thing he was able to think about was fucking her again.

"I say we put in a call to Mr. Nothing then find out where this rehab camp is," he said, forcing his mind away.

"You want us to let one of these slayers capture us?" Luke asked scornfully. "Huge risk."

"No," Chace said with a smile. "I got one. I'll get the

information."

"Let me talk to him!" Max demanded, slamming his fist on the table. "You never hurt a fly, Chace! I can do this."

"I can do it, Max," Chace snapped. "I may not hurt a fly, but I can dangle a slayer over a canyon and threaten to drop her if she doesn't cooperate."

"Her?" Gunner's eyes narrowed. "Wait, it's not the chick who wandered into the bar two weeks ago is it?"

Chace said nothing.

Gunner and Luke exchanged a look.

"Who was she after?" Luke asked.

"Me," Chace said mirthlessly. "Luck of the draw."

"We need to do something soon," Gunner's gaze went around the bar. "Another two disappeared last night. I put out the word that they should travel in pairs at least."

"I know the shifter code is not to commit violence, but at this point ..." Luke drifted off.

Chace felt both of their gazes on him. A flutter of guilt went through him, knowing he'd signed away their only safe haven without understanding that's what would happen once he was human. Mr. Nothing was using him to find the people responsible for killing shifters – but how long would he wait and how much information would be enough for the elusive Mr. Nothing to cash in his end of their deal? What if Mr. Nothing just took Skylar and left the rest of the shifters to their fate?

Suddenly restless, Chace rose.

"I'll find out something by morning and let you know the plan," he said resolutely. "Why don't we keep the bar here and encourage people not to leave for a day or two?"

"You think that's safe?" Gunner asked.

"I think that Max can crush the melon of any non-shifter that ventures close."

Max perked up, straightening in his seat at the mention of the lift of the restriction Chace gave him long ago for being admitted to the bar.

"Can you handle trespassers?" Chace asked him.

"Not a one will live," vowed Max.

"All right. Sounds good." Chace hid a smile and glanced at Gunner, who grinned, understanding Chace's unspoken message to keep Max from going completely nuts.

Chace walked out of the bar and stood for a long moment in the last rays of the late autumn day. He breathed in the ocean air, concerned about the shifters and just as concerned that he'd screwed up by not realizing that they'd be vulnerable without his magic.

It was his mess to fix, the last good thing he'd do before Mr. Nothing ended his suffering.

He willed himself to change and braced himself for the tearing and rebuilding of his body as it took on a dragon's form. He vaulted into the sky and flew, the great wings propelling him forward at dizzying speeds. He'd taken it easy on Skylar earlier, not wanting her too suffer too much during the flight, before he had some answers.

This time, however, he went as fast as his wings would let him, anxious to learn more about what he'd inadvertently stumbled into. Mr. Nothing was right – who else but the strongest could protect the small society he was involuntarily a part of?

He reached the mountaintop across the country in about two hours and landed, starving. Flying left him hungry, which meant he needed to roll out his grill and cook up some food. The air was cold on top of the mountain, and the cabin had turned on a light the way it did every night for him. Smoke came from the chimney, indicating the cabin's magic had done what he forgot.

*She won't freeze. At least, not until I have to dangle her over the cliff's edge again to get some more answers.* Whatever it took to protect his people …

Chace picked up the clothing he'd carried in a talon, pulled it on and strode to the cabin. He opened the door, ready to start the inquisition, when he saw she wasn't hanging in the middle of his cabin like he expected.

He froze, startled, and looked around.

Skylar was lying in his bed, sound asleep on her stomach. Her hands were still bound and extended above her head.

Chace closed the door, checking the magic of his cabin instinctively.

"What the hell?" he whispered to the cabin. "I gave you strict instructions!"

The cabin didn't respond. It never directly disobeyed him, just often found creative ways of doing what he asked of it that bordered on passive aggressive. After a thousand years, he thought they had reached an understanding of sorts. Had the magic taken pity on her, or did she somehow affect it the way she did him?

Approaching the bed, his eyes swept over her, and a familiar stir of desire warmed his loins. He had the urge to touch her once more the way he always did when they were together. And when she kissed him … some part of him melted. Maybe it was because she felt so real, so unlike every other woman he'd been with ever since the curse descended upon him.

*Focus, fool.*

"Skylar," he said.

She shifted.

"C'mon. Wake up."

Rolling groggily onto her side, she eyed him then sat up. Her gaze searched his features intently, as if she wanted to see if he was about to shift.

"How did you get free?" he asked.

She shrugged. "Told the hook to release me, and it did."

*Damn cabin.* "Anyway, I have an idea. You want to take me in, and I need to know what's happening to the shifters who go into your reprogramming camp."

She frowned.

"So. Take me in."

Skylar shifted to lean against the backboard. "You're going to eat everyone, aren't you?"

"First, I've never eaten anyone. Ever." He rose, agitated once more by her insistence he was some sort of monster. "Or fried them. Second, I've never hurt anyone in my life. Ever."

She was staring at him.

"Okay," she said softly. "When you do that, you freak me out."

Chace paced, needing fresh air already. He wasn't expecting to feel her cool hands on his forearm and jerked away.

"Chill, dragon," she told him and took his arm again. "For whatever reason, you don't flip out when I'm touching you. So ... just stand there for a minute." Her cool hands wrapped around his forearm.

Chace resisted the urge to move away before his magic forced him to shift. Instead, he concentrated on what was going on inside him, the inexplicable quieting of his magic. He absently responded to the instinctive impulse to be closer to her and looped an arm around her, pulling her into his body while he concentrated on subduing his magic.

"You just can't ... ugh!" she muttered. "You are so lucky my hands are bound."

"Or you'd kill me?" he asked, amused.

"I'd give it a good try."

"Pretty sure you ran last time we faced off."

She shot him a glare, pushing at his chest while her face flushed.

"I'll let you go, but no guarantees I won't turn into a dragon right here," he said, loosening his grip on her.

She hesitated, uncertainty crossing her features, then rested her hands on his chest. Her plump lips were ripe for kissing, even if she looked ready to cut him to pieces.

Chace gazed down at her, wishing he knew what it was about her that drew him with inhuman need. If he knew, he could turn it off, and his life would be easier. Her lower body was pressed to his, the depths of her blue eyes like the sky. He felt himself tumbling into them the same way he did the heavens.

"Maybe if you kiss me, I'll free your hands," he offered.

Her eyes dropped to his lips and for a moment, he thought she was going to refuse.

As she had on two other occasions, she lifted to her tiptoes and kissed him lightly then started to drop back to her heels. Chace captured her soft, warm mouth with his, his other arm going around her. She tasted of minty toothpaste and her own flavor, which was as sweet and addictive as the nectar of her core he'd sampled two weeks ago. It made him want to listen to his physical urges instead of the warning bells going off in his head.

But he didn't. With regret, he eased away. Her breathing was uneven, her body resting against his.

"You drive me crazy," he told her in a husky voice. He willed the magic to free her, and the manacles around her wrists disappeared.

Her look was slightly dazed, her lips reddened from his kiss.

"Kinda complicated, isn't it?" he asked, as perplexed by what was between them as she appeared to be.

She sighed and reclaimed her balance.

"I don't do complicated, Skylar," he warned her. "Whatever this is ... it's just physical. Something we can both walk away from."

She raised an eyebrow at him and pried herself away. Whatever she was thinking, she didn't say it, instead stepping out of his reach. He felt the loss of her body heat like he'd feel the cold of the air outside the warm cabin.

He didn't like it. Rather than focus on it, he turned to the fire and quickly assessed himself. His magic was calm once more, though his hormones and erection were nowhere near as placated. He grimaced, hating the idea of walking away from her when she seemed willing to sleep with him.

"Back on task," he said as much to himself as to her. "Tomorrow, you're taking me in."

Her silence was troubled, but he didn't dare look at her, not until he'd settled his blood. Every time they touched, her scent ended up infused into his senses, distracting him.

"Got it?" he prodded.

"You're not worried that I'll warn people about what you're doing?"

"Pretty sure I can handle it."

"But you don't kill people, remember?" There was sarcasm in her voice, enough to draw his gaze. Her arms were crossed, her eyes direct. Her features were still flushed from their kiss.

"The way I understand it, I only need to kill *you*," he reminded her.

"If you aren't going to kill everyone, what do you plan on doing there?" she asked.

"What is your obsession with me killing people?"

"It's what you do. You're a dragon."

"Shifters don't hurt people, Skylar. They mind their own business and try to lay low."

"We wouldn't have spent the past thousand years hunting them if that was the case," she argued.

"You haven't. Slayers are a recent thing. I've been alive for a thousand years, and you are the first slayer I've ever heard of, let alone met!"

"That can't be true," she replied, studying him. "They couldn't track you."

"They didn't exist. Now that they do, shifters are dropping like flies. Your people are collecting them for a reason." His anger was rising again. He drew a deep breath.

Skylar's troubled gaze was on the ceiling.

"What?" he asked, reading her expression.

"Nothing. I don't want to take you in, though."

"Look, nothing bad will happen to anyone if you take me in. I'm going to find out what's going on. It's my job to protect the other shifters."

"You're nothing like what they said you'd be like," she murmured.

"What? That I'm a *man* who turns into a dragon and not some soulless monster?" he challenged. "We police our own. We take care of our own."

She appeared torn, as if not wanting to believe him.

"What do they do to you in your training?" he asked.

She shrugged. "Teach us martial arts, history of the slayers, how to track shifters."

"Any sort of extended meditation where you're out for hours and don't recall what happened?"

"How do you know that?"

"Honey, I've been around long enough to have seen it all. You've been brainwashed, plain and simple," he replied.

"Whatever. Let's go." She turned and walked to the door, tugging at it.

Chace watched. The cabin had freed her from her place hanging from the ceiling but wouldn't let her out. At least it was listening to him about not freeing her.

"There's only one way down the mountain," he reminded her.

She stiffened.

"Where we going?"

Her back was to him, her fingers testing the doorknob. It didn't open, and she dropped her hand, quiet for a moment. He almost saw her debating. He'd given her a way out with a hefty caveat.

"Sonoita, Arizona. The Field is in the middle of the desert." She turned as she spoke and leaned against the door.

Chace grabbed his jacket. He ordered the cabin to take them to the new location and strode to the door, not expecting her to block his exit.

"Ready when you are," he said, pausing inches from her, close enough for her scent and warmth to derail his intentions. She gazed up at him, clear blue eyes troubled.

"Promise me you won't hurt anyone," she said. "Unless it's me. That's okay. We're supposed to be enemies."

Chace studied her. He restrained the impulse to touch her. She was uneasy but unmoving despite her fear.

"I promise not to provoke anyone," he replied carefully. "But if someone comes after me …" he trailed off.

She looked away. "Okay. I guess that's fair."

"You decide to trust a monster that turns people into fried chicken?"

"Not much of a choice. Besides" she brightened "maybe the Field can do what I can't and bring you under control before you turn people into fried chicken."

She started to turn, but he caught her arm.

"I can't take this shit," he snapped. "If I was going to kill anyone, it'd be you, and I haven't hurt one hair on your head. In fact, we fucked like we've been lovers for years. You can't keep telling me this bullshit about me being the monster you think I am when you've seen proof of the opposite!"

She stared at him for a moment, her face flushing. For the first time since they'd met, there was anger in her eyes.

"Maybe you should stop insisting that my entire reality is wrong, and yours is right," she retorted. "I don't know what to think about you, Chace, or what's happening or why I keep having these dreams … but I can't think that the only world I've ever known is just … fake!" She stopped, flustered.

"I'm sorry," he said, even more disturbed. She hid her turmoil well. He hadn't considered that debunking her reality was as distressing to her as accusing him of eating people was irritating to him. "But don't you want to know the truth? If not about me, then about you? Because I have a feeling they did more than train you at that place. I think they wiped your mind."

Skylar pulled away from him and yanked open the door. She walked out.

Chace remained in place, torn between pushing her farther and leaving her alone. She knew something was wrong. Was this why she didn't protest too much about taking him in? Did she think he might learn something she needed to know?

"Where the hell are we?" she demanded from outside.

Chace smiled and left the cabin. In the distance, the sun was peeking up over a set of purple-gray mountains. The flat southern desert between them and the mountains was littered with saguaros, mesquite and other varieties of desert cacti and flora.

"Outside of Sonoita," he replied.

"We ... your cabin ..."

"My magic controls the cabin and the bar," he explained. "They go and do what I want." *Most of the time.*

"That isn't in our training, either." Her frustration was in her voice. "But you're not a real shifter. You were turned into one."

"I *am* a real shifter. How do you know all shifters were born the way they are? Your training?"

"You don't have to be an asshole," she muttered.

"Oh, you're here to kill me, and I'm the asshole?" He shook his head, beyond agitated by her. "If you don't want me turning into an angry dragon right now, you might want to take my hand."

She turned at the ultimatum and studied him briefly before quickly crossing to him to take his extended hand. At once, his magic began to settle, this time responding faster to her than before.

"This doesn't make sense," she voiced his thoughts aloud. "None of this does." Her nearness was distracting him, quieting his emotions in a way that warned him the only problem with his plan was going to be the insane attraction he felt towards her.

"Which way?" he asked.

She focused on their surroundings and the different mountain ranges in each direction.

"That's Elephant Head," she said, pointing to a mountain that resembled the smooth, sloped forehead of an elephant. "The Field is at the base."

"Let's go."

She glanced down at their clasped hands, and he sensed she was as rattled by their bodies touching as he was. She said nothing, though, and tugged him in the direction of the mountain.

*Hopefully, this works.*

# Chapter Eleven

S kylar was sweating by the time they reached The Field. Chace's grip on her was firm, and he hadn't said a word to her since leaving the cabin.

Which was good, because she was pissed at him, at The Field, at not understanding why he didn't behave like any shifter she'd ever heard of. His assertion that *she* was wrong about the thousands of years of slayer history was absurd.

Except what he said almost made sense. She'd missed her annual session at The Field, and she wondered if her dreams were connected to missing her monthly and yearly refreshers. Last night was the worst. She was almost grateful to wake up and find a dragon standing beside the bed. The more she thought about the dreams and the possibility that Chace was right about her being brainwashed, the more distressed she became.

She tried to push the dream away, but it was harder when she was hungry, hot and tired. It didn't help that Chace's dragon fire was stirring her body in ways that took away from her attempts to center her focus.

One of the dreams was creeping back, the one where they were running from the farmhouse. She feared looking up, in case the great dragon from the vision was circling them.

*Ginger.* Skylar abruptly remembered her mother's name. She shouldn't have any memories of the woman who allegedly died so long ago.

"What's wrong?" Chace's low, soft voice interrupted her thoughts.

Skylar realized she'd stopped walking and stood with her eyes closed, reliving the tender memory that shouldn't exist. She opened her eyes to see the tans and browns of the desert.

"Nothing," she murmured. "Didn't sleep well last night." She started forward once more, pulling her hand free of his after the few hours walk.

It was easier to push the memories away without Chace's magic fluttering through her.

The Field was visible, a single-story, long, adobe-style building hugging the base of the mountain. Located half an hour from the nearest house, it rested at the end of a dirt road behind thick stone walls. Seeing it made her more anxious than she expected.

"How often do you come here?" Chace asked. There was a note of uneasiness in his voice.

"Monthly for a one-day refreshers," she replied. "Then once a year, we spend two weeks here to get physical check-ups and re-certified in our fields."

"So that's when they brainwash you."

She rolled her eyes, not wanting to argue with him again yet feeling unsettled by the routine visit to The Field. She should be happy for bringing in the last dragon. She was conflicted as much by her attraction to him and her sense of duty as she was by her too-real dreams. Being around him made her doubt her world.

She reached the entrance of the compound and paused, going to the guard shack beside the main entrance. He held out a thumb print scanner, eyes straying to the large dragon shifter standing too close behind her.

"Bringing in a shifter," she said with forced lightness.

The scanner turned green.

"Voluntarily?" the guard asked skeptically, eyes on where the golden lasso should've been.

"Yeah," she said. "Long story."

He nodded slowly and stepped aside. "I'll tell Caleb you're headed to the rehab facility."

"Thanks." Skylar didn't need to look behind her to know that Chace was following. She almost wished he wouldn't, so she wasn't caught between the disappointment of never seeing him again after today and the hope that she could return to her normal, simple world once he was gone.

She crossed a large courtyard edged by official SUVs and went to the thick, metal door leading into the compound's side entrance, the closest to the containment facilities. Pressing her hand to the hand scanner, she waited for the familiar click and opened the door.

"Thank god!" she breathed as a whoosh of air conditioner hit her. The desert sun was horrible, even in autumn.

"You're that eager to get rid of me?" Chace asked, irritation in his voice.

*Far from it.* She hesitated then refrained from responding, instead walking down the hallway. She didn't know what to think about Chace or his claim of wanting to help other shifters escape, and letting her mind even acknowledge how incredibly well he knew how to use his mouth and tongue.

She entered a small vestibule secured by two locked doors. One led into the compound while the other led into the rehabilitation center, an area she wasn't authorized to be. Today, however, her gaze lingered on the door opposite the one she entered, and she wondered what was there, and if it was as bad as Chace seemed to think. True, she'd never seen any shifter after she helped bring him or her in, but she'd never thought twice about where they were resettled or what they went through to become non-threats.

"You did it," Caleb sounded surprised.

Realizing he was waiting for her to speak, she faced him. His dark eyes were on Chace, his body tense. He held one of the golden ropes.

"Caleb, this is Chace, the last dragon shifter," she said. "He's ... interested in being rehabilitated."

Chace said nothing, though she sensed him bristle at her words.

"He came voluntarily?" Caleb asked.

"I did," Chace answered. "You won't need that." He pointed to the lasso.

"It's protocol."

"He means, he can melt it with his magic. They don't work," Skylar explained. "So, you've met. He's all yours."

"Great work, Skylar," Caleb said with a rare smile. "You're here for your monthly refresh?"

"Yep," she said and started away. "Out of curiosity, how long does the rehab take?"

"Depends." Caleb looked from Chace to her. "He's older, so it might be longer."

Though she didn't expect him to say more about the secret program, she couldn't help feeling disappointed by the vague answer.

*What do you expect, Sky?* She asked herself silently.

"If you'll come with me, I'll give you a tour before we start discussing the program," Caleb told the shifter.

She watched Chace join Caleb at the other door, uncertain why her instincts were growing more restless. The farther Chace got from her, the more unsettled they became, as if some part of her knew what lay beyond the door behind Caleb – and that it was not a place Chace was going to return from.

"Follow me, please," Caleb said in a clipped tone. He opened the door and walked through.

Chace paused to look back at Skylar. The direct gaze further distressed the instincts she didn't understand.

"See you soon, Sky," he said.

*I don't think so.* Biting her tongue to keep from saying anything, she watched him step through the doorway. The heavy door swung shut, sealing them both away from her vision. She suddenly wanted to know what was on the other side of a door she'd never looked at twice.

*What's wrong with me?*

Shaking her head, she left the area and strode through the compound to check in with the medical crew that ran the monthly check-ups before she went for her refresher. A nurse led her to a private room.

The routine physical was the same every month. Skylar sat on the table and waited, swinging her legs. A moment later, the door opened.

"Heya, Sky," said the doctor, a young, recent graduate of medical school a few years older than her. "How's life?"

"Good, doc," she murmured, thoughts on her weird two days with the dragon shifter.

"You don't sound like your normal happy self," he said with a smile.

"Didn't sleep well," she admitted. "Then trekked across the desert this morning. I'm hungry and hot."

"That I understand," he said. "Tell me about your sleep problem."

She considered. "Just … weird dreams. Nonsensical really."

"Oh? Like what?" He set down the medical record in his hands to focus his attention fully on her.

*Weird.* Normally, he asked a few routine questions, listened to her heart and walked out. She didn't remember the last time one of the doctor's had really paid attention to anything she said.

When she didn't respond immediately, his eyes went to her bandaged wrists.

"What happened?" he asked, taking them.

"Got caught by a shifter." She winced at his touch.

He unwound the gauze around each wrist to study them.

"These don't look bad. Probably painful, though. I'll have a nurse clean these up and re-bandage them," he said. "Drop by the pharmacy on your way out for some antibiotics."

"Okay."

"Now, these dreams."

She made a show of looking at her wrists, not certain she wanted to share her dreams with him.

"They're nothing," she said at last. "Just of my family."

"But they're upsetting you?"

She shrugged.

He was quiet for a moment then picked up the tablet computer. He jotted something down on it then smiled.

"You're late for your annual refresher, and you've brought in quite a few shifters lately. The yearly visits help us assess stress issues with the job. Maybe you're repressing some angst about work. Perfectly normal."

"Really?" she asked.

"Yep. Just stop by the psych's office on your way out, okay?"

She nodded, somewhat relieved by his nonchalance.

"Take care and see you next month," he said cheerfully.

She smiled. He left and was quickly replaced by a nurse who bandaged her wrists before okaying her to leave.

Ten minutes later, Skylar entered the office of the resident psychiatrist, a fit man in his forties with a friendly smile and dark eyes.

"Skylar!" he exclaimed. "Come on in."

*Do The Field people normally irk me?* She managed a smile, shrugging off her agitation as a side effect of the long walk and no breakfast. The staff at the compound were normally nice, but she didn't recall them being overly friendly before.

"Hmm. I can move a few appointments around this morning. You're late for your annual, so I want to go ahead and treat you," he said, studying notes on a tablet. He sat behind a modern desk, in front of which were two chairs. "On the table. We can do some meditative work."

She glanced at the massage table that served as his meditative table. Never had she dreaded it before, but this time, her instincts were wriggling.

*It's just a mandatory nap, like usual,* she chided her restless mind. Just because the shifter she brought in claimed this was somehow part of her brainwashing ...

Queasy, she went to the table anyway and lay down.

"My wrists are hurting. Might be hard for me to concentrate," she said, holding up her arms.

"Not a problem at all. I've got something that'll put you under in a few seconds." He crossed to the small refrigerator in a corner of his office and withdrew a small bottle of clear liquid. Grabbing a disposable syringe from the top, he expertly opened it and prepped the shot.

"Relax," he urged, approaching. "This is the same thing we do for your yearly."

*I don't recall there being needles involved.* Skylar realized she was gripping the edges of the table tightly enough for her bandaged wrists to pulse.

Skylar's instincts were at a roar, and she didn't understand what was wrong with something she supposedly went through every year. She forced herself not to look at what he did, wanting to believe that the doubt she'd felt around the dragon shifter was a byproduct of his strange magic and nothing more.

"The doctor said you're having strange dreams?" the psychiatrist asked. He pushed up the sleeve of one of her arms then swabbed the injection site with alcohol.

"Yeah," she replied.

"Do you remember what they were of?"

"My mom. Nothing really concrete. Just random images," she hedged.

"If they were real enough to interfere with your sleep, I'd say there's something to them," he observed. "How have you been feeling lately?"

"Good. Just frustrated with the dragon I've been tracking."

"Stressed?"

"Eh, not really," she said.

"The doc says you were a hostage?"

"I guess."

"That can create a great deal of psychological stress, may even have you relating to your captor."

"I think you're right," she said slowly. "I mean, some of what he said makes sense."

"Perfectly natural," the psychiatrist said with a warm smile. "What did he say that made sense?"

"Well …" Skylar was thoughtful for a moment. "That slayers are a new thing, something he hasn't seen in his thousand years."

"You know that to be untrue."

"Yeah, I do," she agreed, mind on the history classes she'd taken during her training. "But he also said we were brainwashed. And then I started remembering things about my mother, about growing up with her, that just aren't possible. I mean, she died after I was born. Why do I remember her?"

"These are the dreams you're having? Of your family?" he asked.

"Yes."

"I can address those during this session."

She glanced at him. The sting of the needle entering her arm made her stomach turn, and she focused on deep breathing. He withdrew the needle and crossed to a biohazard bin to throw it away.

"Close your eyes, Skylar," he said. "This won't take long, and you won't remember the discomfort."

She obeyed. The solution he injected into her felt like it was trapped in her arm, making the muscles around it ache. The place grew warm then uncomfortably hot but didn't leave the small area where it was contained.

"These will monitor your brain activity while you are in the meditative state."

She felt the cold, moist pressure of round monitoring pads on either temple. A machine nearby whirred to life, and she heard the psychiatrist's rustling stopped as he sat.

"As the serum takes effect, I want you to focus on your training," he said. "The history of the slayers, the dragons who have caused numerous deaths in the past two decades, turned people into fried chicken."

*Chace doesn't like fried chicken.* The thought caught little traction before fluttering through her mind and being swallowed in the darkness that was closing in.

Skylar slid silently into a drugged sleep.

# Chapter Twelve

T hus far, the building resembled a science laboratory. Chace peeked into each door they crossed, his senses recording everything from the whir of air conditioning to the hue of the walls to the distant scent of cleaning products and ... something else. Something that made him pause. It was elusive, too faint for him to determine the direction it came from or what exactly it was.

But he suspected it was the scent of other shifters.

"... the medical clinic where we check everyone who comes in," Caleb was saying, pausing at a doorway.

Chace glanced in, seeing a receptionist desk, waiting area and short hallway lined with exam rooms. His gaze lingered on the waiting area, and he almost laughed. He didn't see half a dozen shifters waiting patiently to be reprogrammed.

"This will make the staff more comfortable," Caleb added, holding up a golden lasso.

It was thicker than the one Skylar had possessed.

"Whatever," Chace said, unconcerned. "I burnt the last one to a crisp." He reached for it.

Caleb handed it over, and Chace draped it over his neck.

"Happy?" he asked.

"Very." Caleb's smile was confident.

"Now, tell me what really goes on here," Chace ordered him. "No more of this crap about rehabilitation."

Caleb strode into the clinic, motioning for Chace to follow. Chace did so. He tossed the tail end of the rope over his shoulder to keep it from bumping against his chest with his movement. His eyes scanned the rooms they passed.

They were all empty, but the faint scent was stronger. Shifters had been in this clinic, even if he didn't see them now.

Caleb ducked into one room

"Have a seat," he said. "I'll have a nurse come in to check on you."

"I'll stand." Chace entered the small room and glanced around.

Nothing was threatening about this clinic or different from a normal clinic. Mr. Nothing had warned him, but Chace wasn't seeing the issue yet, aside from the brainwashing the slayers went through.

"How do you rehabilitate shifters?" He tried again.

"We inject them full of a solution that takes their magic away."

Chace's gaze returned to Caleb in interest. "Explain."

"That's all there is to it." Caleb shrugged.

A nurse entered with a smile at Caleb that turned nervous at the sight of Chace.

"He's got his lasso on. You're fine," Caleb assured her.

"You take their magic and just free them?" Chace asked skeptically.

"Not exactly."

The nurse took his arm and wrapped rubber around his bicep tightly then peered at his arm, looking for a vein. Chace felt her tap it then swab him down before drawing a needle out of one drawer.

"What're you doing?" he asked.

"Taking a blood sample for the lab."

"Are you brainwashed, too?"

She said nothing. Caleb snorted.

"I'll take that as a yes," Chace said. He was quiet as she drew two small vials of blood, placed a band-aid on the droplet of blood that remained when she withdrew the needle, then released the rubber from his arm.

The nurse left.

"They aren't brainwashed," Caleb said when she was gone. "They are indoctrinated the same way the slayers are."

"And you? Are you indoctrinated?" Chace asked.

"I'm a loyal member of the organization. No need for indoctrination."

*Pretty sure that's the same thing.* Chace was quiet, studying Caleb. The middle-aged slayer appeared to be waiting for something, his expectant gaze on Chace.

"This all seems … normal," *Even though I know it's not.* Chace voiced. "Are there any shifters here in the program now?"

"Half a dozen. They're all almost ready for reintegration."

"Which consists of …"

"How are you feeling, shifter?"

"Great. Never better." Except his head was starting to spin and his senses dulling.

"No lightheadedness?"

Chace forced himself to shake his head.

"We'll continue the tour." Caleb left the room.

Chace reached up to the lasso, not understanding what was making him suddenly ill. As hard as he tried to grip the golden rope, it seemed to go straight through his fingers. He wasn't able to move it or grab it. Disturbed by the weird magic of the lasso, he trailed Caleb, not wanting the slayer to know something was affecting him.

He sniffed the air again, unable to smell even the cleaning solutions that had been almost overpowering before. The lights of the waiting room, however, had grown in intensity. They were bright enough for him to shield his eyes from them.

"Problem?" Caleb asked calmly from his spot leaning against the receptionist desk.

"Just … fine." The world was starting to spin and the ground shift beneath his feet. "Shit."

Chace hit the ground like a sack of bricks, unable to gauge where the ground was to brace his body. He lay still, the cold floor against one cheek while he focused on not throwing up while his head spun sickeningly. The dark figure of Caleb squatted near him.

"The lassos we give newbie slayers are fake for two reasons: one, because they don't understand how dangerous it is if it falls into the wrong hands and two, because there are only two real lassos. Can't have one going missing on a routine mission."

Chace listened, furious then sleepy. Unable to hang onto his emotions the way he needed to if he was to shift, he lay still, aware of the world around him, even if he couldn't register everything going on.

He was lifted off the ground onto a stretcher. The movement of the lights overhead made his stomach lurch, so he closed his eyes.

They didn't take him far, and the glare of the lights disappeared. He didn't open his eyes again until he was certain they stopped moving. When he did, he found himself in a private exam room. While he wasn't able to see well, he judged that this was not a normal exam room, if the thick metal door was any indication. It was propped open by an orderly in white.

Resting his head back, he tested his strength.

It was gone. His arms and legs met the resistance of thick straps across his body, bands he would've been able to break on a normal day. The lasso had incapacitated his magic in a way far beyond what Skylar's touch did to him.

Caleb entered, followed by another nurse wheeling two IV towers.

"What is this?" Chace asked, lifting his head to try to motion to the lasso with his chin.

"Containment rope. Its core is the hair of a dragon shifter and it's coated in radioactive material and poison, among other things, to create a lethal combination that renders a shifter powerless. Can't take it through the airport, but it'll incapacitate the biggest shifters alive."

*Shit.* Chace had once been warned that brashness and arrogance had a price, a lesson that just didn't stick. Right now, he wished he'd listened to his instincts and Mr. Nothing about these people.

Distantly, he registered the pain from catheters being placed in both hands. He didn't feel the first IV but he did the second. It felt like ice was being pumped into him.

He gasped, unable to combat the coldness moving through his body. It went up his arm and shoulder then to his heart. He felt it slow then stop, the way it had been before he met Skylar, before the ice continued through his body. It didn't just calm his dragon fire, but it felt like it was eating him alive from the inside out.

"You don't want to know that this is," Caleb said. He motioned the others out. "Just know it'll kill you pretty quickly. You'll be reintegrated into a graveyard with the rest of the dead, no longer able to hurt innocent people."

"I've ... never ..." Chace wasn't able to finish. The agony moving through him was too much.

"I'll take this back," Caleb said, stretching across him to reclaim the lasso. "One less shifter in the world." His eyes were hard, as cold as the strange fire in Chace's veins. "Goodbye, shifter."

Chace heard the door clang closed behind Caleb. He closed his eyes, unable to move.

*I hope Skylar is doing better than me.*

# Chapter Thirteen

S kylar awoke with a jerk, the world around her solidifying quickly.

"You dozed off."

She sat, recognizing the shrink's office on the compound. Vaguely she recalled bringing in Chace then having her wrists checked before coming here.

*Pretty sure you knocked me out,* she responded silently. The site where he'd inject her felt swollen like a knot had formed. She glanced at it noticed faint bruising.

"You feel okay?" the shrink asked.

Skylar glanced at him, uncertain why his intent gaze bothered her.

"Hungry," she replied. "How long was I out?"

"Two hours."

"Ugh. Starving then."

He smiled. "Go on to the cafeteria. They should be serving lunch."

She nodded and climbed off the table.

"See you next year."

Skylar didn't respond but left his office, her stomach feeling like it was ready to start eating itself. She touched the tender spot on her arm and flinched. Not only did the light touch hurt, but there was a large bump beneath the surface. She'd never left an annual check-up with a lump like this. It had done as he said and helped her relax.

*I can address those during the session.*

"Maybe I shouldn't have slept through it." The memories were more insistent instead of gone. Was she relieved that she hadn't lost her mother again or upset that she wasn't able to return to her normal life?

Shaking her head, she went to the cafeteria to grab a sandwich and sat down with her tray at a table, staring at the food on her plate.

*Ginger was baking pies. They smelled like heaven, the rich combination of apple, cinnamon and butter drawing Skylar from her room on the top floor of the two-story home they were renting in eastern Ohio. She hopped down the stairs and skipped through the hallway towards the bright kitchen with a yellow ceiling and white walls.*

*She loved the smell, had missed it since they started running again months before. It was almost Thanksgiving, the time of year when her mother cooked. The simple tradition of a pie managed to alleviate the fear and uncertainty she'd felt since the day they left the farmhouse.*

*Life was almost normal again.*

*"Mama, that smells like heaven!" she exclaimed, running down the hallway towards the kitchen. At thirteen, Skylar was tall and lanky and made an effort not to trip over her feet. "Can I please, please, please try a little piece?"*

*She hurried into the kitchen and the pie sitting on the counter. Her mother was nowhere around, and Skylar assumed she'd gone to the restroom.*

*Skylar ventured from the kitchen, listening for sounds of her mother rustling around somewhere in the house. She heard the slam of a car door instead and the sound of someone hurrying up the steps to the front door.*

*Skylar went to a window overlooking the front. Her mother was nowhere to be found, and Skylar studied a black SUV with windows too dark for her to see who was there. Leaning against the window, she recognized the man at her door.*

*Caleb.*

"You waiting for them to leap into your mouth on their own?" a familiar voice asked.

Skylar shook her head, the scent of apple pie lingering with the weird vision. She waved for Mason to join her.

"Weird day," she said. "How you doing?"

"Not bad," he replied. "Here for my yearly. Heard you brought in the dragon."

"Yeah. He didn't put up much of a fight."

"That's amazing!"

*Except it's not.* She rubbed her face with her hands. "I don't know what's wrong with me. I should be psyched."

"Definitely."

She toyed with her food, hungry but bothered by the random memory of apple pie.

"You okay?" Mason asked. "Caleb said you were a prisoner. He didn't hurt you did he?"

"No. I kinda wish he did. I mean, isn't he supposed to be this horrible monster that eats people?" she asked. "Mason, he's ... not a monster."

Mason took a bite of his sandwich, listening intently with his dark eyes on her.

"Guess I'm just tired." She turned her focus to her food, not wanting to think about what was happening to Chace at that moment somewhere on the compound.

"Did you see the shrink?"

"Yeah. Just pumped me full of some shit that is making my arm hurt," she bent the angry arm.

"You normally leave his office pretty happy."

Mason's words added to her sense of something not being quite right.

"Mason, what do you think happens to the shifters when they're rehabilitated?" she asked quietly enough for only him to hear.

"No idea. Never thought about it."

"I didn't either until today. Now I can't stop and I can't stop thinking about my mom."

"Your mom?" he echoed, confused. "But she died soon after you were born, like mine did."

"I know it doesn't make sense."

"I'm not saying that exactly."

She paused in her chewing to meet his gaze. Mason appeared as troubled as she felt, his large brown eyes distant.

"Did you know I had a sister?" he asked.

"Really?"

"Well, I think I did. I've been dreaming about her. *That* makes no sense, since I was an only child and an orphan."

"But you remember her."

"Yeah. Certain events bring back these really just random memories. Like one where we're racing our bikes down a hill." He offered a small, affectionate smile at the girl in his mind. "Then nothing for days then like, a totally different random memory."

"Me, too," she whispered.

"They started a few months ago. The shrink said he'd address it during my yearly and make sure they stop. I don't know if I want them to, Skylar," he admitted. "I kinda like the idea of knowing I had a family."

"Seems too real not to be." Skylar toyed with her French fries. "But I mean, it can't be real. Can it?"

"I don't know," he admitted. "I've been trying to figure it out since the memories started."

They finished eating in pensive silence. Skylar was trying hard not to think of what the memories meant, if real. What were the chances that she and Mason started having them after being bitten by shifters? Was it as the shrink said – an aftereffect of the magic – or was there more?

"Do you think … " she started then stopped, not sure she wanted to go down this road.

"… there might be something else going on?" He finished for her.

"Mason, Chace – the dragon – said that there were never slayers before us."

Mason studied her, weighing her words carefully.

"He surrendered because he wanted me to bring him here, so he could find out what happened to the other shifters."

"Caleb took him to rehab?"

"Yeah. You ever been back there?"

"No. You're not thinking of … what *are* you thinking of doing?"

"I don't know." She sighed. "But what if the shifters we slept with – what if their magic opened up memories we're not supposed to remember?"

"Sounds like a conspiracy." Mason smiled. "Not saying you're wrong, but what is the motivation behind doing that to us?"

"That I don't know."

"You like the dragon more than you should," he guessed.

"He's just not what I expected or what we were told dragons were like," she replied. "If he's right about … some things, then it seems like we might've been misled. But why mislead us?"

"To get the shifters here. Maybe we really are the only ones who can track them. Don't ask me why," he added quickly. "Just theorizing at this point."

"What was the shifter you slept with like?"

"Nothing like what they said. She was really sweet."

Skylar sat back, thoughts on Chace. She hadn't been able to clear her senses of his smoky sweet scent or dismiss the memory of his hands running down her body. His kiss was incredibly good, his soft growl and intelligent gaze snagging her attention even when they weren't touching.

He'd been genuinely puzzled or dismissive of everything she tried to tell him, everything she'd been told her entire life. He'd been gentle with her. Now that she knew the cabin responded to his magic, she realized he had turned the interior of her bonds into fleece when he saw they were hurting her.

Aside from hanging her over the cliff's edge to find out why she was trying to hurt the shifters, he hadn't done anything to hurt her.

Seeing him in his dragon form, however, was enough to make her reconsider anything nice he'd done. He'd been right about everything from the start, but he was a *dragon*! Why was she considering trying to help him or at least, to make sure rehabilitation wasn't as grim as he tried to convince her?

"I need access to the rehab wing," she said softly. "Chace has been almost right about everything. I want to ask him more about dragons and slayers, and I feel like I need to know what really goes on in the rehab center." *I want to learn more about my history.* Somehow, Chace's magic helped jar the memories loose.

"They told us … ah. Right. We can't really trust what they told us."

"Exactly. Who has access?"

"Trainers. Caleb. The shrink. Or at least, their hands do," Mason joked, referring to the palm scanners at the entrance of the rehab center. "We'd need someone to get us access."

"You're headed to the shrink, right?" she asked.

"Yes."

"Well then, I'm coming with you. We need someone to open the door, and I think he'll cooperate."

"You do?"

"Sorta," she said. "I mean, if he doesn't, we just knock him out and take him with us to the door."

"And then when he wakes up?"

"I don't know." She thought back to the serum he'd injected her with. It put her out for two hours. It was enough time for them to find out what was going on and leave, if it came down to it.

"Hopefully he'll just agree to help. If not, then I'll figure out something."

"Wait a minute. You're talking about the possibility of having to walk away. Permanently."

She said nothing.

"Skylar, you can't go down this path without realizing there might not be a way back. Is it worth it to save this guy?" Mason asked in a hushed tone.

"It's worth it to learn the truth. I don't know about him, but these can't be dreams. I have a mother out there somewhere," she said. "He scares the shit out of me. But something isn't right and if this is a dead end, we can grovel and beg for Caleb's forgiveness and let them brainwash us again, if we're wrong. I mean, they need us, right?"

"It's a huge risk, Sky."

"I know." She propped her elbows up on the table and cupped her cheeks. "But I mean, I just want to ask Chace some questions. We don't know that I'll have to leave."

He was quiet for a moment then sighed. "Just questions. Okay. But let me get the doc, okay? We play golf together. He'll probably listen to me more than he would you."

"You're so sweet, Mason." She smiled. "Okay. Go get the doc and I'll wait for you in the vestibule."

He stuffed the last of his sandwich in his mouth and stood. She took his tray and watched him walk away.

Skylar dumped their trash and made her way through the compound to the area where she'd led Chace earlier. She paced, waiting nervously for Mason.

Her friend was right – it was a risk, but she couldn't help the nagging instinct that urged her to find out what was beyond the door where Chace had gone. She wanted to talk to him one more time before he was brainwashed, if that was truly what happened beyond the doors.

Her gaze settled on the palm scanner standing between her and the rehabilitation center beyond. After a moment, she approached it and rested her hand to it, expecting it to light up red, a sign she didn't have access.

It turned green.

Surprised, Skylar debated waiting for Mason then opened the door.

*He'll catch up.* She stepped into the part of the compound where she'd never been before and closed the door behind her. A long, white hall was before her that ended in a T-intersection with a familiar plaque on the wall. The grey plaques were at each intersection and corner of the compound, denoting directions with arrows for what parts of the compound lay in each direction.

She walked to the end of the hallway and read the sign. To the right was the *Central Rehab Center* while the arrow pointing left was labeled as *Dorms.* She went right, suspecting Chace's day wasn't over yet for him to be in the dorms.

The hallway smelled medicinal and was lined with doors, most of which were closed. She peered into the first one she passed with an embedded window. Her gaze swept around a lab of some sort. It was quiet, with two men in white coats working diligently over equipment she didn't recognize.

She continued onward, passed an intersection with a plaque indicating there was a medical clinic, and continued towards the rehab center. Another man in a lab coat passed her without stopping, and she relaxed, suspecting they saw a steady stream of different faces throughout the compound.

She engaged her senses, trying to track the dragon shifter.

His elusive essence was behind her. It was stronger this time than the last when she'd tried to hunt him. With a glance in the direction where Mason would come from, Skylar backtracked then headed towards the medical clinic.

She listened to the instincts this time, not expecting them to guide her to the dragon when they'd thus far just confused her. Stopping in front of a door, she paused to orient herself towards a possible route of escape, in case she needed to make a run for it.

Skylar opened the door where she'd sensed the dragon shifter and stepped into a narrow hallway lined by thick, metal doors identified only by numbers. The shifter's essence was scrambled here and she placed a hand on the first door.

*Reminds me of the bar.* All the doors seemed to emit some sort of shifter magic. She moved to the next, rested her hand to try to tap into the magic behind the door, and then moved on. She'd made it halfway down the hallway when she almost caught his essence again.

Skylar pressed both hands to the door to double check before she slid one over to the wall and rested her palm on the scanner.

The lock clicked open softly. She pushed the door open and entered the small exam room. Counters and cabinets lined each side, and it smelled of disinfectant.

Her attention was immediately caught by the form of Chace. He was strapped to a bed and unconscious, two IVs running to his arms. He seemed pale beneath the golden skin and his veins were an unnatural dark purple against his skin. Though the power of his muscular frame was far from diminished, his uneven, shallow breathing warned her that he was growing weaker.

*We are the dragons' protectors.* Her mother's voice was louder this time, and an instinct unlike any Skylar had every experienced roared to life within her.

She had to protect him. Whatever was going on here, it was wrong, even if she wasn't entirely certain what it was.

Skylar approached him, not understanding why he was on IVs when he'd been perfectly healthy the last time she saw him. Was this part of the rehab program? Why were her hands shaking and the warning bells in her mind screaming?

She crossed to him and looked at the contents of the first IV bag.

"Saline. Okay. Nothing weird there."

The second, however, had a biohazard sign on it and bore the name of a solution with more letters than she cared to count.

"Chace?" she ventured.

His eyes fluttered open. He didn't seem able to focus and his breathing grew more ragged. He looked from her to the second IV, the one with the biohazard sign. He tried to lift his left arm.

"You um, don't like that one, huh?" she asked.

Shifter magic permeated the air around her in a sudden surge as if he was trying to shift. His eyes closed again, and his body went limp.

*I have to get him out of here.* The urge to protect him was almost too strong for her to think logically. It was as powerful as the chemistry between them; it managed to overwhelm years of training the first night they met and did so again now. Skylar tugged the IV tube free of the splint in his arm. She leaned forward and tapped his cheeks until he woke once more.

"It's out," she said, concerned. "What is it?"

"Good." His voice was almost too quiet to hear. "Need ad … ren … lin."

"Adrenaline," she repeated. "Where would I find that?"

His eyes went to one cabinet.

Skylar crossed to it and opened the door, observing the syringes in plastic.

"Looks like adrenaline," she said. "You want one or two?"

"One."

She tore the package open and returned to his bedside, resting it on his chest while she reached for the releases to the straps holding him to the bed.

"No," he said. "Ad … renalin."

"All right." She pushed up his sleeve to get at the meaty bicep.

"Heart."

"What?"

"Shot in … heart."

"Um, seriously?"

"Heart."

Skylar swallowed hard then picked up the syringe. She freed the needle at one end then rested her hand over his heart. His eyes closed again, and she sensed whatever was wrong, it was getting worse.

She set one hand on his chest and practiced hitting his heart a few times.

"Okay. Just … don't freak out on me, okay?" she said.

He was unconscious.

She drew a deep breath then plunged the needle into his heart. With a grimace, she pressed the plunger until it was empty then yanked the syringe free.

Nothing happened.

"Chace?"

His breathing slowed and then stopped.

Skylar crossed to the cabinet and snatched another of the syringes. She tore it open with her teeth, braced a hand against his chest and plunged the second into his heart. She emptied it out then tossed it aside, waiting.

About to grab a third, she just opened the cabinet when he gasped.

Skylar whirled and froze.

Chace's face was red, his muscles bulging. He strained against the straps. They snapped open, and Chace rolled, landing on the floor on his stomach.

"You okay?" she asked uncertainly.

"What … did you do?" he managed in a strained voice.

"One didn't work, so I used two." She backed away as she spoke.

He uttered a string of curses. His skin rippled, the muscles bulging and changing beneath his skin. Shifter magic filled the air.

"Shit!" She glanced around. There was no room for a dragon, let alone *her* and a dragon. Spinning, she went to the door and tried to open it. It didn't budge. There was no palm scanner inside. "Bad news, Chace."

She faced him again and pressed her back against the door. Wings were budding from Chace's back, his body convulsing.

*Dear god … just calm down, Chace!* She pleaded silently.

"Come … here," he rasped.

"I don't think that's a good idea."

"If I turn … will probably kill you."

"Maybe there's something to calm you down in here." She went to the cabinet again and wrenched it open, starting to pull out the bottles it contained.

Chace's arms wrapped around her from behind, and he leaned his body weight into her, pinning her between him and the counter. His breathing was harsh in her ears, his body shaking. She seemed to be the only thing keeping him up. He radiated heat, and she quelled her impulse to pull away at the strange sensations at her back. He held her against him tight enough for her to feel the muscles and bones of his body moving.

His breathing started to grow steadier, though the unnerving movements continued.

"You can control my magic," he said in a voice that sounded more human. "How?"

"I don't know," she replied. "I didn't know I was doing it."

"I need more of it," he said. He shuddered. "Whatever it is, if I don't get more of it, I'm going to shift."

"What the hell do we do?" She racked her mind, trying to figure out how to help or at least to prevent him from crushing her if he transformed into a dragon in the small space.

"Kiss me."

"Right now?" she asked with a startled laugh.

"It's worked before."

Skylar twisted in his arms. She didn't wait for him to ask again but took his face in her hands and kissed him. Chace wrapped her in a bear hug, his lips hungry and mouth demanding. She wrapped her arms around his neck, submitting quickly to his intensity.

He kissed her long and hard, until she was breathless and her body burning with desire. Heat built in her lower belly then raced through her while the signs of his shifting slowed and stopped, replaced by the erection pressed against her.

Breaking away, he leaned into her and rested his hands against the counter, his head on her shoulder.

"I need more," he said, the strain clear in his voice.

Skylar saw one tiny wing start to free itself from his shoulder. Chace's body shook with effort. The last thing she wanted was to be turned into a pancake.

"More than one way to fry a chicken, right?" she said. She pushed him away to give herself room to move then stripped off her shirt.

That caught Chace's attention. His head lifted, his eyes starting to focus. One of his hands went to her bare abdomen while the other continued to support him against the counter.

She unsnapped her bra, and the large palm drifted upward to cup one breast, his thumb lightly grazing her coral nipple until it was hard.

Skylar stroked his erection through his pants.

His body began to absorb the wayward wing.

"Good, dragon," she whispered.

Chace kissed her once more, his hand sliding into her pants. Any thought she had of teasing him until he was no longer in danger of shifting fled at his hunger and the tickle of his shirt against her sensitive breasts.

"I need to be inside you," Chace said. "It calms me."

Skylar fumbled with the fasteners on his jeans, finally pushing them down. Chace finished the process but staggered, not yet well enough to hold himself up fully, and he fell, dragging her with him. Her knee hit the concrete floor, but the pain was distant, her attention on him. He broke her fall, his muscular body between her and the floor.

"You okay?" she asked with a small laugh.

"Only a concussion," he muttered. "Fuck me, Sky, before I kill us both."

She kissed him hard then shifted to shimmy out of her pants and straddle him. Chace's dick pressed against her wet opening, and she leaned forward to kiss him.

Adrenaline and knowing they were surrounded by people like Caleb, who might just walk in at any minute, thrilled her, made what could only be a quickie an incredibly erotic experience.

Chace lifted her hips to position her body and lowered her onto his erection.

Closing her eyes, Skylar groaned as he filled her sacred space, fitting inside her in a way that sent pleasure swirling through her already.

"God you feel so good!" she murmured in awe, not understanding what made even a quickie with him so much better than any other sexual escapade she'd ever had.

"So do you." Chace's hands went up her sides to her breasts once more, and he twisted her nipples gently then slid one hand to her face. He pushed his thumb into her mouth.

She opened her eyes and looked into his eyes, swirling her tongue around his thumb and sucking hard while holding his gaze. His baby blues were dark with need, his pupils dilated and displaying the tiny flames of his dragon magic.

"You are the sexiest, most beautiful woman I've ever known," he said. "I have to warn you – my stamina is not what it should be right now. But I'll make it up to you."

She continued to suck on his thumb and began rocking her hips against his, alternating between undulating her lower body and tightening her sheathe around his thick dick, doing her best to milk and massage him.

His hand left her mouth. He took her hips, pressing her onto him with more force, and sending a ripple of new sensation within her. Skylar shuddered, loving the way he felt inside her, and let his hands guide her hips. The friction between their bodies was intense, the tension within her growing, but not as fast as Chace's. His body went rigid beneath her.

Wanting to see his face when he came, Skylar focused on him. The muscles of his chest and arms were bulging, his breathing hard and fast. His eyes were closed, his jaw clenching and body arching ever so slightly a second before he climaxed.

True to his word, Chace's muffled cry of release was quick this time, and he held her in place while his erection convulsed within her.

His body went from tense enough to snap to utterly relaxed within seconds, his grip on her hips falling away, and even his features losing some of the signs of illness from the drugs in his system. Pink bloomed in his cheeks once more. All signs of strain were gone, and his magic was calm. Hidden, leaving him in some level of peace while he rode the waves of his orgasm.

Skylar watched the changes in his body, amazed that she was the one causing them. It touched her at a deeper level than she expected, in the part of her where her newfound instincts to protect him were growing stronger.

His eyes flickered open, and she smiled. She was panting and beyond aroused from their lovemaking, her body aching for the release she'd just given him.

"Sorry," he muttered.

"Why?" she asked. "My plan worked didn't it?"

He chuckled. "Something like that. You aren't satisfied though."

*I've never felt so satisfied.* She didn't know what to say or if telling him that watching him come was as incredible as her own orgasm would sound stupid. But it was.

"We need to get out of here," she said with some regret, wanting to stay with their bodies connected, even if they were lying on the cold, uncomfortable floor of an exam room.

She moved off of him and stretched for her bra, putting it on. A glance at Chace renewed her concern. He was still having problems, though not as bad.

He pushed himself up drew her to him with one hand, kissing her deeply. His taste and scent were invading her senses again, a dangerous invasion.

His fingers slid between her legs to dip inside her core then make their way to her clit.

"Chace," she objected.

He kissed her harder, robbing her of breath and words while his fingers worked their magic with her clit, swirling and stroking, with pressure that was sometimes light enough to tickle and sometimes hard enough that she groaned. Unable to bear the tease, she moved against his hand, trying to hurry the orgasm that was building once more. Chace's fingers slid inside her to stroke her G-spot while she rubbed the swollen clit against his palm.

"Oh, god, Chace," she murmured, breaking off the kiss to lean into his body.

"It's only fair," he whispered, nipping her ear. "I get off seeing you come. It's so sexy."

She buried her face into the nape of his neck, intoxicated by his scent. His thumb slid to her clit, intensifying the sensations, and her world exploded. She collapsed against him, shuddering and breathless.

He held her against his chest, the warmth of his skin and strength of his frame a welcome barrier between them and whatever awaited them on the other side of the exam room door.

Skylar struggled to catch her breath and rein in her senses, overwhelmed by Chace's passion. His body was solid and unchanging once more, though he still shook from the strain and drugs in his system. She took his face in her hands, running her fingers along his roughened jaw and warm skin. Under the harsh fluorescent lighting, he appeared haggard, with dark circles beneath his eyes and a chalky hue to his features.

The heartbeat that hadn't been present when he was hooked up to the IV was back, his pulse rapid and throbbing in the side of his neck.

"One shot next time," he said huskily. "Let's get cleaned up and get out of here."

She rose with effort, her legs shaky. The two of them made use of wet wipes they dug out of one drawer then dressed hurriedly. As her blood calmed, she began to realize what she'd done, not in making love to him, but in freeing him. Her gaze slid to him, and she watched the effortless – if still strained – movement of his body.

This time, it almost scared her how attracted to him she was. How she was able to forget about the threat to his life – and possibly hers – and lose herself in his body.

*Skylar, you can't go down this path without realizing there might not be a way back.* Mason's words returned to her. Looking at Chace, she found herself doubting she was ready for that one-way trip, no matter how much she loved being in his arms and how off-balance she felt not knowing the truth about her own history.

It wasn't the right time to start down this path. Not yet. Not until she found out all she could from Caleb, Chace and anyone else who held the secrets to her past.

Skylar crossed to the door.

"We're locked in," she said.

"Not for long." He brushed his lips across her cheek before pushing away from the counter and walking to the door.

As she watched, he placed his palms on the door. The metal beneath his hands grew red and hot, until she was able to feel the heat he channeled across the room. Abruptly, the door popped and caved.

Chace shoved it open and strode into the hallway.

"Which way?" he asked brusquely.

*This is a mistake.* She stared at him, heart beating hard.

"Skylar."

"Right," she managed. "Just head down the hallway, left at the intersection and – "

His gaze sharpened and fell to her. "You're going with me."

"You need to get out of here fast. I might slow you down," she lied. "Go ahead."

He walked into the room and took her arm, pulling her with him into the hallway.

"Why does this always end with you kidnapping me?" she complained.

"Now is not a good time to piss me off."

She glanced up at him, sensing his tension and the tightly held magic that was close to snapping. Skylar held her tongue and let him take her with him down the hallway. She pointed the direction they needed to go and within five minutes, they were in a courtyard at the center of the compound.

At once, she felt the rush of magic as he started to shift. He released her.

"We're good, right?" she asked, stepping back quickly. "You're free, I'm not totally complicit, we can just part ways once and for all."

His response was a bellow, a half-human, half-dragon sound that rang in the confined space. He morphed and changed before her eyes, terrifying her the way he had before.

She was too enthralled by the changes to react when they were done. Without giving her a chance to run, Chace leapt into the air, hovering in the courtyard, before he snatched her in a talon.

Skylar shoved at the thick claw, cursing him under her breath. The compound dropped out from under her as his powerful wings carried them with ease into the air. She was about to squeeze her eyes closed and pray when she saw their destination – the cabin.

He dropped to the ground and released her, morphing into his human form before she climbed to her feet. Her eyes swept over his naked body, the wide shoulders, rounded ass and long thighs. Without looking at her, he strode into the cabin.

"If you're safe, then I'm just gonna take off," she said.

"I will come after you," he called over his shoulder, disappearing into the cabin's depths. "In dragon form."

"Dammit." Skylar trudged towards him. In the distance, she heard the sounds of sirens from the direction of the compound. "Magic cabin sounds good about now."

She hurried in and closed the door behind her just in time to see Chace buttoning jeans.

"Are we going somewhere else?" she asked somewhat anxiously.

"Already there."

"Where?" She was afraid to look out the nearest window.

"Better question is why you broke me out."

"That wasn't entirely my intention," she admitted. "I meant to just ask you a few questions but then things just went the way they did."

He sat down on the edge of his bed and gripped his head.

"You okay?"

"Lucky I'm alive after that shit."

"Sorry. I didn't realize it took a minute."

"Not the adrenaline." He lay back on the bed, displaying the length of his abs and chest. "Your boss was working on killing me."

"You couldn't be in the rehab program?"

"There is no rehab program," he snapped. "There's no reintegration into society. They kill us, plain and simple."

Skylar was quiet, watching him. She didn't want him angry so soon, not when he'd just shifted back into a human. He was struggling, apparent from his uneven breathing and the tremble of his hands.

"Come here." His voice was husky from exertion and strain.

The idea of him setting his hands on her to calm down thrilled her and concerned her. He wasn't in control, and she was afraid of what happened if he wasn't able to rein in his magic, even with her help.

He held out his hand. She crossed to him and sat on the bed, taking it. With his perfect body stretched out before her, she was unable to resist the urge to touch him and skimmed her other palm along the ridges of his abs and up his muscular chest.

His breathing became steady beneath her touch, and she almost smiled at the sight of the erection forming in his jeans. She slowed her movements and let her free hand drift downwards, over his lower abs, and slid her hand under the band of his jeans. She stopped short of reaching his thick, stiff dick and tickled the skin above his groin wickedly.

Skylar glanced at his face. He was calm and quiet, all signs of him needing to shift gone. She removed her hand from his jeans and rested it on top of his erection, stroking him gently.

"So my touch calms you but something more sexual is faster," she observed. "Is that with every woman?"

"No. Just you."

She paused, not expecting the response or the strange flutter it sent through her.

*He's my dragon.* The thought made her uncomfortable for reasons she didn't understand. What they had was more than physical … it felt permanent.

"You, um, should probably drink as much water as you can to flush your system," she advised, disturbed. She rose.

"Wait, that's it?" he asked, opening his eyes to stare at her. "You're not gonna finish what you started?"

She rolled her eyes at the familiar words she'd uttered at him not long ago.

"Just trying to help calm you down," she said cheerfully. She turned away before he could see her interest and crossed the cabin to the kitchenette area, where she poured him a glass of water. She placed the glass on the nightstand nearest him then returned to the kitchenette. Being near him while beyond turned on was dangerous, especially with the unfamiliar, powerful emotions floating through her that she needed to suppress somehow.

"You haven't eaten in a while, I take it?" she asked, recalling that she'd only just gotten breakfast at close to one o'clock.

"No," he said. "Haven't gotten laid either."

"Wah, wah," she replied. She went through his cupboards and fridge and pulled out bread and lunchmeat for sandwiches. She didn't stop to think twice about making them for the monster that had basically kidnapped her twice within the span of a week.

It was the protective impulse, the one that flipped out seeing him lying in the hospital bed. She didn't understand it or why she – a trained slayer – felt the need to help the creature she was supposed to capture. It had something to do with her dreams. The answer was there in her memories and had been trying to warn her.

She made him three sandwiches and herself one then took a

plate with the offering to the bed. Apprehensively, she sat on the corner of the bed and set the plate down close to him, like she would a feral animal.

He lowered his hands from his head and sat. Skylar watched the taut muscles of his abs contract, admiring the ease with which he moved.

"You cut the crusts off," he said, gazing at the food.

"No one likes crusts."

"I do."

"Then you can make your own next time."

He snorted but devoured the crust-less food and downed the water. Some coloring returned to his face, though his features were still drawn. Rubbing his face again, he looked around.

"So we're just going to roam the earth in your magic cabin?" she asked, glancing uneasily towards the window. "I, um, would really like to go home."

"You can't."

Skylar stood and crossed her arms, glaring at him.

"Don't look at me like that," he said with a faint smile. "You're the one who broke me out. Don't think home is the safest bet for you."

"It'd be fine. They'd just brainwash me again and all would be forgiven."

"So you believe me now about your people being screwed up."

"I don't know what to believe, but I want to find out more," she said carefully. "I want to know …" *if I still have a family out there somewhere.*

The idea she might wasn't something she'd ever considered before. The thought was almost too large for her to digest. In her dreams, she had a mother, one who was afraid enough of something that they began running.

It was hard to consider the dream a memory without dwelling on the great, royal blue dragon she'd also seen in the vision. It wasn't rational to believe her mother existed but the dragon did not or that her mother had baked her pie but not told her they were protectors of dragons.

"What is it?" Chace was gazing at her.

"Nothing." Too aware of the two feet of space that separated them on the bed where they'd made love, she stood and walked away, sinking into a chair in the living area. Her injection point still hurt, and she rested a hand on it. The skin felt hot.

"Are you hurt?" he asked. "I didn't think to ask if I scratched you or anything when flying."

"No, you're uh … gentle, aside from the whole kidnapping thing."

He smiled, the sparkle returning to his gaze while the warmth of life returned to his features.

"The shrink injected me with something. Ever have a shot that feels like it's just burning a hole in your arm?" She peered at it, perplexed.

"What did they inject you with?" The wariness in his voice made her sit up straighter.

"Something to make me sleep."

"So they could've injected like a tracking device or something in you?"

"Maybe." She sighed. "I swear if you bite off my arm …"

"What in the name of everything holy will it take for you to understand that I've never hurt a fly in my life?" he growled.

She ignored him. She didn't want to believe that about him. Or that she'd been brainwashed and had a family out there somewhere. Or that everything she'd ever known was just *wrong*.

"Let me see." He knelt beside her chair, bringing his warmth and scent into her personal space again. Without asking, he took her arm.

Skylar found herself caught up in admiring the hue of his eyes and the long, feathery eyelashes lining them. His skin was the perfect shade of gold, like a ripe peach, while his bare upper body reminded her that in either form, he could've done a ton of damage to her, if he wasn't the pacifist he claimed to be.

He rested his warm hand over the spot, and she hissed in pain. His gaze flickered up to hers.

"I think this needs to come out," he said.

"What needs to come out?" she asked.

"What my magic is telling me is that whatever they put into your system, you somehow stopped it. Trapped it right there." He withdrew his hand.

She stared at the spot on her arm. The way he explained it made sense. The ball that formed as soon as the needle went into her and had halted the spread of the solution's fire.

*Is this why I still remember the dreams, when the shrink said I wouldn't after the session?* Her body was protecting her. Or was it his magic?

She met Chace's gaze. Confusion and desire raced through her. Whatever was going on, it all started around the time she met him.

"My guess is that they tried to brainwash you again." He rose and crossed to he kitchenette, pulling free a sharp knife from the block on the counter. He returned to his spot at her side.

"Whoa. What are you doing?" she asked, pulling away when he reached for her arm once more.

"Whatever it is, it needs to come out."

"Let's not cut open Skylar today."

"Skylar, it could make you sick," he returned. "Like it'll fester."

"Why do you care?' she asked, baffled.

He lowered his hand and gazed at her, appearing as surprised as she felt.

"I'm not a monster," he said at last. "No matter what they tell you at your *reprogramming* center."

The mocking tone made her flush.

"Where, by the way, they kill shifters instead of reintegrating them into society." He snatched her wrist and gripped it tightly.

"I still can't believe that," she said, tugging unsuccessfully at her arm.

"What do you think he was doing to me? That shit was killing me,

Skylar."

*I know.* Even if she hadn't been able to pronounce let alone identify what drug they were injecting into him, she'd felt how wrong it was. Admitting it, though, was a step towards acknowledging that her entire world was a lie. *I'm not ready for that.*

"This might hurt," he warned her. The dragon shifter was moody again. He flipped her arm to expose the spot where the shrink had injected her.

She squeezed her eyes closed and held her breath, waiting for the pain. It was sharp and hot. He pierced the skin deep enough to reach the bubble beneath.

Gasping, she ventured a look then stared openly.

A grimace was on Chace's face. He leaned away from the black goo oozing from her arm and dripping onto the floor.

"What the fuck is this?" he demanded.

"I don't know." Seeing it made her want to ask him to cut out any part of her body that touched it.

Chace released her wrist and dabbed a finger into the liquid draining from her arm. He studied it.

"Oh dear god!" she exclaimed.

The black goo shifted and moved around his finger of its own recognizance, as if it was alive.

"Get it out!" She shook her arm to hurry the flow of the contaminant.

"Easy," he said calmly, resting a hand on her forearm. "Now we know how they've been doing it. It's magic of some sort."

"Out, out, out!" she chanted, pushing at the wound. "This is disgusting!"

"It's okay." His gaze was warm, the entertained smile on his face gentle. "We're taking care of it." He dropped the knife on the coffee table then reached forward, swiping away a tear she didn't feel from her cheek.

Embarrassed, Skylar wiped her face on her shoulder. The black stuff only supported a reality that was becoming harder to dismiss.

Her breathing was harsh, her heart pounding hard. It wasn't just the goo upsetting her but the idea that she no longer knew what parts of her life were real and what parts were the creation of an organization she thought had raised her since the death of her mother.

"It just hurts," she mumbled, feeling like an idiot for crying.

"I'll let it pass this time. But for the record, I know when someone is bullshitting me."

She snorted but didn't look at him, not wanting to be drawn into his intensity and warmth. It was easier to keep her emotions balanced when he wasn't touching her.

"I'll get this cleaned up." He rose and moved away again. Smoked honey wafted towards her with each of his movements, and she sucked in a deep breath, tasting and smelling him.

She shuddered, a shiver working its way through her, before her gaze settled on the black stuff again. Any pleasure she took out of being near Chace died when she saw what was on her arm.

*I have to warn Mason.* Her only real friend the past few years, he was going through what she had. He'd understand.

Chace handed her a paper towel. She squeezed goo out of her arm. Blood trickled out and she stopped then held the towel in place until it stopped bleeding. Quickly, she tied her hair up in a loose bun on top of her head so as not to get blood or magic goo in it then leaned over to help him clean up.

"It's running away," she said, horrified.

"Trying to." Chace was quickly mopping up the goo then tossing soaked towels into a trash bag. "Put a bandage on. Make sure none of this junk gets back inside you."

*Ugh.* She stood and went to the first aid kit on the table. Blood formed a stark red trail against her pale skin, and she caught a drop before it had a chance to reach the floor. She wrapped her arm quickly. Caught up in her task, she didn't hear him approach.

"What is that?" he asked, a hushed note in his voice.

"What is what?" she asked, turning to face him.

"Your tat."

She glared at him. "Like you don't know."

"I wouldn't ask if I did." He took her arm and turned her once more, tracing the tattoo on the back of her neck lightly enough to make her shiver.

"You marked me after we slept together. I assumed so you can keep tabs on me," she grumbled.

"I didn't do this," he replied. "I'd remember giving someone a tattoo."

"Seriously?" She pulled away. "It's a magic tattoo, Chace, like the one on your chest."

"So you're a dragon?" he asked.

Skylar spun, sensing he was messing with her. Her retort died on her lips at the sight of his genuine confusion.

"Sometimes I feel like we're talking two different languages," she said. "This … thing appeared on my neck where you bit me the night we …" she cleared her voice.

Interest flared to life in his gaze.

"Anyway, two weeks later, I've got a magic tattoo."

"I've never heard of this," he said. "Maybe we should cut that out, too."

"What? No." She took a step back when he raised the knife. "Whatever was in my arm was just plain evil. This isn't." She touched the tattoo, not at all certain what it meant, but sure it wasn't bad.

"So how did the mark of a shifter dragon get on your neck?" he asked, irritated.

"You put it there."

"I know you believe that to be true, but you also thought you were slaying monsters that eat people," he pointed out. "Any intention of finishing what you started earlier?" He took her hand and placed it on his crotch, where she was able to feel how hard he was.

Skylar looked away, feeling claustrophobic with him there and trapped by her attraction to him and the strange emotions. He was everything she didn't need right now, all wrapped into one delicious, sexy package that was beyond a doubt too real for her to pretend she was a normal slayer doing her job.

She pulled her hand away from his body with effort.

"Can you go fly around or something for a while?" she muttered. "I have a headache."

"Whatever."

The moody dragon shifter snatched up the trash bag filled with magic goo and stormed out.

Skylar breathed a sigh of relief, uncertain why her insides were churning like they did when she suspended in his talons again, convinced she was about to fall to her death.

"Calm down, Sky," she murmured. "We're slowly getting the answers." *Too slowly.*

It struck her then that the only time her past was remotely clear was in her dreams, when her mother spoke to her. She hadn't learned anything else about herself outside of them.

Too wired to sleep, she searched through the kitchen cabinets for any booze or sleeping aids.

"Hey, uh, cabin. You got any sleeping pills? Downers? Drugs?" she asked.

Something rattled behind her, and she whirled in time to see an orange prescription pill bottle fall off the nightstand beside the bed.

"Thanks, I think." Crossing to it, she picked it up curiously. "So dragon-boy has sleep problems, too. Interesting. *Take one at bedtime, two if needed. Do not exceed two in twenty-four hours.* These things look awfully small to work well."

Skeptically, she poured herself a glass of water and then dumped four of the tiny pills into her hand. Tossing them into her mouth, she downed the glass of water and went to the bed.

*Tell me everything I need to know about me,* she commanded her mind.

As soon as she settled on the bed, sleep swept over her.

# Chapter Fourteen

**B**eing around Skylar was too much of a distraction. Chace had never been so aware of someone that he noticed when even a single hair was out of place or *felt* the distress that clouded her blue eyes. The tension between them made it harder for him to think straight when all he wanted to do was take her in his arms the way he had previously.

She definitely didn't want anything to do with him right now, which left him restless and turned on.

He torched the magic that had polluted her body then went to the only other place where he found solace. Landing behind the bar right as the sun began to set, his body morphed back into its human shape. He stood for a moment, gaze on the sky. He was tired and weak from whatever it was Caleb had used to try to kill him.

"Dragon shifter?" A woman's voice came from a few feet away.

He turned. The statuesque blonde with large breasts and long hair didn't seem comfortable. Her eyes darted around them, and she was clenching her hands together.

"Who's asking?" he asked warily.

She held out a familiar appointment card, and he relaxed. Chace approached her and took it, pretending not to notice how she inched away. His magic was agitated; it made the air around him hot enough for a sauna.

"Thanks," he said. "Stay out of the bar."

She said nothing but took another step back then turned and hurried around front, where she was probably parked.

Chace read the card.

*Five minutes. Same place as last time.*

He shoved it in his pocket and took off at a trot towards the ocean, the sunset at his back. The dark blue sky stretched before him, sprinkled with stars. Twilight always reminded him of the Viking funerals he'd attended as a youth. They were frequent during the volatile period when he was born, the result of wars and a famine that had hit his village. Rather than disturb him, the connection to his past calmed him. At this time where day transitioned into night, he was able to pretend that the modern world didn't exist, that he was still home a thousand years before.

*Some things never change,* he thought to himself, eyes on the darkening horizon while he jogged down the dirt road. The ocean air was cold, the way it was at home, and the flavorful scent of the sea worked into his senses.

By the time he reached the place where Mr. Nothing wanted to meet, he felt centered again, despite the frustrating woman and mystery he wasn't able to figure out.

Mr. Nothing was there, leaning against a boulder, waiting.

It was one of the few times Chace had seen his features. They were bathed in the brilliant, orange-pink light of the dying sun. Mr. Nothing was a man in his prime with black hair peppered with silver and blue eyes, porcelain skin and chiseled features. He was slender but solid, built more like a runner than the thicker, weight lifting crew Chace ran with. He wore all black, as usual.

"You rang?" Mr. Nothing asked drily. His eyes were colder than the sea, his penetrating gaze too steady to be friendly.

"Got a few questions for you," Chace replied.

"Did you find her?"

"I did." Chace chose his words carefully, not at all certain why Mr. Nothing would want Skylar but certain it wasn't a good reason.

Mr. Nothing was too … cold, self-serving, to have good intentions. "There's something not right at all about these slayers," he started. "Or what they're doing to the shifters. But you knew this, didn't you?"

"I suspected."

Chace regarded him closely. Mr. Nothing appeared genuinely interested, as if he really didn't know what Chace would discover when sent on the mission to capture Skylar and find the location of the others.

"How did you know where to look for what was wrong?" Chace asked. "I didn't. None of us did. We just knew the shifters were disappearing."

Mr. Nothing crossed his arms.

"It's only fair we share information," Chace said, amused by the silent refusal. "Like you said, we're both on the same team here in wanting to protect the shifters. The more you tell me, the more I can help."

There was a stony silence, one Chace didn't think was going to end the way he wanted, when Mr. Nothing's arms dropped and he looked out towards the ocean.

"A … friend of mine was taken. I started digging into the disappearance but hit a brick wall. I'm from a much older caste of shifters than you, a nocturnal generation who cannot be exposed to full daylight," Mr. Nothing said. "It limited my ability to investigate."

"So your friend disappeared one day, and you stumbled on these slayers."

"Yes. I tracked down Skylar and a few of the others, but what I was able to discern with my limited abilities made no sense."

"Yeah, I was baffled at first, too," Chace admitted. "Until I realized that they've been brainwashed."

"Brainwashed?" Mr. Nothing looked at him with a frown. "By whom?"

"If you're asking who's behind the whole thing, I have no idea. If you want to know where it happens, that I know. But I don't think the master puppeteer behind all of this is located there, just the worker-bees who are probably all brainwashed." Chace paused, pensive. "Since you've been around much longer than me, who do you think has that ability and bears a grudge against shifters?"

"I don't know. We are solitary creatures by nature." Mr. Nothing's response was too quick to convince Chace it was the truth. "You found Skylar?"

"Yeah. There are dozens of these slayers there. Why are you interested in just one?" It was Chace's turn to cross his arms.

"My business," Mr. Nothing replied. "She was brainwashed, too?"

"She seems to be coming out of it. Slowly. Or at least, sometimes she seems reasonable." Chace shook his head. "From what I learned, they go in annually for their reprogramming, where I'm guessing their minds are wiped."

"What about the shifters they're collecting?"

Chace grunted and bent the arm where the IV to the drug Caleb said would kill him had been inserted. The wound caused by the catheter was healed, but the ghost-like sensations of liquid ice being pumped into his veins hadn't left him yet.

"They're killing them," he said. "I don't know why."

"Straight out killing them? Not trying to take their powers or brainwash them?"

"Doesn't seem that way. They were quick to incapacitate me and hook me up to some drug that was supposed to wipe me out."

"You went there?" Mr. Nothing's surprise and intrigue were short-lived before his shuddered façade returned. "You've been to this rehab facility?"

"Unfortunately."

"Where is it?"

Chace cocked his head to the side, studying Mr. Nothing. Their deal had been for Skylar, who was in Chace's cabin. Even if Mr. Nothing went to the facility, he wouldn't find the girl he was looking for.

"Southern base of the Santa Rita Mountains in south Arizona," he answered. "When you get Skylar -"

"Our deal is done. I'll turn you human."

"That's not what I wanted to ask," Chace replied. "What happens to the rest of the shifters?"

"You gave up the right to know about our kind when you decided you didn't want to be one of us anymore," Mr. Nothing replied sharply.

Unease rippled through Chace, a sense of both guilt in knowing Mr. Nothing was right and alarm that he was abandoning the adoptive family he'd known far longer than his own human family.

"And the other slayers who were brainwashed?" he asked.

"Also not your business," Mr. Nothing said. "But if the person behind this is who I suspect it might be, he'll be among the slayers or worker-bees to monitor and control what's going on. My guess is that he's someone Skylar knows."

"Why her?"

"Again – "

"None of my business." Chace's anger stirred and with it, the need to shift. "So bring her to you and this is over for me."

"Exactly. You'll no longer be forced to exist among us."

Chace bit his tongue. He bore the shifters no ill will, and if he was a normal one, he was certain he'd feel differently. He simply was sick of living under a curse that made him a freak among humans and shifters alike.

"Let me know when you have her," Mr. Nothing said.

Chace gave a curt nod, unwilling to cut the strings to his shifter family as abruptly as Mr. Nothing wanted. He wanted out, but he wasn't going to leave them in danger, and he didn't dare risk giving Mr. Nothing what he wanted and then *hoping* the mysterious man took care of the shifters.

No, Chace wasn't going to become human again with a conscience clouded by the knowledge he hadn't helped those he cared about when he could. Likewise, he wasn't certain he wanted to turn over Skylar or even if he dared ask Mr. Nothing any of the questions he had about her, the magic goo or her tattoo.

"Before I go," he said slowly. "One more question. I've never known a non-shifter to bear a shifter mark. Is it possible, or was this done by those brainwashing the slayers?"

Mr. Nothing's gaze sharpened. "What're you talking about?"

"A human slayer, total non-shifter, has a tattoo like a shifter. Did those people do it to her?"

"Skylar?"

Chace didn't understand the flare of fire in Mr. Nothing's gaze or why he had the sudden urge to stop talking.

"Never mind," he replied and began to turn to leave.

"Wait," Mr. Nothing called. "Is it Skylar who's marked?"

Chace hesitated and then nodded.

"What does the marking look like?"

"A shifter mark."

"Yes, but *whose*?"

"Why?" Chace demanded. "What does it mean?"

Mr. Nothing was silent, though his teeth were clenched tightly enough for his jaw to tick.

"You tell me first this time."

No response.

"See ya 'round," Chace said and started away.

"A shifter marks his heart with a like sign."

Chace froze. "What do you mean?"

"We only have half a heart, and it cannot beat on its own. When it's whole ..." By the thoughtful note in Mr. Nothing's voice, he was remembering something far more pleasant than their current discussion.

"I don't understand," Chace said. His own heartbeat was distracting him once more, beating fast, as if he was being chased and not in mid-discussion with Mr. Nothing.

"It means, the shifter has found the other half of his heart."

Chace said nothing. He forced himself to nod but didn't dare dwell on the information too long. He'd attributed the beating of his heart to something Mr. Nothing had done when they made their deal, not to … this, whatever *this* was. The other half of his heart? Did that mean he had to kill her and claim it? Or was there something much more to Skylar's arrival into his life, something that made his gut heavy and his chest tight.

The idea he'd met the woman he should've ended up with – at a time when he was calling it quits on life – made him a little ill. Yet hadn't he suspected as much the moment he touched her in the bar?

*You put it there.*

For once, the brainwashed slayer stuck in his cabin was right about something.

"Now. Your turn," Mr. Nothing said. "I need to know whose mark is on Skylar." There was emotion in his voice. Chace wasn't able to identify it. Anger or maybe disappointment and frustration.

"I'll let you know," he said casually. "Next time I run into her. I just got a glimpse." He had no reason to trust Mr. Nothing, but he had no reason to lie either, except that his instincts were warning him not to reveal this secret.

"Very well." Mr. Nothing was looking at him unhappily. "My patience is growing thin, Chace."

"Then go get her yourself," Chace snapped. "Oh, right. You can't."

"No, but I can get another shifter to bring her in."

"Good luck." Chace snorted and walked away, this time not giving Mr. Nothing the opportunity the chance to stop him. For once, Mr. Nothing had said more than Chace wanted to hear.

He stripped and shifted into his dragon form then leapt into the air, carrying himself far, far away from the mysterious, nocturnal shifter and his strange claims about Chace's heart being whole again.

*Why is it beating after a thousand years?*

He didn't feel ready to admit the truth: there was more to Skylar than someone he was physically attracted to.

It took a while for him to calm enough to want to shift and even then, his heart was still beating too fast. It left him concerned, even when he landed in a puff of snow in the isolated mountains of Alaska. It was dark, though the bright snow rendered the night brighter than it would have been otherwise. Fat flakes floated to land on his wings and body, soon covering him in a coat of white.

Momentarily intrigued by the sensation, he let the snow build up before tossing his head and flapping his wings to dispel it. He shifted quickly into his form and yanked on his clothes. His dragon form was well insulated, unaffected by the cold or snow. His human form was shaking and chilled by the time he shoved his feet into his boots. He hurried towards the cabin, whose warm light spilled out of wide windows onto the snowy landscape.

Not at all certain he was ready to talk to Skylar, he at least wanted a glimpse at her tattoo again. Maybe the people where she'd been brainwashed had commissioned it, and it hadn't grown out of magic like Mr. Nothing claimed.

He carefully didn't think about the fact that his heart started beating after he met a certain dragon slayer.

He stomped his feet on the porch to clear the snow from his boots then opened the door, not expecting to find his prisoner lying on his bed asleep once again. The cabin was toasty and cozy, the burning hearth keeping the small space warm

Chace pushed off his boots and went for socks, gaze on the woman asleep on her stomach on top of his bed. Something seemed off, but he didn't understand what. More concerned about the chill that sank into his skin outside, he pulled on a sweater and made a pot of coffee before crossing to the bed.

None of his moving around woke her, and he didn't bother trying to keep quiet.

She was out.

His gaze fell to the nightstand, where a familiar pill bottle sat. Years before, Gunner wrote him a prescription for sleeping pills. The panther shifter was a former physician, one of the many professions he'd picked up over a few hundred years. He'd forgotten about them until now.

Chace picked them up and realized the top was loose. By the mountain of white pills, it appeared as if most of them were still in the bottle, indicating she wasn't trying to kill herself. And yet, she hadn't bothered to take her shoes off or slide under the covers before she went to sleep, either.

There was no way to know how many she'd taken, and he read the expiration date grimly. They expired five years before.

"What the hell are you doing?" Chace asked the sleeping woman, perplexed. Concern he didn't want to feel spun through him and for a moment, he didn't know what exactly to do.

Kneeling on the bed, he pushed her hair aside and tugged down the back of her shirt to get a better look at her tattoo. If the brainwashers at the rehab center did it, they did a damned good job. From what he was able to see, it was identical to his.

Chace traced his fingers over the soft skin at the back of her neck, unable to subdue his growing worry.

She'd been upset when he left, but if she meant to kill herself, she'd have to take a bottle full of the pills. Then again, they were expired.

But if she was out, he didn't have to deal with her.

This thought made him feel the guiltiest, and he rested a hand between her shoulder blades. Her body moved with her deep breathing, and the warmth of her skin through the shirt reassured him that she was at least alive. He removed his hand, grateful to know she was asleep and not dead.

It did nothing to help him navigate his feelings, though.

*… the shifter has found the other half of his heart.*

He really, *really* hoped that didn't mean what he suspected it did. It was why the attraction between the was so quick and intense, why he hadn't been able to drop her over a cliff even knowing his people would be safer with her gone. It was why his chest was tight gazing down at her and hoping she hadn't taken resorted to pills, because of something he said.

Agitation made his nails blacken and start to grow.

"Not now!" he grated.

He rested his hand on her back again, unable to understand what it was she did to him to help him calm. He felt no different, no telltale sign of foreign magic moving through him or burst of warmth. His body simply … calmed.

The urge to shift calmed then retreated, and he blew out a breath.

He didn't remove his hand but sat, pensive. The tattoo meant they were connected somehow on a level he didn't feel ready to explore. If she was able to control his magic, could his magic affect her, too? Taking a chance she wasn't trying to hurt herself and hoping she woke up in the morning was going to drive him crazy with worry.

Chace closed his eyes and focused. She'd claimed all she did to get the cabin to obey her earlier was ask it to.

"Wake up, Skylar," he whispered.

He felt no exchange of magic, no flush of heat the way he did when he shifted. Resting his other hand on her back, he concentrated harder.

"C'mon. Wake up for me, honey."

He waited for a long moment and began to think it wasn't going to work.

"Dammit!" Her groggy mutter startled him.

Chace rolled her onto her back quickly and touched her face then checked the pulse in her neck. He pulled down the skin beneath one of her eyes to get a look at her pupils. They were dilated, but she was awake and moving.

She swatted at his hand and blinked rapidly, planting the meat of her palms on her eyes.

"Why did you do that?" she groaned. Her saucy tone made him smile. Relief replaced his worry.

"Do what?" he asked, resting his hand on her stomach. The heat of her body stirred his blood, but he focused on her rather than the fact she was already in his bed.

"Wake me up."

"So it worked," he mused.

"It was like someone knocking down the door to your cabin with a jackhammer."

He chuckled. "Good to know."

"I was so close …" She drifted off, troubled, and then sighed.

"To killing yourself to get away form me? That ain't happening," he snapped.

"No. To the dreams."

"What dreams?"

She said nothing but sat up, dazed.

"What dreams?" he demanded again.

"God you're so moody," she retorted. "It's none of your damn business." She started to climb over him to get out of the bed.

Chace caught her hips and twisted, flinging her down on her back.

"Ooowwww. My head hurts!" she complained, gripping her temples.

"I don't care. If I hear one more person say it's none of my damn business …"

"Chill, dragon." She reached out and rested one cool palm on his arm. "Whenever you get moody, you freak me out."

He drew a deep breath, darkly amused. His emotions calmed again along with his magic. They sat in the quiet, him trying hard not to pry or be pissed at her, while she lay still with one hand on his forearm.

As if able to sense when he was calm, she withdrew her touch and sat up once more, meeting his gaze.

"So what was so important you just had to wake me up for?" she asked. Her pupils were back to normal, her face flushed with either frustration or desire.

He had the urge to taste her plump lips again and lean closer until he was able to smell her skin.

"I thought you were trying to off yourself," he said, motioning to the pill bottle.

"If I wanted to kill myself, I would've downed the bottle or better yet, jumped of whatever mountain you put us on this time," she pointed out.

"The thought crossed my mind. Just wanted to be sure."

She arched an eyebrow at him. "*You* were worried about me?"

"Why do you say it like that?" he growled. "Your brainwashers teach you dragons don't have feelings?"

"Something like that," she replied. "If you were so worried, maybe you'd stop kidnapping me."

"I'm probably the only one keeping you alive right now."

A frown flickered across her features.

"Back to the dreams," he said. "Why is it so important that you'd swallow expired meds? And if you tell me it's none of my damn business again, I swear I'll freak you out good and turn into a dragon right here."

Uncertainty crossed her gaze. As if to prevent him from following through, she rested a hand on his arm again then touched his jaw with her fingers.

"You cannot kiss your way out of this," he told her firmly.

"Why not?" she asked, smiling. "It seems to work."

"Not now. I've got a lot on my … mind."

She leaned into him, and any thought he had of needing to resist her – and hopefully prevent whatever it was Mr. Nothing claimed existed between them – were swept away. Skylar kissed him lightly, her hair tickling his cheek and her scent washing over him.

"Come on, little dragon," she teased. "Afraid of a kiss from a mere human?"

He captured her lips with his in response, not bothering to check his passion. If she wanted to mess with him, he wasn't about to back off. He'd been relatively good the last couple of times she kissed him, but even he had his limits.

Chace drove her back until he was laying on top of her, their hungry kissing quickly elevating into heavy petting. Skylar met his passion with her own, devouring him with similar need.

# Chapter Fifteen

Hours later, she lay on her side and cuddled with him, too sated to move. Their arms were wrapped around each other, their groins pressed together with her thigh held tightly between his. She'd never met someone with Chace's passion and intensity, both of which were tempered by tenderness that made her trust him in every way in bed, even if she didn't outside of it.

They made love like they were made for each other. There was no hesitation or awkwardness, and she almost swore he was in her head and knew where to touch and when.

Their foreheads were pressed together, and they breathed the same air, laden with the scent of their combined skin and their lovemaking.

"About those dreams," he whispered huskily.

It was hard to remember they shouldn't trust one another, when she was wrapped in his heat and intoxicated by his scent. The cabin lights were out, the crackling of the romantic fire peaceful.

"I don't think they're dreams," she murmured.

"I don't understand."

"They're memories. Trapped somewhere in my mind." She tensed, expecting him to utter one of his blatant *I-told-you-so's* about her being brainwashed.

He said nothing and began running his fingers through her hair.

She closed her eyes at the gentle touch, relaxing once more.

"I have a mother. Or had. I'm not sure," she said, replaying the dreams though her mind. "Caleb took me from her about six years ago, when I was thirteen. I'm not sure what happened then. The dreams just kind of … stop."

"Caleb is an asshole."

"Yeah."

"Tell me about your mother."

She hesitated. "There's not much to tell."

"Skylar." His growl was low, barely human.

"If you hadn't waken me up earlier, I might know more," she retorted.

"Excuse me for caring about your life." His tone was dry.

Skylar chewed on her lower lip. It was swollen from his kisses, and she shifted forward to plant her face in the nape of his neck, where his scent was strong. His smoky-honey flavor somehow eased her into calm once more, like a drug she needed more and more of. Her physical satisfaction, combined with his scent and nearness, helped her think more clearly than she'd been able to since meeting him.

What bothered her more? That he admitted to caring about her or that he was the only person she knew on the planet right now who wasn't lying to her or brainwashed?

"She's beautiful," she whispered. "Big blue eyes, long, dark hair. She has a smile that just melts you from the inside, and she makes good apple pie."

"Like you. Except for the pie. Do you cook?"

She snorted. "No way."

"We can buy pie then."

*Sometimes, this guy scares me for a reason other than because he's a dragon.* It was too easy to fall into his arms and want to stay there, to imagine herself surrounded by his warmth every day and know that there wasn't anyone on the planet who was going to tangle with a dragon.

Even Caleb.

"What else?" he asked.

"Just glimpses mostly. Pieces of my past or what I assume might be my past. They don't make sense though. Kinda like flipping through a photo album. The pictures are clear, but there's so much missing from the story. From *my* story." The tremor in her voice bothered her. She cleared her throat.

His arms tightened around her, and she snuggled against his chest.

"What do you see?" he pressed.

"Why?"

"Just curious."

For the first time since they began making love, a trickle of unease went through her.

*I don't know this guy. At all.* It didn't bother her when her hormones got involved, but when she had time to think, she had trouble making sense of him.

"I told you about my mother. Now I want to ask you a question," she said.

"Hmmm."

"You said you're not a normal shifter. Why not?"

He drew a deep breath. She listened to his heartbeat and nuzzled his skin with her nose, smiling at the tickle caused by the small hairs that littered his chest.

"I was placed under a curse a thousand years ago," he replied. "Pissed of someone who knew how to use magic. I was a stupid, stupid kid."

"Oh, wow," she said. "I didn't know magic existed outside of shifters."

"I'm guessing she was a shifter. Probably an ancient one, one of those damned nocturnal shifters." By the distracted tone in his voice, he was thinking hard.

"What'd you do? Cheat on her?"

He was silent.

"Turn her dog into fried chicken?" she joked, not liking the sudden tension of his frame.

"You were close the first time," he said tersely. "Anyway, she made me into this so I'd suffer."

"When does the curse end?"

"I don't know."

She shifted her head back to see his expression in the low light of the fire. Flames and shadow danced across his noble features. His gaze was distant, stormy. For a long moment, she was mesmerized by both the flames reflected in his blue eyes and the ones that danced in his pupils.

"It has to have an end," she murmured. "Curses always do."

"This isn't some Disney movie fairytale," he replied. "There's no happy ending, no running off into the sunset or waking up one day to find it's all a dream. Just me and the curse. Forever."

Skylar pitied him in that moment, hearing the pain in his voice. An eternity alone as punishment?

She shimmied even closer to him and returned her face to his neck, where his scent grounded her.

"I bet there is a way to break it," she said. "Or someone who can help you."

"Maybe." By his short response, he was ready to leave the topic.

"One of the things my mother told me in a dream … or memory … ugh." She sighed.

Chace pressed warm lips to her forehead in a sign of support that made her heart flutter.

"She said I'd get my own dragon someday," she finished. "I think that's you."

He said nothing.

"I don't understand what it means. It's why I took the pills, to try to learn more from my memories about this and about who I am. Or was. Or should be. Whatever."

"I can't imagine what you're going through," he said gently. "I may be cursed, but I know who I am and where I'm from. I don't know what it would be like to have that part of me taken."

"Yeah kinda sucks," she admitted. "But maybe it's not such a bad thing. I mean, you're miserable remembering your curse. Maybe I don't want to remember what's happened to me. I can start from fresh, right now."

"Your past is a part of you. It'll come back to bite you. Might as well know what's gonna get you."

*You're so jaded.* She kept this observation to herself, wanting to believe her life wasn't as bad as it sounded out loud.

"What did your mom say to do with your dragon?" he asked.

"Fly around the world? Make fried chicken in an eco-friendly way?" she joked. "No idea, Chace. I haven't gotten to that part of my memory. Or maybe, that part is permanently gone." *Like my mother might be.* "Speaking of brainwashing … what on earth are you doing sleeping with a slayer?"

"Damned if I know," he said with a sigh. "I can't get enough of you or far enough away to stop wanting to fuck you again."

"Ditto," she murmured. "I'm surprised you're not more upset about yesterday, about what Caleb tried to do to you. I thought you would've fried him good."

"I still might. You keep distracting me," he said pointedly. "My plan is to raze the place. Set the entire rehab center on fire and everyone in it."

She propped herself up on one elbow to see his face. "Chace, the slayers like me don't deserve to be hurt. They can't help what they are," she said, alarmed.

"They're destroying my kind. You're snapping out of it, but they might not."

"You don't know that. My friend Mason was going through what I am. He remembers his sister, who shouldn't exist, according to his file."

Chace studied her. "Do you know how many shifters are dead

because of this little operation? Close to five hundred."

"By your rationale, I should be one of those you fry. I turned in over a dozen, Chace, not knowing what was going to happen to them."

He grated his teeth together, and the fire of his pupils grew brighter, bigger.

She placed both hands on his chest and pressed him onto his back, straddling his muscular hips. She rested her palms on his lower abs, marveling at the firm ridges beneath taut golden skin.

"Calm," she ordered with a worried smile. "I'm sorry the shifters are getting hurt, but more death isn't going to fix this. So you need a Plan B."

"No."

"How many times have you told me that you've never hurt a fly?" she challenged. "You're not going to set fire to people who are innocent of any purposeful wrongdoing."

"There's nothing innocent about slayers."

"Does that include me?"

He stared at her, jaw ticking. The depth of his anger and pain was clear. She didn't blame him for wanting to set the world ablaze, but neither did she believe he had a right to take innocent lives.

"I'll stop you," she told him.

"How?"

"I don't know. But I'll figure it out," she said. She ran her hands up his abs and chest and down his thick biceps and roped forearms. Skylar took his wrists and pinned them by his head with a grin. "I'll just kiss you again. You melt every time I do."

He snorted, some of the tension fading.

She kissed him deeply, wanting to taste him again so soon after they'd just made love. She rested her body on top of his, aware of the erection growing against her lower belly.

"You can't kiss this problem away," he whispered, pulling away.

"No, but I can help you realize that hurting slayers isn't the way to go." She said, meeting his gaze. "You want to help your shifters. I want to help those like me. I still don't understand what's going on, but I don't think your plan is the right one."

He tugged his wrists loose from her grip and wrapped his arms around her.

"You're brave, until you see my other side," he said. "I don't think you fully understand what your dreams told you about what it means to have your own dragon."

"No, I don't. But I'm getting closer to figuring that out, too," she replied. "Maybe it's this. Us. Or maybe I'm meant to help you somehow."

"No to both." His tone was firm. "This ... *us* ... is a one-night stand that turned into a few nights. I will do whatever it takes to protect the shifters, even if that means someone gets hurt."

*Not someone. Me.* The words stung, their hidden meaning hitting her harder than she expected.

"I'm running out of time. I've got to act soon," he added more quietly. "Which is why you'll tell me everything you know about other slayer rehab centers or training centers or even where every single member of the organization lives."

"That won't happen," she replied, unsettled by the force of his words. "You've got eternity, don't you?"

Chace rolled her onto her back and settled between her thighs. One of his hands traced her skin from knee to hip while the other pushed stray hair out of her face. The tenderness was gone, replaced by purpose and resolve.

"It will happen," he said. His dark blue eyes were piercing, the hard body pressing her to the bed a distraction she didn't need.

She did what she'd done whenever he started to scare her and reached up, taking his face and pulling it down to hers.

"Kiss me."

"You can't-"

She didn't let him finish but kissed him hard, fast and deep, opening herself to him in an invitation she knew he wasn't going to walk away from. Chace started to resist then gave, his emotion bursting into hunger even more intense than before. Skylar relaxed, aware she was about to go on a ride much different than before, rougher, more primal. She let his passion sweep her away.

*Tomorrow I'll figure out what to do.*

# Chapter Sixteen

Skylar eased out of bed. Morning sunlight streamed through the windows and sheer curtains, and she paused, touched by how peaceful her surroundings were. It was cozy and quiet, aside from Chace's soft snoring. The fire was low, and the natural chill in the air made her want to crawl back into the warm bed and curl up with her dragon once more. She imagined them cuddling in bed, making love once more, then getting up for a late breakfast that included hot cocoa and scrambled eggs.

Her skin pricked from the cold, and she shivered.

*We have a nice breakfast and then we go to war.* Shaking her head, she got dressed as quietly as possible. She didn't know how serious Chace was about torching the rehab center, but she had a feeling that kisses weren't going to discourage him this time.

"Cabin, can you take us back to Sonoita?" she whispered.

Nothing happened. She gave it a moment then crossed to the window.

The snowscape outside had been replaced by the tans and browns of the desert.

She gasped, amazed the cabin had not only listened, but moved them thousands of miles without so much as a whisper.

*Cool but freaky.* She glanced at Chace. He was on his belly, arms crossed beneath his head, sound asleep.

She'd been disappointed when her dreams didn't take her back to her memories after the rough sex with Chace. He'd been aggressive yet gentle, and her core and thigh muscles felt bruised from the unusual positions and movements.

Pain made her chest clench, and she tried to tell herself that she wasn't leaving for good. Just … making sure no one got hurt when he decided to torch the rehab center. Unable to determine exactly which team she was on, she knew that protecting people who had done nothing wrong was never the wrong answer.

*This feels like farewell.* Her instincts were in mourning, the pain almost making her double over.

No part of her wanted to leave.

Was this what her mother was trying to tell her in the short memories? That she had to stay with her dragon to protect him?

Or was there something more, something deeper, in the duty she had to Chace? Something more permanent?

Skylar looked away from him. Her fingers twitched with the urge to touch his hair and skin once more, to taste his mouth and run her tongue along the long shaft of his erection before suckling and swirling her tongue around its head.

Frustrated with the images in her mind, she opened the door and quietly left the cabin. The desert air was cool but not cold, and she was grateful not to be somewhere cold. She enjoyed the outdoors too much to be trapped inside. Guessing Chace wouldn't want her to leave, she set out at a quick jog through the desert, towards the southern end of the Santa Rita Mountains.

Long before she was able to see the compound, she smelled it burning. Her pace quickened to a run and then to a dead sprint when she was near enough to see the damage.

The fire had long been put out, and what remained of the compound smoldered. Wisps of smoke floated towards the sky. The innermost section of the compound was melted and charred, the outer buildings burnt and gutted but their walls still standing.

A few vehicles were outside the compound at a safe distance, and she made out the rows of bodies covered in white sheets that lined one side of the dirt road leading to the center. On the other side of the road, what looked like a triage station was set up under a small tent.

Her first thought was that Chace had followed through on his threat. It was quickly replaced by the realization that he'd been with her all night. While she didn't know much about dragons, she didn't think he could be in two places at once.

Her lungs and legs burning from the run, she stopped a quarter mile away from the facility and doubled over, sucking in deep breaths. Her mind flew between trying to remember if Mason and Dillon were scheduled to be at the center and who else could've melted the walls in place, if not Chace.

Both Caleb and Chace claimed there were no other dragons left, yet the evidence before her suggested otherwise. When she was able to catch her breath, she started forward at a trot, scanning the area with her gaze.

The facility was located in the middle of the desert for a reason, to keep its activities under the radar. Unfortunately, that meant there were no ambulances within two hours, and no fire stations either. Not that someone like Caleb would call a normal emergency service. No, it was the reasoning the slayers were taught to be self-sufficient, so they'd never draw unwanted attention to themselves.

She glanced up at the sky. The morning sun had chased away the darkness of night, while the slender shape of the moon and some stars remained in the west. Her eyes skimmed over a bird circling far overhead, dismissed it, then returned.

*Birds don't have tails like this one.* She slowed, staring at the creature soaring far, far above the desert. It was the size of a large plane from the distance, dipping and diving gracefully in the early morning sky. Sunlight reflected off the wings, which flashed dark blue, and created small rainbows that splashed into the sky around him and then were gone.

Skylar sucked in a breath, suddenly aware of where she'd seen this dragon before.

*Mama, where is he going?*

She knew this creature somehow. He'd been with her and her mother, the day they ran from the farmhouse. Were they running from him?

No. He'd been protecting them. They were running from Caleb.

Skylar racked her mind, struggling to pull the memory free completely.

"Sky! My god, we thought you were dead!" Mason's voice yanked her attention away.

Her gaze dropped, and she saw him and Dillon jogging towards her. Both had dark circles under their eyes and were covered in soot.

"You okay?" Dillon asked, concern on his face.

"Yeah," she managed. "What happened?"

"What the hell do you think?" Dillon was tense. "We're lucky we only lost twenty."

"Oh, god. Any of our friends?" she whispered.

"Walk and talk, Sky. We need to get back and help," Mason urged.

They took off at a jog, and she joined them, taking in the damage the closer they got.

"None of our classmates, thank god," Dillon answered. "Dad's okay, too. He was at home in Phoenix when this went down."

"Who ... or what did this?" she asked.

"Dragon shifter. One we've never seen before." Mason sounded frustrated. "Not the Teal Dragon."

"How ... who ... we had no idea there were two," she managed, unable to understand how a dragon from her youth had remained hidden from someone like Caleb.

"You!" Caleb's bellow made them all jump. His face a mask of controlled fury, he marched towards them, eyes on Skylar. "The only one who can track and stop them just happens to be gone during the attack?"

"Whoa, Caleb, let's just calm down," she said, backing away. Skylar held up her hands. "I'm sure the security footage from yesterday –"

He tackled her and shoved her onto her stomach, twisting one arm behind her hard enough that she felt the muscles burn and start to tear. She gasped. Tears of pain sprang from her eyes.

"Dad!" Dillon exclaimed. "Stop it!"

"You think I don't know you freed the son of a bitch?" Caleb leaned forward to hiss for her ears only.

Her heart slamming into her chest, Skylar was still, trying to stay calm while pinned beneath the furious trainer. Small rocks dug into the side of her face, and her hair was tangled in a small cactus. She didn't dare complain or move.

"Twenty of your colleagues, Skylar. *Twenty!*"

She flinched at his sharp tone.

"I trained all you kids. And you let them die!"

"Dad!" Dillon said again.

"Step away, son," Caleb snapped. He leaned forward once more. "The only reason you aren't dead is because you're the only fucking person on the planet who can track the monster that did this!"

"Caleb, don't," Mason sounded calmer than Dillon.

Skylar watched him lean over and grip Caleb's arm. Caleb yanked away, but Mason took his arm firmly while Dillon moved to do the same to his other. The two men pried the enraged trainer off her.

She pushed herself up. The muscles of her shoulder were hot and tender, but she dared not complain when Caleb was still incensed.

He shook himself free of the two.

"Do your fucking job and find that dragon!" Caleb snarled at her.

Skylar said nothing. She waited for him to turn away before testing her shoulder with a grimace.

"Sorry, Sky." Dillon's voice was unusually hushed. He knelt beside her. "Is your arm okay?"

"I'll be fine," she murmured. "He's right. I should've prevented this. Somehow."

"He's not right," Mason objected. "Sky, you had no way to stop this. You wouldn't have been able to sense the dragon was here until the place was on fire. It's not how this works. Caleb knows better. He's just upset."

The sound of metal against metal drew all of their attentions back to Caleb. Enraged, he was beating the back window out of an SUV with a crowbar.

She winced, aware that probably would've been her, if she wasn't the only dragon tracker.

"I'll try to calm him down," Dillon said and rose, darting towards his father.

Mason watched him. "You okay?" he asked when Dillon was far enough away. "Like really?"

"Think he tore something in my shoulder," she said. "But yeah. Better off than you all." She searched his face. "Mason, I'm so sorry. I should've been here."

"You couldn't have done anything," he said, dark eyes compassionate. "Good thing we got a solid look at your dragon yesterday on the security cameras when he grabbed you."

"The one upside to being kidnapped I guess." *Aside from the amazing sex.*

She wanted to warn him. She wanted to take Mason and Dillon away to see if the magic clouding their minds cleared enough for them to understand what was going on. Was there some truth to the lies the rehab center had fed its slayers? If not, then why had the blue dragon committed an atrocity that Chace claimed was forbidden for shifters?

Looking out over the smoldering building, she realized she was going to have to make a difficult choice soon, without having any more insight into what was really going on than she had at the moment. Whether or not Chace wanted an outright war or he was simply angry when he spoke about torching the rehab facility, the dark blue dragon had just raised the stakes. Chace would be hunted

LIZZY FORD

down like an animal, now that there was proof that shifters were monsters.

*We are the dragons' protectors.* She struggled with the persistence of her dream. What if it really was just a dream and not a memory?

What if the blue dragon had gone crazy or was rabid or had decided to take the fight to the slayers and humans? Chace had come close at the storage facility he torched, but he'd done it to draw her out.

The blue dragon wasn't playing games.

*She* would have to hunt him down, since there were no other dragon slayers. And what did it mean for Chace?

*My dragon,* she knew. She didn't understand which way was up with the rest of her world, but no part of her doubted this simple truth. No matter how compelled she was to him in his human form and how much his dragon form scared her, Chace was hers to protect, if not more.

But she couldn't let him or any other dragon hurt the brainwashed slayers, either.

"What's wrong?" Mason was concerned.

She glanced at him and forced a smile. "Got a lot on my mind."

"You were with him again last night?"

Skylar stood, not certain how to respond.

"It's okay. I know your dragon didn't do this," he said. "Things aren't as black and white as Caleb makes them out to be. By the way, sorry I got there too late yesterday to keep the Teal Dragon from carting you off."

"I wondered where you were," she said, suddenly recalling that Mason had been missing in action the day before. "They were pumping him full of this awful stuff to kill him, I think."

"The shrink told me." He looked away. "He managed to stall me for a while and finally I left and realized that my palm print opened the door to the rehab center. You were being carted off by that point, though. Didn't look entirely voluntary, either."

"Call me crazy, but I don't like flying without a plane or parachute," she said.

Dillon was headed back towards them. Mason fell silent with a glance at her. She understood the look warning her that their friend didn't know about either the doubts or discussions she and Mason had about their organization.

"I think he'll be okay," Dillon said, distraught. "I called my mom to come get him. The rest of the injured will be moved by van. And, I think we need to get out of here, Sky." He looked at her pointedly. "I don't think my dad is gonna take seeing you around well."

"I know." Why did she feel so guilty, even knowing she wasn't able to prevent some crazy dragon from burning down their compound? "I'll figure out how to make this right."

"Sky, don't put so much pressure on yourself," Mason chided.

"For once, I agree with soft-hearted, wussy Mason," Dillon added. "Dad had no right to say those things. You couldn't have stopped this. No one could."

"Thanks, Dillon." Her ex-boyfriend's kindness made her feel worse. "Where we headed?" She glanced towards the direction she'd come. If Chace decided to track her down, now was not the time or place to be seen with a dragon or for a dragon to be around at all. It didn't help that her skin smelled of him, and she was having a hard time focusing on the guys when her mind was on how close Chace's cabin was to the compound.

Would his magic cabin know to move him, if he failed to wake up? She doubted that slayers like Caleb were going to wait for her to lead them to the right dragon. They were out for blood and would do whatever it took to corner a dragon.

"To track a dragon," Mason said. "You guys wanna get cleaned up first?"

"Yeah." Dillon rubbed his face, exhaustion replacing his distress. "And coffee."

"Sounds good," she seconded quietly.

"C'mon then." Mason started towards one of the black SUVs.

Dillon trailed while Skylar brought up the rear. Her eyes went to the compound once more. She didn't want to imagine the chaos of the attack or what it meant for the slayers and shifters as a whole. The slayers no longer needed brainwashing after this event.

A faint trace of magic made the back of her neck itch. She scratched it absently and looked in the direction from which it came.

She couldn't see him, but Chace was nearby. What was he thinking? Was he silently brooding about not being the first to torch what remained of her world? Or did he know that this could only end badly for him?

*He knows this isn't good for us.* No matter how much he wanted to deny there was something between them, she at least knew she had a duty to protect him, without knowing how or why. The instinct was too strong for her to walk away from him. Their fates were intertwined at some level.

"Hurry up, Sky!" Mason urged. He lifted his chin towards the remaining vehicles.

Caleb was glaring at her hard enough that she quickened her step. Chace had *no* chance, if she got herself killed today.

"Coming," she said. *I could really use some dream guidance right now.*

# Chapter Seventeen

L ying on a small hill a short distance away, Chace watched Skylar get in the SUV with two other slayers, grappling to control the urge to snatch her up and take her away from the mess before him. He wanted to put distance between them, but he also didn't want her getting brainwashed again, before they both got some answers.

If nothing else, he finally had confirmation of what kind of shifter Mr. Nothing was. By the looks of it, Mr. Nothing had probably flown directly to southern Arizona after they spoke last, in order to destroy the compound.

*I feel like shit.* Chace knew the nocturnal shifter was hard to read, but he didn't expect Mr. Nothing to do this. When he was calm enough, Chace let himself acknowledge that Skylar was right. The brainwashed slayers didn't deserve to be treated the way they treated the shifters.

Last night weighed to heavily on his mind. He wasn't able to think straight without an errant thought of how beautiful she looked when her skin glowed in the firelight or the way her body moved beneath his. Their combined scent had even managed to become engrained in his long hair while the memory of her whispering his name made him feel possessive of another person for the first time in his life.

Made him wish he hadn't made a deal with Mr. Nothing, so he could see where this was going.

At least, that was the initial reason he set out after Skylar when he woke to find her gone. The moment he stepped outside, his sensitive nose picked up on the smells of burnt buildings, metal and flesh.

The SUV drove away, and Chace continued to watch. He received no small amount of satisfaction out of watching Caleb throw a tantrum and smash up the back window of another car. He didn't pity the man, despite knowing how true Skylar's words were.

The slayers were brainwashed fools, but they weren't killers. The people within the compound were a different story entirely. Skylar's shrink knew what they were doing to the rest of them, and wasn't possible that this elaborate of an operation was operated by two people. No, the cadre of the rehab center knew what was going on.

This was why he felt no mercy towards the bodies lined up along the side of the road.

Chace rolled onto his back for a moment, comforted by the blue sky above that reminded him of Skylar's eyes.

*Dammit! Stop thinking of her!*

He had much larger concerns. The slayers weren't going to need to be brainwashed to come after shifters now, not after the deaths of their colleagues and the leveling of their operations center. Chace and the shifters were about to become openly hunted animals instead of those that were quietly tracked. How far could the spooked shifters be pushed before another snapped and went bat-shit crazy, like Mr. Nothing?

How much longer before Mr. Nothing turned him into a powerless human, since he had torched the compound he tasked Chace with finding?

*I've got Skylar.* The reminder disturbed him, more so because seeing what Mr. Nothing was willing to do did nothing to make him believe that Skylar was going to be safe with the ancient shifter.

But he could trade her, perhaps for more time, to ensure he was able to help the shifters. Or perhaps for a promise from Mr. Nothing not to hurt anyone else in the hopes that the slayers would gradually lose interest in the shifters.

"What aren't you telling me, jackass?" he muttered, mind on Mr. Nothing. "I know you know who is behind this."

*Someone close to Skylar,* Mr. Nothing had said.

Whenever their paths crossed, she was with the same two slayers, and Caleb claimed to have trained her.

Caleb was the natural choice. Seasoned, guarded, smart.

Chace pulled out his phone to text Mr. Nothing. He knew from experience that the texts were always received, even if Mr. Nothing never returned them. He sent beautiful women with appointment cards instead.

*We need to talk.* He texted.

Replacing the phone in his pocket, he eased away from the hill and strode back to the waiting cabin, which was a few thousand miles away from where he'd left it. Irked that Skylar was able to use his magic somehow, he reached the cabin and immediately willed it to move somewhere far from the compound, in case the slayers searched the surrounding area.

His next stop: the bar. He willed it to move, too, to the foothills of the remote mountaintop in Arizona where the cabin was. The shifters alone were able to know where it was, and he wasn't about to put it on a mountaintop where he wasn't able to go on his daily ride with the others.

Chace stripped quickly and bundled up his clothing as usual then strode out into the open area outside the cabin. He morphed quickly and dived off the mountain. Wind roared through his ears, into his nostrils and ruffled the fur lining his scales. He relished the sensation, his wings folded for better aerodynamics. Just before he was about to plunge headfirst into the ground, he released his wings and soared upwards, twisting and turning, diving and climbing.

He couldn't escape Skylar's sweet scent, but he tried, flying until his blood settled. At last, he floated lazily down to the bar, circling it multiple times before finally dropping to all four feet a short distance away.

Gunner waited for him, arms crossed as he leaned against the front post where his bike was parked.

Chace transformed into his human form and tugged his clothing on as he walked towards his friend.

"Heard there's some trouble," Gunner said, watching him.

Chace grunted in response and finished pulling his shirt over his head before answering.

"Lots of trouble," he said. "As in, if things were bad before, they're about to get worse." *And if I don't talk to Mr. Nothing, you all might lose the bar, too.*

"We were right about Mr. Nothing," Gunner observed. "What the hell made him fry the people tracking us?"

"I think he meant to finish them off and managed to piss 'em all off instead." Chace rubbed his mouth. "I need to find Mr. Nothing. We've gotta warn the shifters, too. I am so fucking frustrated right now!"

"All right. Calm down," Gunner said. "You're not one to flip out over nothing."

Chace drew a breath. "You know how you said not to make the deal with Mr. Nothing?"

"Shit."

"Yeah I didn't realize what all I was giving up. The bar is connected to my magic. When it's gone, there's no refuge for the shifters."

Gunner grew pale beneath his olive-hued skin.

"The slayers now have a real reason to come after us all, thanks to Mr. Nothing, and I gave up the only place we're safe."

Gunner spoke, but Chace was distracted by his thoughts. He wasn't able to dismiss Skylar from his mind. He was about to lose his magic and his bar. Absently he touched his chest, above the heart.

His heart was whole, according to Mr. Nothing, and he wasn't able to determine why exactly that bothered him as much as the bar situation.

*It means the shifter has found the other half of his heart.* What the hell was he supposed to do about that?

"Yo." Gunner waved his hand in front of his face.

"Yeah. Sorry." Chace focused on his friend.

"Like I said a hundred times already, why don't you go find Mr. Nothing, and I'll warn the others. Sound like a plan?"

"He's nocturnal. He won't be out until tonight," Chace replied. "This is my fault, Gunner. I'll help you warn the others. It's the only thing I can do."

"I've got our handy phone tree in the bar. Let's start making the calls."

Chace nodded.

Gunner strode into the bar.

With another look around him, Chace followed.

Notifying the other shifters took a solid two hours. They began to trickle in by pairs for the emergency meeting Chace had called. When the last of them arrived just after sundown, he took a count and frowned.

"Four more gone," he said to Gunner, mind going to the rehab center and the pain he'd gone through while there. "That place deserved to be destroyed."

"I agree," Gunner said. "I can't believe they tracked down so many shifters over the years."

"I know." Chace's stomach churned just thinking about it. "I have a feeling they've declared outright war this time. I don't think they're taking them to any rehab center, just killing them on sight."

"What's the plan?"

"If my magic is going to be gone soon, then I want to move the bar one last time to see if we can delay discovery until I figure out how to fix this," Chace replied.

"You plan on trying to reason with Mr. Nothing a second time?"

Gunner was amused. "Enough is enough. We'll figure out something else. I've known him for a few hundred years and never once had the desire to trust him."

"What else can I do?" Chace demanded. "This is my fault. It was … arrogant of me to think there weren't more consequences for my actions. Just like it was stupid for me to walk into the rehab center without thinking twice about walking out. I've been alive a thousand years and feel like I haven't learned anything."

"You have," Gunner reassured him. "Some lessons are harder. I got my own demons with learning lessons." Darkness flickered across his face.

Chace didn't ask. They'd been friends too long to doubt one another, even if neither had learned the entirety of the other's past.

The movement of someone entering the bar caught both of their attentions, and they looked, hoping it was another shifter. Instead, a buxom brunette in a tight black dress was making her way to the bartender. Chace saw her pass a familiar appointment card to the bald man then leave hastily when she saw Max headed towards her.

"Go find Mr. Nothing. I know you won't sit still until you do," Gunner said, nudging him forward with his elbow. "I'll handle things here and see if we can't prep people for the worst."

"Thanks." Chace slapped his arm and strode out, too edgy to protest, even if he knew he should. He crossed to the bartender, who held out the card as he approached.

Chace took it.

*Fifteen minutes. Your cabin.*

Expecting the short timeframe, Chace waved towards Gunner and strode out of the bar.

He had transformed into his dragon shape by his fifth step out of the door to the bar and flung himself into the sky. His grueling pace rendered him almost breathless by the time he'd climbed to the oxygen-thin elevation where his cabin was. He circled the mountain to confirm Mr. Nothing was waiting for him in the area near his cabin.

Chace began transforming before he was on the ground and dropped the last few feet. He yanked on his pants then approached Mr. Nothing, pausing to catch his breath.

"It's too late, if this is a desperate attempt to not become human. It takes effect at dawn," Mr. Nothing told him.

"I don't want to change the terms of our initial deal," Chace said. His body was too wired from emotion for him to feel the chill of the night air. "It struck me that the girl wasn't part of our original deal. I wanted to amend our agreement."

Mr. Nothing folded his arms across his chest, suddenly tense.

"I'll bring her to you," Chace added reluctantly. "But I want you to protect the shifters the way I have the past few hundred years, by giving them a refuge. If my magic can do it, yours can, too."

Mr. Nothing was quiet.

"I'll turn her over before dawn. You pissed off the slayers by destroying their center, and they're killing faster now. The shifters have nothing but the bar as a refuge."

"You should've known that before you made your decision. Your selfishness put everyone else at risk."

"I also found the center where they were being killed," Chace retorted, hating how right Mr. Nothing was.

"My generation of dragons is much different than yours."

"I'm trying to make things right. Do you agree to my terms or do I just hide Skylar in a deep hole where you can't find her?"

"You learned nothing from acting brashly." Mr. Nothing muttered a curse. "I should say no."

"But I have a feeling you won't."

It was Mr. Nothing's turn to appear frustrated. Chace waited.

Part of him hoped Mr. Nothing refused. At least then, Skylar would be safe. But a small voice told him that he had to turn her over, at least temporarily, to save the others. At dawn, his entire world changed one last time after a thousand years under the curse.

It wasn't right to escape and leave more skeletons behind him than necessary. It didn't seem right to sacrifice her, either, but he tried hard not to think of what he felt when he was with her, how smooth and soft her skin was, her faint womanly scent mixed with the peaches of her shampoo ...

"I agree," Mr. Nothing replied with the same reluctance.

Chace's heart felt like it dropped to his feet. It made sense to trade one life for a hundred.

But it felt wrong, too.

"Okay," he whispered. "I'll bring her to you by dawn. Where do you want to meet?"

"Maine coast, where we met before. I'll be waiting."

Mr. Nothing started away.

"Wait," Chace called. "You won't hurt her, will you?" The question sounded stupid out loud. What did he expect would happen to her?

"Not your concern at this point." Mr. Nothing kept walking. He spread his arms and leapt off the edge of the cliff.

Chace cursed loudly. Moments later, the massive blue dragon soared overhead.

He watched it go, distraught by what he'd done.

Chace walked to the edge of the mountain and sat with his legs hanging over the ledge, pensive

He had a victory, the only good thing to come out of the choice he'd made a couple of weeks ago. He had a promise from Mr. Nothing, the oldest dragon and most powerful that he knew, to take care of the shifters.

The victory was as cold as the wind whipping up the cliff face. He didn't fully understand what was between him and Skylar or even if it was sustainable beyond physical attraction. Being with her left him calm and centered. She felt so different from anyone else he'd ever dated or slept with.

Did it matter? He'd sold her out, good cause or not. Was this the ultimate price of all his bad decisions? He lost the part of him that made him feel whole?

# Chapter Eighteen

The knock at her door jarred her awake. Skylar sat up straight and tossed off the blankets, halfway across the room before she fully registered what she was doing. She shook her head and blinked away what remained of her sleep.

It was midnight. She tied her hair back and made her way through the dark apartment, pausing to flip on the kitchen light so she could see better. She'd been inventorying her new equipment before bed and laid it out on the table to keep from forgetting anything when she set out early the next morning. The thick golden lassos and weapons assured her she had the necessary tools to handle whoever – or whatever – was at her door.

She slid the chain into place on her door then opened it, looking up into stormy dark blue eyes.

"Chace?" she exclaimed. "What're you doing here?"

"You wanna let me in before the slayers in the lobby figure out I'm here?" he responded roughly. His air was tense, his gaze flickering around the hallway as if he expected slayers to leap out of the shadows lining the walls.

She hesitated, heat blooming in her belly at his scent and the familiar size of his muscular body.

"Or I can just morph into a dragon right here in the hallway."

"Not my problem," she told him. "You shouldn't be here in the first place!"

"Who else can take you to the blue dragon?"

She closed the door, thinking briefly. She should be jumping at the chance to find the man who killed twenty of her coworkers. If the news came from anyone else but the sexy shifter she couldn't keep her thoughts or mind from straying to …

With a frustrated sigh, Skylar unlocked the door and opened it, stepping away to let him in.

"I see you were expecting me," he said, gaze going over her body with interest.

"Whatever." She wore a tank and underwear, no bra. She tried to keep her voice steady, even though her body was growing almost fevered from his nearness. "Like you haven't seen me naked before."

"No complaints here."

She rolled her eyes at him and went into the kitchen, eyeing the golden rope.

"You've got my attention," she said. "Where's the blue dragon?"

His gaze was on the table. He leaned against the doorway, crossing his arms. His chiseled features were calmer than he'd been in the hallway, his blue eyes no longer flashing with fire. His jaw was shaded by a day or two of hair growth, and there were shadows beneath his eyes.

"Two lassos. Two remaining dragons," he observed. "So you really aren't planning on stopping at the blue dragon."

Skylar didn't answer. She'd never felt endangered around Chace, but she had began to feel a little … uncertain about much of her life. If she was truly brainwashed, then were her emotions really hers?

"I guess that answers that," Chace said tersely. "Is it safe to assume whatever was between us is over?"

She looked up at this. Her mouth was suddenly dry, and it was hard to breathe deeply.

"If that's the case, just lasso me now and take me in," he goaded, raking both hands through his loose hair.

"Maybe I should," she retorted, as much to convince herself as him. She crossed to the table and rested her hand on the lasso. It was silky beneath her fingertips, its long fibers smooth.

Skylar's emotions and thoughts were all over the place. Technically, she needed to take him in, before he, too, blew a gasket and wiped out a building full of people. The power of one dragon to destroy lives had never been clearer than it was less than a day before. She'd left the arms of one dragon to see what the temper of another had done.

Except she hadn't been able to swallow the idea that Caleb and the others killed shifters. It wasn't right. The blue dragon, yes, needed to be stopped.

But Chace? Whose worst crime was starting a building on fire to get her attention?

*He doesn't deserve to die.* This thought was followed quickly by another, one driven by the instinct she wasn't able to understand. *I have to protect him.*

"Hard to condemn someone to death just for being different, isn't it?" Chace whispered.

She blinked out of her stupor and realized he was standing behind her. The heat of his body was at her back. He moved forward until their bodies were just touching and covered the hand she rested on the lasso with his. Too aware of his warmth and nearness, she froze.

He removed their hands from the rope and to her lower belly. His slid away from hers, under her shirt, and her stomach quivered at the touch. His other hand went to her hip.

"You didn't come here to tell me about the blue dragon," she said, seeking some semblance of control over her raging hormones.

"I did. Mostly," he replied. "And to say farewell."

"What do you mean?"

"I don't want to talk about it. But I'll … take you to him. Just might be the last time I can see you."

"Because I'm still a slayer?" she asked. His words tore her up more than she expected. She didn't know what to think when they were together, but she didn't want them to be permanently a part, either.

"No." He said nothing else. He pulled her back against him firmly while his hand traveled down, slipping beneath the thin fabric of her underwear.

Her breath caught. "You're here to *show* me farewell."

He nudged her head aside and began kissing her neck, then down her shoulder.

Skylar twisted in his hold and gazed up at him, distracted by the large hand that was roaming over her ass.

"Really. What's going on?" she pressed. "I don't want a farewell."

"No?" He searched her gaze.

"I have no idea what I want, but it's not for you to be gone. Permanently gone." *I think.*

"Almost sounds like you like me, slayer," he observed, moving close enough that her thighs were pinned between him and the table.

"I don't know what I feel."

"How can you be so ..." He gave a frustrated sigh. "...you. I guess."

"Openly conflicted while you're hiding all kinds of secrets?" she asked, amused. "Why don't you just stop thinking and kiss me?"

She didn't have to ask twice. He kissed her hard. His arms tightened around her, and he slid the hand on her ass downward, dipping into her core.

"You were expecting me tonight?" he teased.

"Shut up and take your clothes off, dragon," she replied roughly.

He leaned back and released her enough to pull off his shirt, followed quickly by his pants. She peeled off her tank and underwear, barely managing to toss them aside when he grabbed her and kissed her with enough intensity to push her back against the wall.

His thick dick pressed against her, and her belly was ablaze with need. Her core was wet enough for her to be uncomfortable.

Everything about him was rough, raw, from his demanding kisses to the pressure of his touching. He was branding her, claiming her.

*Or maybe, afraid to lose me?* Unable to identify where the random thought came from, she dismissed it, more interested in the sensations flying through her body and the feel of his warm skin and hot mouth.

He lifted her onto his hips and pressed her against the wall, his hard dick pressed to her core. She wriggled against him.

"No teasing this time," she warned him.

"I won't," he said, withdrawing.

He studied her features, as if wanting to memorize her face. Freeing one hand, he pushed her hair back from one side of her face then traced a finger down the side to her chin.

"You okay?" she asked, not expecting the pensive look that crossed his face when their naked bodies were pressed together.

"Right now, yeah," he said hoarsely. "Could change later."

Her instincts wriggled, warning her that something was really wrong.

"Then let's enjoy ourselves," she said and took his finger in her mouth, sucking it hard.

He smiled, tenderness in his gaze. He pulled his finger free and traced it down her neck and stomach, towards where their bodies were pressed together.

"You have to trust me, if I take you to the blue dragon," he whispered, kissing her lightly. "Can you do that?"

"Yeah," she murmured and then took his lower lip between her teeth.

His finger stroked her clit hard, and she arched with a gasp. He made light, lazy circles around the aching button.

"You sure?" he whispered. He kissed her neck.

Skylar's heart felt like it was going to explode from the adrenaline and need that lit her blood on fire.

"Right now, I'd trust you with anything," she managed.

His finger left, and he gripped her bottom, positioning her. He withdrew enough to align their bodies and slid his dick into her until they fit together perfectly. He filled her core, and her body adjusted to his size

Chace hissed, his muscles bulging with the amount of control he exerted.

"You said anything. You mean it?"

"With all my heart." She moved against him and wrapped her arms around him, pulling their bodies closer.

He kissed her and began moving in and out of her, pressing her against the wall and helping support her with his hands.

"I love being inside you," he said.

"Shut up, dragon."

He chuckled huskily and began to pump faster. Wrapping an arm around her, he maneuvered them to the kitchen table and wiped it clear with his free arm, then lay her on it. She kept her legs around him and gripped his ass, urging him to move faster in and out of her. The cold table beneath her was only a distraction for a split second, until his hot mouth found her breast and began alternately nibbling and suckling one then the other.

His control was slipping, his nips almost too rough, his hands branding her once more. He slid out of her body and dropped to his knees, trailing his palms down her body and legs. He propped her feet on his shoulders and pulling her lower body to the edge, until the heat of his mouth reached her.

She groaned at the incredible sensations of his fingers and mouth working her clit and G-spot, driving her close to climaxing with expertise that left her unable to think of anything but where he'd lick or touch next.

Just when she was about to shatter, he stopped and stood, holding out his hands for her to take his arms.

She groaned in objection, needing her release, but held out her hands and let him pull her up. He hefted her onto his hips once more, sinking into her swiftly enough for her to shudder. She kissed him hungrily, and he walked them into the bedroom, clutching her hard enough that she wasn't able to rub her aching clit against him.

"You owe me one," he told her and lowered her across the bed. "Talk about teasing. At least I let you come."

If she weren't so uncomfortably turned on, she would've laughed. Instead, she reached for him. He rested on top of her then rolled for her to be on top.

"Go to it," he said with a wicked grin and pushed her away, towards his straining erection.

Skylar glared at him, frazzled.

"I have a better idea," she snapped. She climbed off him, circled the bed to where his head was then climbed on top of him, settling her clit at his lips while she took the head of his erection into her mouth.

"One of my fave positions," he said in approval. He gave her a hard lick to underscore his point.

She rested on top of him, focused on making him come. She teased the soft skin of the head then took all of him into her mouth, gripping him hard with her lips as she moved the length of his erection. Wrapping a hand around his shaft, she squeezed hard and began using her mouth and hands in sync while stroking the sack beneath his large dick.

"Oh, yeah," he murmured. "It won't take long with you doing that."

"Then you better get to work!" she snapped.

His fingers moved inside of her. He sucked on the nether lips then traced them lightly with his tongue, teasing her, before he circled the clit lazily.

She groaned.

"Don't get distracted," he whispered.

Skylar struggled to focus on pleasing him with the exquisite sensations he was causing her own body. She sucked on him hard, grazing his head with her teeth and alternating between her mouth and hand to stroke his shaft relentlessly until she heard him groan.

Her body grew tense from his gentle manipulation, and the head of his erection in her mouth grew larger, its shaft thicker.

Once more, right before she climaxed, Chace stopped, this time rolling her off him. She muttered a curse at him, but one look at his face said he was too close to his own orgasm for the control necessary for him to tease her again.

She beckoned him to her body. He flashed a grin and pushed her over onto her stomach, pushing her thighs together. He worked one arm beneath her shoulders, the other around her hips to lift them for his entry.

"Cross your ankles," he whispered.

She obeyed.

Chace plunged into her. "Oh, god you're even tighter." He moved in and out of her once more, faster this time.

His breathing was hard in her ear and the friction of his movement causing more intense sensations than she'd ever experienced. The rough bedspread was torture against her sensitive nipples, and the arm he held under her hips moved downward until two of his fingers were positioned to stroke her.

But he didn't, instead holding enough distance between her and them to prevent her from so much as brushing anything that might send her toppling into an orgasm.

"Chace!" she gasped, overwhelmed.

"We'll come together." His voice was harsh, his strain clear.

The climax was building deep within her with his increasing speed and the repeated deep penetration of his erection. Skylar gripped a pillow with one of her hands.

"Ready?" His words were barely human.

"Yes!"

He stroked her once, hard, and she arched, sensing something she never thought possible: a double climax getting ready to break. The tension deep within her sheathe, coupled with the more exquisite sensation caused when he touched her clit, made for a potential explosion she wasn't certain she could handle.

"Skylar!" Chace cried as he reached the last shred of control. He stroked her hard and fast, in rhythm with him plunging into her body.

Her body flushed as if with fever, her toes curling a moment before the orgasms broke. Too intense for her to cry out, all she was able to do was ride the waves of ecstasy that wracked her body hard enough to jar her clenched teeth. The climax made her core more sensitive, enough that she felt his dick inside her in detail. His fingers continued working her, finally wringing a cry from her.

Chace came hard next, his panting heavy and his body shaking. He dropped on top of her, and they lay still.

"Even … after that, I want more of you," he breathed, kissing her cheek.

Skylar focused on catching her breath, still lost in the waves of pleasure working their way through her system. The intensity of the experience sapped any strength or desire to move from her.

"That was amazing," she said when she'd recovered enough to speak.

He eased off her enough to nudge her to roll over. She did so, gazing up at him. He settled between her legs and began licking and nibbling on her breasts.

"Again already?" She laughed.

"I'll enjoy you while I have you."

The instinct returned, the one that said that not only was he serious about saying farewell, but that something … not good was going on, too.

"You can have me whenever you want," she said, testing him.

"Now." He moved up her body to kiss her with hungry that should've been sated. He was already hard, and he entered her fast, hard.

Her body tender from the orgasms, her breath caught, and she broke away, trying to orient herself before plunging again into the intense pleasure of their lovemaking.

Chace found her lips with his, not giving her the chance to recover before sending her toppling again into his body. With his scent intoxicating her, and his thrusts already taking her close to climax again, any desire she had to figure out what her instincts were trying to tell her faded.

He was more demanding this round, his hips working as hard as his mouth. She dug her nails into his ass and held on for dear life, aware of her body growing tense in a sign she was about to have her third orgasm in less than fifteen minutes.

*What the hell has gotten into him?*

Did it matter? Sex with him was incredible. Tonight, it was otherworldly.

Skylar rode his intensity to three more orgasms over the course of an hour, while he showed no signs of letting up. He never tired of manipulating her body into new positions and going down on her, of savoring every inch of her with his mouth and hot hands. He didn't let her recover long between, just enough for his orgasm to subside and his dick to grow hard again before he teased her into a frenzy or plunged into her with desperation. His lovemaking was primal and consuming in a way she'd never experienced.

At long last, he stopped and rested on top of her, breathing hard. Skylar released her ankles and lowered her legs to the bed once more, wrapping her arms around him. She shook from pleasure and exertion, her muscles quivering.

"Are you okay?" she whispered in a voice hoarse from crying his name.

"I don't know," he murmured, capturing her nipple with his mouth and sucking hard.

She shivered in response, certain she didn't have anything else in her.

"I don't' want to leave," he added.

"Don't."

"We have to. Gotta find the blue dragon."

There was a note in his voice that warned her something really was wrong.

"He can wait, can't he?" she teased.

"I set up a meeting … for you."

"Oh." She ran her hands through his hair then pressed her lips to his temple. "We'll meet him and rendezvous here."

Chace didn't react for a moment. He got up without looking at her and walked out of the bedroom into the kitchen.

She watched him, no part of her wanting to move.

"We have to go," he said abruptly, as if they hadn't spent the past few hours making love.

"You gonna tell me what's going on?" she asked, concerned.

"You just have to trust me."

"I do, Chace."

The sounds of his rustling paused then resumed.

*Damn moody dragons.* She groaned as she rolled out of bed. Her wobbly legs barely held her up, and she grinned at the disheveled woman gazing back at her. She looked rough but felt fantastic, if sleepy.

Skylar got dressed slowly and left her walk-in closet to see Chace seated on the edge of the bed, pillow in hand. He was fully dressed once more, his hair neat and tied at the base of his neck. In his other hand was a set of handcuffs and a pillowcase.

"Did you change your mind about leaving?" she asked, gaze on the two items.

He snorted. "I may have told him I captured you."

"Ah. Okay. Cuff me."

"Okay?" Chace twisted to look at her. "Just … okay?"

She searched his strong features, not understanding the question he wasn't asking. Crossing to him, she tugged the pillow free and tossed it, then settled onto his lap.

"You told me to trust you," she reminded him, wrapping his arms around her. "So … yeah. Okay."

His arms circled her, and he squeezed her ass, pulling her body closer to his. She rubbed her cheek against his roughened one, wishing she knew what was disturbing him enough that he thought they'd never see one another again.

He hugged her hard, and she reciprocated, relaxing in his arms. The tender moment grew long and peaceful, a far cry from the desperation of his lovemaking. His hair tickled her chin, and she breathed in the scent of his neck, loving it more every time she smelled him.

"We can capture the blue dragon then go for pizza," she suggested.

"You're thinking of food at a time like this?" he asked with a surprised laugh.

"I'm thinking of *you* and a pizza," she corrected him then added in a whisper. "You're my dragon."

He squeezed her harder. "I'll always be your dragon, no matter what happens. Even if you hate me one day."

"You can't hate your dragon," she said. She leaned away to see his face, touched by the deep sorrow in his face. "I can't hate you. Ever."

He held her gaze, the warmth in his beautiful blue eyes glowing in a way that told her she was as much his as he was hers. Seeing his despair troubled her on too many levels. His suffering was deep enough to scare her.

"We have a pizza date," she said with forced lightness. "Let's get the stupid blue dragon so we can hang out."

"Okay," he said and kissed her forehead chastely.

She climbed off his lap and smiled at him, hiding a tremor of fear and dread.

Whatever was going on, she suspected it had to do with the blue dragon. A part of her began to think she wasn't meant to walk away from their meeting alive.

*I trust you, Chace.*

# Chapter Nineteen

*I*t has to be this way. Chace repeated the words until they became an absent chant. In his dragon form, it was impossible for his delicate senses to ignore her scent or the idea that this was the last time he may ever be this close to her let alone spend the night making love to her the way he had.

He landed lightly at the spot where Mr. Nothing had indicated he should, close to the ocean. He chose a large, flat rock, so as not to make Skylar's life too much more uncomfortable. The hood and ropes were enough for his conflicted conscience.

*It has to be this way.*

Refusing to dwell on what Skylar was probably thinking or feeling, Chace focused instead on assessing his surroundings. He smelled Mr. Nothing. The ancient dragon shifter was around somewhere, even if Chace wasn't able to pinpoint where exactly. They were otherwise alone.

He released Skylar and shifted into his human form, pulling on his clothing quickly to prevent the ocean chill from soaking into his bones. He heard the crash of the sea against rocks in the near distance. Stars lit the isolated area, the only light visible for miles.

"Still with me?" Chace asked her and gently helped her stand.

"Yeah." Her voice was muffled. She didn't sound scared or worried, as if she really did trust him the way he'd asked her to.

It made him feel worse.

Skylar shivered, and he moved closer to her until the warmth of his body helped chase away the cold night.

"Is he here?" she asked somewhat apprehensively.

"He's close. Not sure exactly where." Chace looked around once more for some sort of movement in their vicinity.

Skylar shifted closer to him, and he instinctively looped an arm around her shoulders.

A whoosh of air stirred his hair, and Chace looked up, making out the form of a large dragon hovering overhead.

"He's here," he said, dropping his arm. "Ready?"

"Yep."

There was no hesitation in her voice, and he wondered if any part of her suspected what he planned on doing.

*It has to be this way.* The lives of the shifters were at stake, and Mr. Nothing had *seemed* like he wanted Skylar alive. If she was alive long enough, then Chace could figure out how to keep his magic, save the shifters and rescue her.

Or maybe he was once more the fool when dealing with a dragon shifter older than him.

"By the way. You were awesome tonight," she whispered.

"As opposed to the other times?" he asked, amused.

"No. I just mean tonight you didn't seem like you were holding back. You did the other times we were together. Wild Chace is just ... incredible." There was warmth in her tone that made the dread in his belly grow heavier.

"For the record, you're not too bad in the sack either," he teased.

She elbowed him.

"Best I've had in a thousand years," he added more quietly.

"Seriously?"

"Seriously." He watched Mr. Nothing descend, aware he was about to be out of bargaining chips.

"You know, Chace …" she hesitated. "My mother told me that I was supposed to protect my dragon."

"I don't need protecting."

"I think you do. Not just from my uh, kind either. I think there's some other way she meant for me to help you. Sometimes, I almost have it. Then it's gone in a puff of smoke." She grew troubled. "Do you think the memories will ever come back? Or maybe you can help me unlock them again?"

"I don't know." Chace rubbed his mouth, apprehension in his blood. "I kinda doubt I can help."

She was quiet, expectant.

"But I'm not a born shifter," he forced himself to say something more. "I probably couldn't help anyway." *Even if I wasn't planning on betraying you tonight.*

"Maybe after our pizza date, we can do some research," she suggested.

"Yeah." *I'm a piece of shit.* Chace's heart was beating hard enough to alarm him, his chest almost too tight to speak.

The nocturnal shifter alighted behind a few boulders and emerged a few moments later, dressed in his typical dark clothing.

"Stay here. I want to talk to him first," Chace said to her. "He's expecting me."

"Okay. Be careful." She sounded anxious.

He stepped away. His body was fevered despite the cold air, his anxiety growing by the second. He glanced over his shoulder at Skylar.

She was tense but obedient. He almost wished she'd flee or fight him or somehow make this easier. The golden rope was tucked in her pocket, the sole source of hope he had that she wasn't going to be vulnerable with Mr. Nothing.

Chace met Mr. Nothing at the halfway point, far enough away for her not to hear them.

"This is her?" Mr. Nothing looked past him.

"It is," Chace replied. "Per our agreement …"

"In exchange for this one, I'll maintain the shifters' refuge and cease all attacks against the slayers."

"Can I ask why her? Why not Caleb, the lead slayer?" Chace asked.

"You said she is the first to break through the brainwashing. I need someone with a strong mind."

"Not to torture or kill or …"

"Why does her fate concern you?" Mr. Nothing's tone took on a scornful note. "You will soon be more human than she is."

"I know. But that doesn't mean I like seeing innocent people hurt."

"I won't, unless she forces my hand."

Chace folded his arms across his chest, not liking the words.

"Dawn is in an hour," Mr. Nothing said. "I'll give you until then to move your cabin where you want to remain permanently."

"Can I ask you one more question?"

Mr. Nothing waited, blue eyes almost silver in the pale light of stars.

"The woman who put this curse on me in the first place was like you, wasn't she?" Chace asked. "From some ancient line of shifters."

"Most likely. The older a shifter becomes, the more powerful. But also the harder it is to survive, since the magic grows too strong for most shifters to handle. To turn someone into a shifter, she had to have been over five thousand years old."

"Wow. So you're about the same age, if you can make me human?"

"Close," Mr. Nothing said vaguely. "We were raised in a world where the dragonkind were welcome. We had a society, mentors to teach us about our magic, humans who helped protect us. Those were lost with most of the ancient shifters."

Chace was amazed by the information after a thousand years of being generally ignored by Mr. Nothing when he asked about the dragon shifters.

"Now. Get out of here. One hour, Chace. At dawn, you will be human again." Mr. Nothing brushed by him and crossed the boulders that separated them from Skylar.

Every muscle of Chace's body tensed, and every instinct cried for him not to let Skylar go, especially not with Mr. Nothing.

He turned away, his emotional turmoil calling forth the magic that was forcing his body to shift, even when he didn't want it to. Chace dropped to all fours. His clothing split and tore, but for once, he didn't care. He wasn't in control of the emotions or his shifting or even his life anymore.

He'd made a choice and was about to go on his last flight ever and leave behind the first woman who made him feel in a thousand years, who made his heart whole and beat again.

He leapt into the air before his body was fully transformed. His wings struggled for a split second before they'd unfolded and lifted him into the night sky. He hovered, needing to know that Skylar was okay, before he left her for good.

Mr. Nothing didn't speak or linger long. He stood in front of Skylar, pensive, before stepping away and shifting.

Chace watched him unhappily, wishing he'd said something else to Skylar before walking away. *Farewell. Thank you.* Anything.

Mr. Nothing's wingspan was one and a half times the size of Chace, another indication of just how old he was. From above, his wings and scales were blue-black in the moonless night, silent as they unfurled around a body slightly bigger than Chace's.

Skylar still hadn't moved or spoken, unaware of what was going on and waiting patiently the way he'd told her to. Chace breathed in deeply to catch her scent, at once hungry for her and tormented by the knowledge of what he'd done, of how trusting she was.

Mr. Nothing lifted himself off the ground with the long wings and carefully swept her up in one clawed talon.

"Chace?" Skylar cried, startled.

A tremor went through him, ruffling the scales down his back. Two thoughts clashed in his thoughts.

*It has to be this way.*

*She belongs with me.*

The blue dragon vaulted into the sky, passing Chace in a blink and continuing upwards at a dizzying rate.

A bellow of frustration worked its way free from the depths of Chace's chest, along with a plume of fire that crackled in the air around him. The sudden burst of fire and light faded without torching his pent-up emotion.

Chace flung himself toward the heavens, unable to stand by while someone else took away his Skylar. His eyes searched the night sky for movement.

Mr. Nothing had vanished.

Chace extended his senses, seeking any sign of where the blue dragon was. It didn't seem possible that the creature was just … gone. Nothing on the earth could move with the speed necessary to outrace his senses!

And yet, the blue dragon had.

Mr. Nothing – and Skylar – had completely disappeared.

Loss hit him hard and deep, sinking beneath the emotions and distance he'd tried to put between himself and Skylar.

*What the fuck did I just do to the other half of my heart?*

# Chapter Twenty

The speed with which they flew drove Skylar near unconsciousness. She hung limply in the massive talon, unable to register much more than the roar of the cold wind by her ears. The hood was torn off by their speed, giving her a view directly below. Air made her eyes water until the ocean and sky looked the same, further baffling her senses. She closed her eyes and stopped trying to orient herself.

Something bad had happened, if Chace hadn't said anything to her before snatching her up and fleeing. She'd heard the low murmurs of two men speaking followed by the sound of breaking bones and tearing sinew, an indication Chace was changing into his dragon form.

*Maybe my instincts were off.* Hope surged within her. By the way he'd made love and spoken to her, she had an uneasy feeling that he was setting her up for something. Though what, she didn't know. He'd given her the lasso, which she was able to use against him as well as the blue dragon.

Were they being chased? Was this the reason behind the breakneck speed?

Uncomfortable and helpless, she ducked her face behind a claw, trying to shield it from the cold air. The talon offered some warmth, and she wasn't able to move her body to curl up or otherwise try to consolidate her body heat. She was shaking.

After a short while, she sensed their pace was slowing. It wasn't enough for her to want to expose her face to the elements, but it gave her hope that maybe they weren't being pursued.

Their speed slowed again, and the dragon began circling, a sign he was preparing to land. Huddled in his talon, she lifted her head enough to see where they were.

The first rays of sunlight pierced the dark blue skies to the east. The horizon was lined with yellow, and she got a better view of what was below them. They were headed to an isolated island in the middle of the ocean whose biggest terrain features were a building and a long beach. No other sort of land was anywhere in sight, and she ducked her head again, eyes quickly watering from the coldness of the air.

Moments later, they landed in the soft sand of the beach. She was released, and she rolled onto her belly, shaking too hard to move far. Her hands and feet were numb from cold, her stiff limbs not far behind. She rested her cheek against the cold sand and closed her eyes, comforted by the soothing sound of waves racing up and down the beach.

She guessed they had flown south, if the humidity of the air and its early morning warmth was any indication. Dawn lit up the eastern sky. The sun peered over the horizon. Bright pink and orange clouds drifted westward towards what remained of night. Sunlight warmed her face, and she closed her eyes to the brightness.

Her shivering gradually stopped, and her mind started to clear after the quick flight.

"Are you well?"

It wasn't Chace's voice.

*So much for a pizza date.* A pang of heartache almost took her breath away. She spent a moment to test her strength and reclaim her wits. The dragon was in its human form, which would make it easier to capture.

With a deep breath, Skylar pushed herself onto her knees then twisted until her back was to the sunrise.

A stranger crouched a few feet from her, watching her closely with sharp blue eyes. The ocean breeze ruffled black hair peppered with silver, the only sign of his age. He was otherwise fit and trim with olive-hued skin and a runner's body clothed in black.

A vision from one of her dreams returned full force, almost knocking her to the ground with its intensity.

*Skylar stood on a hill overlooking a large farm that was ablaze, from the old farmhouse where she'd spent her summers to the cornfields that ran in each direction as far as she could see. Her gaze followed the billowing smoke upward toward the sky. The great blue dragon circled high above. Sun glinted off his dark scales, creating small rainbows around him.*

*"Mama, where is he going?" she asked.*

*"C'mon, Sky. You have to get out of the open. They'll see you!" her mother replied.*

*Skylar retreated from the hilltop to the car waiting down below on a dirt, country road. Her mother was shaking, her face covered in soot.*

*Skylar looked down at her hands and saw them, too, covered with soot and streaked with blood. The sight left her rattled.*

*"Are we going home now?" she asked anxiously.*

*"No, baby. We can't go home. They'll find us there. We just have to keep moving," her mother said and got into the car. "Get in, Sky."*

*She obeyed her mother and climbed in. "Will he be okay?"*

*"If we get far enough away from him, yes," her mother answered, tense. Her eyes flickered to the rearview mirror. "They figured out how to track the protectors, baby. That means we have to go as far from him as possible."*

*"But how can we protect him from so far away?" Young Skylar*

*grappled with the issue.*

*"He will find us when it's safe, when he's figured out who is taking away the protectors and hiding them."*

*"But ... I'll miss ... him." Despite her mother's calmness, Skylar wasn't able to stop the tears.*

*"It's okay, baby," Ginger said softly. "I promise. Your daddy won't let anything happen to you and neither will I."*

She shook her head to clear the vision.

"Father," she said before she could stop herself. "You're my father."

"You remember."

She barely heard him. Skylar stared at the man before her. He was much less ... fatherly than she expected. There was nothing soft or caring about him. He was tense as if for battle with eyes colder than the blue sky they'd flown through to get there. And a *dragon?*

"Is this a joke?" she demanded, baffled. "Did you, like, scramble my brain or something?"

"I'm the only one who hasn't scrambled your brain." His smile was small, one of bitter amusement.

"But you're a dragon."

"You're a dragon protector. You don't shift, but you have dragon blood running through your veins."

"You fried innocent people!"

"There was nothing innocent about the people I fried," he snapped. "They kidnapped you when you were thirteen and spent years brainwashing you. You weren't the only one. All of the slayers went through the same thing. Only a protector can track a shifter, so who better to use to kill off the shifters?"

"That's absurd," she said. Even as she said it, she knew his words built upon what Chace had told her and the memories that were emerging. The only truth that made sense was the one she didn't want to be real. "You're saying the last six years of my life have been fake!"

"Pretty much. You've got a lot to relearn about the shifter community and your own history." The blue dragon shifter stood, squinting towards the sun in clear discomfort. "I'm nocturnal by nature. I'll be in the house, when you're ready to talk."

Skylar watched him walk away, almost relieved he was leaving her alone. Her body wasn't right yet, and her mind was about to explode. If she was a dragon, she'd burn the island to the ground.

But she wasn't. She was a dragon protector, born to another protector and a dragon.

"This is just fucking insane." It made her head hurt, and she gripped it, trying to rationalize everything she had learned the past few weeks. How could everything she'd ever remember knowing be a lie?

On one hand, she wanted to follow him into the house to demand answers.

On the other, she was afraid of what she'd discover.

Her eyes swept over the home of the dragon on the isolated island. He didn't live in a cave like she expected but in a modern, low, concrete bunker-style house with floor to ceiling windows looking out over the beaches and ocean and a sliding glass door that led directly onto the beach on which she stood.

She made herself comfortable on the beach, lying on her back and staring at the sky. Her mind was trying to reconcile her dreams with her reality and the stranger she knew to be her father with the monster who fried twenty people she thought she'd know for years.

Her last dream-like memory had been when she was thirteen of Caleb coming for her and her mother disappearing.

Skylar resisted the urge to run in the house and ask after her dream-mom. She stayed on the beach, staring at the blue sky as the sun rose. She didn't try to focus her thoughts but let her emotions collide and coalesce as she attempted to process her new world. She felt no connection to the blue dragon, even if some part of her acknowledged his relationship to her. Understanding why he hadn't fried her did little to help her wrestle with the truth that Chace had given her up.

*This* she felt, deep enough to hurt. Had he known that he was turning her over to her father, or was he just getting her out of the way? There had been regret in his lovemaking, an aching despair that led her to believe he didn't know she'd be safe with the blue dragon.

Assuming she was safe. *He's not exactly the friendly type.*

Skylar clenched her hands behind her head, wishing she understood exactly what had transpired between Chace and her father. She prayed with no small amount of desperation that Chace had known she was going to be safe at least. Before this moment, she hadn't realized just how hard she'd fallen for him. It was far more than physical; it was primal instinct that had drawn her to him.

The idea he had abandoned her – that he didn't feel the same – was more painful for her to consider than the remains of her shattered life.

It was noon before her patience grew too thin for her to stay on the beach. The humid morning had turned into a balmy, hot early afternoon. Accustomed to a dry heat, she hated the idea of sweating when just lying around.

Skylar reluctantly approached the concrete and glass structure. She hoped the door was locked, giving her a reason not to go in and face reality, but it wasn't.

She walked into the cool interior. The open floor plan was large and minimally decorated. A modern living area was along the curved edge of the windows and house while a kitchen of stainless steel everything sat in the middle of the rounded wing of the house. The colors were likewise cool, as if to offset the hot climate outside. Crisp white walls and ceilings, light grey furniture, tarnished silver fixtures, and light blues and greens in the rugs and pillows.

While she had no guess as to what dragons did in their down time, she didn't expect to find this one reading on an electronic reader, seated in the living area with a glass of water on the accent table beside the light grey couch.

It was yet another reminder that nothing she'd been told about dragons had yet to be proven accurate.

He didn't move or address her as she crossed to the living area. Skylar set down on the chair facing him, the enormity of her situation settling across her shoulders.

The dragon shifter met her gaze. For a long moment, she wasn't certain how to start. After all, this was her *father*, the man she thought had died before she was a year old.

"So …" She cleared her throat. "You don't seem happy to see your alleged, long lost daughter."

"I spent ten years trying to find you and you turn up brainwashed. Not entirely certain happiness is what I should be feeling."

Her face grew warm. "Right. What do I call you? Don't think *daddy* is going to work for me."

"Gavin."

"Okay. I'm Skylar." She paused. "Aren't I?"

"Yes." He offered an almost-smile.

"Okay, Gavin. What is my mother's name?"

"Ginger."

*Ugh.* "Where is she?"

"I don't know. I'm assuming dead. They probably killed her to get to you."

It was one memory Skylar was glad she didn't recall. While she wanted to know what happened, part of her didn't want to go through remembering seeing her mother dying.

Was this the next dream she'd have? She'd seen Caleb come to her house. Did he slaughter her mother then kidnap her?

Skylar rose, unable to sit still with such a thought.

"How are you so … you're a sociopath, aren't you?" she demanded. "You've got no emotions."

"I've had ten years to deal with this. Dragons as old as I am tend to have more self-control than normal people," he replied. "My focus was finding you."

"How old are you?"

"A little over five thousand, give or take a century."

"How many kids do you have?"

"Just you."

She eyed him in disbelief.

"Shifters can take mates. I had hundreds of protectors who watched over me, but the only one I loved was your mother. I never wanted kids. You were a surprise," he added with a look of mild accusation.

"That shit ain't my fault," she retorted. "I'm not fully convinced this is the truth anyway. I mean, obviously, if I can be brainwashed once, I can be twice." *Or maybe more.*

Gavin stood and breezed by her. "Follow me," he said curtly.

She hesitated, watching him stride through the kitchen and down a hallway into the depths of the house. After a moment, her curiosity got the better of her, and she trailed him.

He went to a guest bedroom and was pulling scrapbook-sized containers out from under the bed and setting them on top. His movements were quick and effortless but jerky – a sign he was experiencing some sort of emotion.

"The first thirteen years of your life are here," he said in the same brusque tone. "Should be enough proof to convince you." He didn't wait for her response but left, the sizzle of anger in the air around him.

Skylar heard him retreat down the hallway. She considered the containers, dread in her stomach. Did she really *want* to remember?

She went to the bed and sat, drawing one of the containers to her. Popping it open, she pulled out one of the two scrapbooks it contained and pushed the heavy cover open.

She smiled at the definitely feminine writing and artsy display on the first page.

*Sky's five!* It read and was surrounded with stickers, paper cut outs and other scrapping embellishments in bright shades of pumpkin and yellow.

Her heart pounding, Skylar flipped to the first pages. An image of her at the age of five – grinning with icing smeared across one cheek

– seated in front of a cake and wrapped in her mother's arms was on one side. She studied her mother, a beautiful woman with chiseled cheekbones and a brilliant smile. They shared the same shade of brunette hair and cerulean eyes.

The picture on the opposite page was of her sitting on one of the wings of the blue dragon, apparently having a tea party while he dozed. She was bundled up, and the skies in the distance were grey.

She almost laughed at the bizarre sight, not understanding how she'd been so calm around the massive, otherworldly creature when so young.

Turning the page, she saw all three of them: the stoic shifter with his almost-smile, her mother grinning and herself. Gavin's arms were around the petite Ginger while Ginger's were around her.

She turned the pages, taking in the photos, the pre-school graduation certificate and tassel, and her mother's cute, quirky commentary with growing alarm.

Skylar's heart was soaring. She didn't recall any of this old life, and she was almost glad. She didn't want to imagine what she *should* be feeling by rediscovering everything she'd lost.

She closed the scrapbook then opened the next. Her mother had made a new one for each year of her life, so she opened all the boxes and put them in order then started flipping through them from the beginning. She saw her as a newborn in her exhausted mother's arms in the hospital and one of Gavin, who seemed uncertain holding her but was smiling. The pictures were numerous in the first book, her mother's scrapping clearly that of a beginner. But Ginger's joy was clear in every page and comment, and the pages were cluttered with pictures and stickers.

Skylar finished and went to the next book, then the next. It was almost like learning about someone else's life. She knew the girl in the pictures was her, but she didn't remember any of it.

The more scrapbooks she flipped through, the more she realized that she wasn't able to recall anything from her youth, aside from the memories that appeared in her dreams. There weren't even any false memories to replace the real ones. There was just … nothing. As if she'd been born when she was seventeen. The first memories she recalled were of being trained by Caleb, meeting Mason, Dillon and the rest of the staff at the Field two years before, and learning everything she knew about dragons and shifters.

The pictures in the thirteenth scrapbook stopped less than a quarter of the way through. The rest of the pages were blank. The last was of Skylar on the front porch of the farmhouse from her dream.

She closed the book, a sense of loss making her ache. She didn't recall her first thirteen years, but there was at least proof of who she was and what she'd gone through.

There was nothing for the four years after the final picture in the last scrapbook. Like she had fallen off the face of the earth.

*Or spent four years being brainwashed.*

She opened the last scrapbook again, looking for some sign of what happened to the girl whose life she'd followed for the first thirteen years. She flipped through the empty pages, hoping there was a picture or something she'd missed, one last piece of her mother and the life she didn't remember.

Tucked between the last pages of the scrapbook was a piece of notebook paper folded into thirds. It was well preserved, though the ink had sunk through the paper and left marks on the pages of the scrapbook. She unfolded it, recognizing her mother's loopy, cheerful handwriting.

*Gavin,*

*I hope you're doing well. I know you're alive, and that's enough for me to sleep at night. Sky and I talk about you all the time. She misses you as much as I do.*

*I think they're getting closer. I've noticed people following me again. I wish I knew how to give our daughter the life she deserves. I can find out nothing from the other protectors except that more of them are disappearing. It's too much of a risk to keep talking to them, but that makes for a really lonely life right now. Hopefully, it changes soon.*

*Sometimes, I get so tired of running. I'm praying you can find the shifter you're looking for, and we can build the island getaway we talked about. Then Sky will be safe, and we'll be together again.*

*Until then ... know I'll do whatever I can to protect our baby girl. Keep safe, my love.*

*Ginger*

Something splashed onto the letter, and Sky wiped it away quickly to keep from destroying what might've been the last written letter from her mother. She swiped tears from her eyes next, not expecting the short letter to affect her as it did. It left her with many questions but also the knowledge that her mother and father had loved each other deeply.

"Not sure how," she murmured, thoughts on the cold, distant Gavin. She re-read the letter, touched by her mother's hope and also her despair, a poignant combination Skylar was beginning to experience as well.

She started to put it away then stopped and closed the book. The letter wasn't addressed to her, but she felt more connected to the two people within it than she did with any of the pictures.

Skylar tucked it into her pocket and straightened. After not moving for hours, she grunted at her stiff body. Stretching lightly, she replaced the scrapbooks in their containers and gently pushed them under the bed.

Her head was hurting, maybe from spending the day hunched over the scrapbooks. A wave of dizziness hit her, and she felt suddenly weak, off balance. The episode passed. Attributing it to her insane day, she pushed herself away from the wall that caught her when she almost fell.

She found the bathroom next then made her way through the house, stopping to stare when she reached the kitchen.

The rounded wing of the house lined by windows held almost a 360-degree view of the ocean. The sunset was brilliant, coloring the white floors, walls and grey furniture in bright fuchsia, oranges, and purples. The red-orange sun was perched on the distant horizon, about to sink into the depths of the sea.

She searched for Gavin with her gaze and found him standing on the beach facing east, where night had begun to claim the sky.

She slid open the door to the beach and approached him, uncertain what he was doing. He seemed to be listening or maybe, using his dragon senses.

"I think I know the answer to this question, but is this your secret island sanctuary?" she asked, once again uncertain how to fill the awkward silence.

"It is." He glanced at her and shook out his arms, frame relaxing. "Took me a long time to build. It's off the radar of everyone: humans, shifters, protectors, slayers."

"I take it you were too late to save Ginger." *And me.* But she couldn't say it out loud yet, wasn't quite able to accept the surreal world she'd witnessed within the pages of the scrapbooks.

Gavin said nothing.

She sensed it was a sore point.

"Why couldn't you find the people chasing her?" she asked.

There was a silence. She didn't think he was going to answer.

"My generation of shifters is nocturnal. The people after you and your mother knew this. They moved around during daylight and hid too well after dark. There wasn't much I could do," he replied slowly. "Chace made more progress in his few days of scouting around than I could in six years."

She winced at the dragon shifters name. As if rediscovering her history wasn't enough to confuse her …

"You were working together?" she ventured.

"I wouldn't say it like that. He had something I needed and I had something he wanted. We made a couple of deals, until everyone was happy."

"He had me, and you had … what?"

"Magic he doesn't have. The old generation of dragons were more powerful, which was why we were limited to night activity."

"I thought he hated magic."

"He does. He needed mine to become human again."

She absorbed the information. It was plausible, given the trouble Chace seemed to have controlling his power and the story behind him being made into a shifter.

"Could be worse," she reasoned. "Did he know who you were when he traded me?"

"That I'm a dragon or your father?"

"Father."

"No."

"Ouch." She frowned, stung by the idea Chace had traded her for something as selfish as being made human again. Wasn't there some part of him that cared for her? How did he just turn her over to the creature that fried her coworkers?

"Can't trust the new generation," Gavin said.

"Guess not."

"He mentioned you're marked by one of the shifters."

"Yeah. And?"

"If it's in a decent spot, I'd like to see it." Gavin faced her.

"*That* sounded dad-like," she said, rolling her eyes. "Will you tell me what it means?"

He nodded.

She turned her back to him, looked at the sand and lifted her hair to reveal the tattoo. She waited for him to say something. When he didn't, she turned to face him once more.

Her father was gone. The blue dragon was back, his long wings propelling him silently into the darkening sky.

"Damn, moody dragon shifters," she grumbled. "What is wrong with you people?" It came out as a strangled shout, the words burning their way through her tight throat.

*So much for learning more terrifying truth tonight.* Clearly stuck on an island, Skylar went inside.

She stood in the cool interior, facing the way her father had flown off. The sky grew darker as she watched, and she couldn't help the sense of concern that made her stomach churn.

"Why the hell is it so cold in here?" She shivered, an odd feeling sinking into her. She didn't feel right, but she didn't know why.

Skylar sat on the couch and picked up the glass of water her father had left on the stand beside the couch. She took a deep swig then coughed, swallowing hard enough to make her eyes water.

"Vodka!" she managed. "Maybe we are related."

Whether it was the alcohol or the stress of her day, she suddenly felt drowsy. Skylar stretched out on the couch.

"Let's not kill the shifter your little girl thinks she might really like," she whispered to her father before drifting into an unnatural sleep.

# Chapter Twenty One

W hen the sun set on the day Skylar disappeared, Chace felt no different than he had when he parked his cabin permanently on the southern Oregon coast. The small beach he'd selected as his home was private, hedged by massive pine trees. Pines and the sea filled the air with a mix of scents he found soothing.

He sat on the beach, watching the sun sink beneath the line of the horizon. With the soothing sounds of the beach and the cool, fresh air, he should've been calm.

But he wasn't. He'd been troubled all day, at first by the permanency of what he'd done to himself and then by the knowledge that he'd sold out the one woman who made him feel whole.

"What goes around ..." he murmured, aware that long ago, someone else had condemned him, too, without a second thought about how he might feel.

He dreaded stepping into the cabin that had been his home for hundreds of years. While he felt no affects of Mr. Nothing's magic, the cabin seemed drained of life. He didn't notice the gentle hum of magic or how warm and welcome the magic always was until all those things were gone.

The cabin had turned chilly soon after he moved it one last time, the colors of its interior muted, the coziness replaced by the sense that it was just … small.

By becoming human once more, he thought he'd be regaining what he lost, not mourning the loss of so much more.

*I feel sick.*

He had to move on. Forget Skylar. After all, the chances of him seeing her again were close to none. If she survived Mr. Nothing, she'd hate him forever. He deserved it, to die old and alone, without ever hearing her attempts at ill-timed jokes or experiencing her sweet body again.

"You're a hard man to find."

Chace twisted, startled by the reminder he was no longer able to sense others approaching. He recognized the slayer behind him without understanding whether or not he was a threat.

"I'm not a shifter anymore," he said. "Sorry to disappoint."

"Who told you that?" Dillon asked.

"Long story." Chace shifted to face him. The slayer war armed, his gaze was sharp.

Dillon considered him for a moment.

Chace didn't explain, more interested in why a slayer was tracking him down now, when he was no longer a dragon.

"All right. Then I'm assuming you don't know. There's no such thing as turning someone into or back from a shifter. It's in your blood. I don't know what anyone told you to the contrary," Dillon said. "Some people's gift manifests early while others just never have that catalyst that makes them turn the first time. Their power is buried. A lot of people are born shifters and die without ever knowing that. Their magic just stays … hidden. In any case, you were born a shifter and will die one. The magic is just caged inside you."

"Whatever. It's over now."

"Wrong again." Dillon frowned. "You shouldn't be so flippant about this, Chace. I mean, yes, you had a chance to live as a normal human, assuming your gift never awoke. But the potential was always there anyway. You mouthed off to someone who provoked it, and then you made a deal with Gavin to silence it. These were not well thought out moves, like dragging Sky into all this."

"Gavin. So he has a name." Chace rose. He carefully avoided talking about Skylar, unable to keep his emotions out of it if she came up. Unease fluttered through him, more so knowing that the slayer had tracked him down for a reason. "What do you want, Dillon?"

"What I did want …" Dillon sighed. "You were supposed to take down Gavin, not turn Skylar over to him and walk away."

"What?" Chace's mind raced as another thought emerged.

*Someone close to Skylar,* Mr. Nothing had said.

Dillon scrubbed his face with both hands.

"You're behind all this," Chace said in a hushed voice. "Not Caleb." A new emotion shot through him, one he hadn't felt in hundreds of years. "You have a vendetta against Mr. Noth … Gavin."

"You had to give him Skylar." Dillon paced. "A plan a few thousand years in the making and you manage to destroy it in a few days. But. Maybe I can fix this."

"Hel-lo," Chace snapped. "You gonna talk to yourself or you wanna let me in on what's going on? Is he going to kill her?"

"Kill? No. He's hidden her away somewhere I can't find her." Dillon blew out a breath.

"What do you want with Skylar?" Chace bristled despite wanting to pretend his torrid affair with her never happened.

"It's her father I'm after."

"Which is …"

"Gavin."

"You're shittin' me." Chace laughed loudly. Mr. Nothing's strange insistence that Skylar be handed over to him suddenly made sense. "That's why he wanted her? Because you brainwashed her, and he was trying to get her back?"

"She's a particularly nifty pawn to have," Dillon admitted. "You're of no use to me like this."

"Human?"

"With your gift caged."

"Not buying that."

"You don't have to," Dillon replied. "I'll prove it to you. Either your magic will reawaken and you'll survive this trial or you'll just die."

Chace eyed him, not liking the sound of it. Dillon took a few steps back. Seconds later, the familiar crackling of breaking bone and soft tearing of muscles filled the air. Chace found himself reaching for his magic, only to find an empty hole inside him.

He started around the shifter, towards the cabin, where he had a few knives and a gun.

Dillon's transformation was complete before Chace reached the top of the beach, and he stopped, transfixed by the creature before him.

Dillon was a griffin, a creature with a wingspan as wide as Chace's and talons just as big. From there, all similarities ended. His horned beak was large enough to snap a man's leg in two, and the powerful lion's body was the size of a truck. Eagle eyes were as sharp as the clawed feet.

As a dragon shifter, Chace understood that magical creatures existed. But he never expected this particular animal of legend to be real.

Dillon leapt into the air and charged him. Chace's human reflexes were too slow to react; he had little more time than to shield his face before he felt the claws wrap around him tight enough to hurt. One sharpened talon tore into his arm, and he stared in surprise at the wound.

It didn't heal automatically, and the pain was so much more than he recalled. Blood ran down his arm and over the clawed foot, dripping downward into the forest that was quickly growing distant.

Chace watched with a mix of horror and fascination. Flying was very different as a human, and helplessness tore through him as he realized what exactly it was to be human again.

If Dillon dropped him, if he went too high or too fast …

Chace closed his eyes and calmed himself. The peace and solitude he was accustomed to finding in the skies was gone, replaced by fear. A part of him acknowledged that he deserved whatever happened after turning over Skylar, no matter what Dillon told him about Skylar not being in danger.

The air grew cold enough for him to start to shiver and then colder. His nose became numb, followed by his ears and toes. Tiny particles of moisture pelted his face. When he opened his eyes, he wasn't able to see beyond the white clouds into which Dillon had flown.

Clutched in the talons of the otherworldly creature, Chace thought again of Skylar. He'd done the same to her and couldn't helping thinking that he'd find a different way to carry her next time, one far less uncomfortable.

*Like there will be a next time. I'll never see her again.*

Distressed by the reminder, he closed his eyes again, no longer caring where Dillon took him. Instead, he focused on clearing his thoughts and awaiting the inevitable: his death at the claws of a slayer.

The air chilled even more, until his cheeks went numb, too, and his body shook out of control.

It was some time later when Dillon's speed slowed, and he began circling, preparing to land somewhere.

Chace roused himself, irritated to find his eyelashes were frozen together. He swiped his face against Dillon's rough claw and blinked rapidly. They were descending out of the clouds towards a snow-covered tundra next to a grey sea. Ice was everywhere, freezing much of the water in place and coating the snow below.

Grimly he realized that Dillon wasn't going to just drop him out of the sky for a quick death. No, the slayer-shifter wanted him to freeze to death. To what end, Chace didn't know, except that Dillon wasn't quite right in the head.

Dillon dropped him a good ten feet from the ground, far enough that Chace's breath was knocked from him when he hit the hard tundra. He gasped until air reached his lungs. Blood smeared from his wound onto the snow beneath him. He pushed himself up, dizzy and disoriented from the flight.

"That didn't do it," Dillon said, frustration in his voice again. "I figured the flying might trigger something."

"I'm telling you. You're wrong about this." Chace looked around. Cold didn't begin to describe the grey-white world around him. Snow sank through his jeans, cold enough to burn the skin beneath.

He rose, shivering.

"What you know about your lineage could fill a peapod," Dillon snapped. "You don't feel any different?"

"No."

"No urge to light a fire to keep from freezing to death or change into a dragon form so you can fly away or stay warm?"

Chace laughed. "I do want a coat."

"You and Sky ... you have the shittiest senses of humor."

"I love her humor. It's so inappropriate. But no surprise. She's wild like me."

"You don't know anything about her."

"I do," Chace said. "She fucks like a dragon, that's for sure."

Dillon's head snapped around towards Chace. Chace didn't need the experiences of a thousand years to recognize the hot jealousy on Dillon's face.

"You know, I am feeling something," he said. "Kinda like ... hmmm." He pretended to consider. "Oh, yeah. It's what I feel when her thighs are wrapped around my head. Satisfaction."

Dillon's punch caught Chace off guard. It was too fast for him to see let alone block, a reminder that he no longer had the agility, power and speed of an immortal shifter.

Chace landed on his back in the snow and spit blood from a busted lip. He laughed. With the pain of the punch and the burning chill of the wetness sinking into his clothing, it was the only thing he knew to do.

"Look, Dillon. You can kill me or stick around and let me talk about how much I enjoyed fucking your girl," Chace said. "Or you can just … get the fuck out of here and leave me to my fate."

Dillon's face went red, and his eyes flared with inhuman fire. Chace saw his skin ripple beneath the emotional turmoil as the shifter began to transform involuntarily.

"I hope your death is painful and slow!" Dillon all but spat. He dropped to all fours, his clothing tearing. His body contorted and expanded until the mythical griffin stood panting before Chace.

Dillon lifted himself into the air and paused, watching Chace climb to his feet.

"Have a good life, Dillon," he said with sarcastic cheerfulness Skylar would approve of.

The griffin smashed a wing into him, slicing the side of his head open.

Chace went down again, this time struggling to control the agony working through his system. Blood ran into one eye and down his neck, the only warmth in the otherwise unforgiving cold of the Arctic.

The griffin soared away, disappearing into a cloudbank.

Chace wiped his face and sat, grimacing at the pain. He looked around, unable to stop shaking. Blood splattered the area to his left, the stark red against snow disturbing him for more reasons than one.

"Well, Chace, this is what you wanted," he muttered. "To become a human and end it all."

Resting on his knees, he touched the wound on his head gingerly. He didn't expect to be dropped off at the North Pole by a griffin and left to freeze to death. No, that was never part of the plan in becoming human, growing old and finally dying, the only way to end the pain of watching those he loved die while he remained immortal.

He looked around, unable to pinpoint when the plan had become so unappealing. Or when he'd decided he didn't want to be human or to die alone.

He wanted Skylar. Whether or not protectors lived forever like shifters, he had no idea. But did it matter, if he spent at least another eighty years falling asleep beside her each night and waking with her each morning?

"Too late now," he said aloud. His voice was the only sound, aside from the wind that had already numbed his face.

With no coat or way to escape the cold, he debated his next move. He could sit and bleed to death or he could try to find shelter.

*And bleed to death while warm?*

It struck him that he didn't know the first thing about how to dress a wound. He had healed automatically for almost his entire life, and this particular knowledge from his first twenty-six years or so as a human was lost.

"Shit." He rose. This time, his anger was directed at himself, pure fury for not appreciating what was before him before he'd traded her to the blue dragon. Hadn't he made a similar decision a thousand years ago?

Hugging himself, he started walking away from the sea. He was lightheaded already and soon, his body started to feel too heavy to go far. He looked around the white world for some indication of where to go: a path, smoke from a hidden chimney. Lights.

Nothing. Dillon had dropped him off in the middle of nowhere on purpose.

Chace gritted his teeth against the biting cold and trudged forward. His toes were soon hurting from cold and wet, the thick strands of his hair frozen.

He paused again and looked up at the sky.

"If I had it to do again, I probably wouldn't have made those last few major life decisions," he told the heavens with wryness. "Or maybe, I just would've stayed in the cabin with Sky and told the rest of the world to go fuck itself." It was the best solution yet, one that seemed so obvious, he didn't know why it took freezing – or bleeding – to death in the Arctic for him to realize.

*So much for second chances.* He was dizzy and becoming weaker, the blood on his skin and clothing frozen.

"What did the dragon who cursed you say?"

For a moment, he thought the voice was a figment of his imagination, a sign he'd become delusional with pain and cold.

Chace turned with effort, not expecting to see Gavin's dark form before him. The shifter didn't look cold, but he appeared angry.

No. Furious.

"I heard a rumor it wasn't really a curse," Chace said. "And you didn't really cure me of it."

"Did you hear why I didn't give a shit who I had to lie to?"

"To get your daughter."

"Exactly."

"I get it." Chace shook his head to keep focused. "You here to finish what the others started?"

The muscles in Gavin's jaw ticked, and fire was in his eyes. He strode forward and smashed a fist into Chace's nose.

Chace went down hard enough that he didn't feel like getting up again. The world blurred and swirled like the snowflakes falling from the sky.

"That is for marking my daughter," Gavin said, crouching beside him. "As much as I want you to freeze to death out here, I can't let you."

"Because she likes me?" Chace asked curiously. He dabbed at his nose and pushed himself up, too cold and numb to feel the wetness creeping into his clothing this time.

"Because she's the other half of your heart," Gavin grated. "Which means if you die, so does she."

"So you're essentially my father-in-law."

The dragon shifter rose with a curse and paced a short distance away.

"What did the shifter who unlocked your magic tell you?" he demanded once more.

"So it's true," he murmured. Chace hesitated. He hadn't told anyone the whole story in a thousand years. Gavin's words confirmed Dillon's claim – that he had always been a shifter. He didn't know how to feel about it after believing for so long he didn't fit in. "I was born a shifter."

"There's only one way to become one."

"Then why am I not like other shifters? Why do they die when I don't?"

"Dragons are the most powerful of the shifters. It's why you have control of the bar and your cabin, why you can survive what would kill others," Gavin said impatiently. "Now. What did she say?"

"Why does it matter now?"

"Tell me."

Chace got to his feet once more, wobbling. "She said one day I'd learn that arrogance and selflessness can't coexist. I'd learn to care for someone else more than I do my own concerns. That I'd relive her heartache for the rest of my years."

"Did you?"

Chace frowned, not expecting the personal question.

Mr. Nothing – Gavin – was glaring at him, clearly disapproving.

"You won't let me die," Chace guessed. "You didn't spend so long trying to find your daughter just to let me kill her by freezing to death. I'm assuming you're trying to figure out if I'm deserving of her."

"You're not. You'll never, *ever* set foot near my daughter again. Ever, Chace," Gavin snarled. "Now answer my question."

The intensity of the shifter's declaration hit Chace hard. It wasn't undeserved; after all, he'd traded Skylar with no guarantee she'd be safe. He lied to her to get her to go with him docilely then turned her over, never knowing she was the daughter of the man he went to meet.

He betrayed her, the way he had the dragon shifter a thousand years ago who awoke his gift out of anger when she'd been spurned. Skylar was too good to want revenge, too smart to trust him again, too much a part of him for him to walk away.

"No," he whispered. "I didn't learn anything." Sorrow filled him, accompanied by anger. "She made my heart whole, and I sold her out."

"Exactly. There should be no question as to your suitability to be anywhere near my daughter."

Chace said nothing, uncertain how to respond. The reality of what he'd done sank into his mind like the cold did his skin. He wanted to agree and make things right by simply leaving her in peace.

"I can't just … walk away," he replied.

"You don't have to. You were too weak a thousand years ago to awaken your own magic. All I have to do is keep you as far from her as I can." As he spoke, Gavin stepped away to give himself room to shift. "You'll never fly again, Chace, and you'll never find her either. You don't deserve someone like Skylar."

The anger boiling in Chace's chest grew. He didn't deserve to feel it, to want to interfere with Skylar's life anymore than he already had.

*I'm her dragon. She's my Sky. We belong together.*

In the seconds while he thought, Gavin had shifted into his other form. The massive blue dragon was beautiful and graceful, its beating wings causing the snow to fly around them both.

Chace was snatched up in talons the way he had been not long before and taken into the clouds. Cold assaulted him while blood dribbled from his head, nose and arm. He was feeling nauseous, more so by the force of their breakneck speed. Snowflakes pelted him hard, while the darkness at the edges of his mind tried to take him.

Did his mind want him to sleep or die?

If he died, so did Skylar. He owed her the ability to stay alive, if nothing else.

Afraid to close his eyes, he blinked rapidly against the moisture and wind. Much faster than Dillon had flown, Gavin soon broke free of the clouds and was flying at top speed over the ocean. The air currents grew warmer, the night sky replacing the white light of clouds and snow.

Stars blinked overhead, reflected in the depths of the ocean below.

Barely aware of the world around him anymore, Chace hung

limply in the dragon's talons and waited for them to land.

At long last, they did, back on his beach, next to his cabin.

The dragon set him gently onto the sand, and Chace lay still, gathering his strength to move. A fire started near him, and he lifted his head to see the bonfire Gavin started nearby. The small effort was enough to make him nauseous. He rested his head on the sand again, hurting.

"The shifter who fucked you up a thousand years ago was right to do so. She failed, but I won't," Gavin said in a hard voice. "If any part of you cares for my daughter, you'll do whatever it takes to survive."

Chace closed his eyes briefly, hearing both the threat and the promise in Gavin's voice. He drew a shaking breath and tested his body, dismayed by what he learned.

He was in bad shape.

Wind whipped by him, and he opened his eyes in time to see the blue dragon take flight.

Fear flew through Chace, and adrenaline forced the darkness at the edges of his mind to retreat.

Gavin was seriously leaving him, even knowing Skylar's life was tied to Chace's.

Chace struggled into a sit. Sand mixed with the blood in his hair. His blurry gaze settled on the cabin. Only twenty feet away, it may as well have been twenty miles. His body didn't respond when he tried to stand.

He focused internally instead, seeking the part of him that Dillon and Gavin insisted was there, the magic of a shifter deep within him.

If it was, he wasn't able to find it. Opening his eyes, Chace eyed the cabin once more.

*If any part of you cares for my daughter, you'll do whatever it takes to survive.*

He'd failed to conquer his selfishness a thousand years before and again with Skylar. With both despair and anger boiling over in his blood, Chace pushed himself to his knees. Grimly, he realized he'd had it easy as a dragon. This time around, he wasn't going to make it, if he didn't learn his lesson.

"Here I come, Skylar," he said then gave a strained laugh. "Maybe."

Chace drew a deep breath and climbed to his feet. At the very least, he knew Skylar was safe with her father. If it took him one step at a time and an eternity, he'd find the other half of his heart, no matter what the blue dragon told him.

Besides, no dragon worth his fire ever, *ever* missed a pizza date with a beautiful woman.

*I'm not about to start now.*

# ABOUT THE AUTHOR

Lizzy Ford is the author of over twenty books written for young adult and adult paranormal romance readers, to include the internationally bestselling "Rhyn Trilogy," "Witchling Series" and the "War of Gods" series. Considered a freak of nature by her peers for the ability to write and release a commercial quality novel in under a month, Lizzy has focused on keeping her readers happy by producing brilliant, gritty romances that remind people why true love is a trial worth enduring.

Lizzy's books can be found on every major ereader library, to include: Amazon, Barnes and Noble, iBooks, Kobo, Sony and Smashwords. She lives in southern Arizona with her husband, three dogs and a cat.

## Connect with Lizzy:

### WEBSITE:
www.GuerrillaWordfare.com

### FACEBOOK:
www.Facebook.com/LizzyFordBooks

or find her on TWITTER!
@LizzyFord2010

www.ingramcontent.com/pod-product-compliance
Lightning Source LLC
Chambersburg PA
CBHW031727170626
46808CB00005B/1916